FORAGER

Forager Series: Book One

Updated 7th May 2015

Copyright © 2013 Peter R Stone

All rights reserved.

This is a work of fiction. The characters and events portrayed in this book are fictional. Any resemblance to actual persons or actual events is purely coincidental.

Cover Art by Peter R Stone

Chapter One

The Custodian G-Wagon was the last thing I expected to see when I strolled into the Recycling-Works yard. As usual, I was a couple of minutes late for my shift. My boss, a tall, balding guy whose once-impressive muscles were slowly turning to flab, was talking – more like bowing and scraping – to the Custodian sergeant. Three privates stood beside the G-Wagon with their Austeyr assault-rifles slung over their shoulders. The Custodians wore their usual camo-pattern fatigues, bulletproof vests, and helmets.

Panic surged through me with such intensity that I had to fight the urge to flee. They could be here for one reason and one reason only, and that was me. I must have slipped up somehow. A slip up that allowed them to discover the secret I had gone to such lengths to hide my entire life. Now they would haul me away to the town's Genetics Laboratory, where the geneticists would cut me apart to study the mutation I carried thanks to nuclear fallout. Whether they would euthanize me before or after they dismembered me I didn't know, and that's what worried me. That and the whole dying part.

It occurred to me that I could try to make a run for it, but in a walled-off town canvassed by ceaseless Custodian patrols, where would I go?

I glanced about frantically for my workmates and spotted them slouching beside our battered old truck, their eyes darting about nervously. They were unnerved by the unexpected arrival of the Custodians too. Despite their ignorance, I'm sure a whole host of minor misdemeanours they had committed were flying through their minds as they wondered if they were the reason for the visit.

Custodians, the paramilitary police force tasked with protecting the town from internal and external threats, were hardly the guardians their name implied. In reality, they spent most of their time curtailing the people's freedoms and enforcing the Chancellor's strict laws.

Noticing I had arrived, my boss, Trajan Barclay, nodded deferentially to the sergeant and hurried over to me, puffing from the effort. "There you are, Ethan."

"What's going on, Boss?" I asked, unable to stop the quiver in my voice. "Why are they here?"

"Beginning today, they'll be accompanying you on your foraging trips," Trajan explained as he glanced back at them nervously.

"For what reason?" I demanded.

"Due to increased Skel attacks on our foraging parties, Custodian Command has decreed that all foraging teams will be accompanied by Custodian squads from now on."

I shuddered. Just the thought of the demented Skel nomads was disconcerting, and encountering them out there in the abandoned ruins of the city of Melbourne gave me recurring nightmares. Nightmares of their mad eyes, fetid breath and body odour that reeked of decaying flesh, and of their suits of armour made from the bones of the dead.

The disgusting savages did not work themselves, but constantly raided civilised towns and settlements to steal supplies, food and livestock, and abduct captives to be their slaves. It was from the bodies of the slaves – none of which lasted long – that they took the bones to make their armour.

On the few occasions they ambushed my workmates and I, we always managed to drive them off or slay them, using prohibited weapons we found while foraging. Weapons that were at this moment hidden in our truck. Lucky for us the Custodians never inspected the truck; otherwise, it would be a prison sentence for us all.

"Boss, we don't need Custodians to keep us safe, we're more than capable of looking after ourselves," I protested as a profound sense of relief flooded through me – the Custodians were not here for me! My secret had not been discovered.

"This ain't negotiable, Ethan," he snapped, glaring at me from beneath bushy eyebrows, "And don't give them attitude or lip. Custodians ain't known for their patience. Now come, let me introduce you."

Fuming inwardly, I followed my boss over to the Custodian sergeant.

"Ah, excuse me, Sergeant King, this is Ethan Jones, the leader of this foraging team," Trajan said.

The sergeant had about five years on me, I reckoned, and was one mean piece of work. He had a six-foot tall, well-proportioned, muscular body (unlike mine – I was still in the lanky stage.) His face was pockmarked and leered at me as though I had just been dredged up from the gutter. "As I'm sure your boss has informed you, Jones, we'll be accompanying your team on your foraging missions from now on. But don't mind us, just go about your business as usual. Our purpose is to keep you boys safe out there, not to get in your way."

I bit back the first dozen retorts that popped into my head, like: *what a load of a baloney! What do you take me for? I wasn't born yesterday,* and a selection of one or two word responses that normally never graced my lips. I finally settled upon, "Understood, Sergeant."

"I trust you have some system for determining where to forage each day?"

The way he accentuated the word 'system' sent thrills of fear surging through me again. Perhaps I had been too quick to think the danger had passed. "Ah, yes, past experience has given us a pretty good indication of where to look." This was true to a limited degree. "But today we're gonna continue stripping out the apartment block we hit in Carlton yesterday."

"Alright then, lead the way," the sergeant ordered before he strode back to the G-Wagon.

My workmates met me before I reached our truck, their faces full of questions and complaints. I held up my hands to forestall them. "Stow it, guys. We'll just have to get used to it, 'cause there's nothing we can do about it. Now hop in the truck."

Michal, our driver and my best friend, clambered into the truck first. He had to duck his head just to get through the door since he easily topped six-foot-four –

and at nineteen, I suspected he hadn't finished growing yet.

Shorty and Leigh climbed into the backseat behind him, chattering away like a pair of old women.

David reached up to pull himself into the cab after them, but hesitated, glancing back at the Custodians. Of Chinese ancestry, David was our Mr. Fix-it, an absolute whiz with anything mechanical, whether putting them together or pulling them apart. Like me, he'd deliberately flunked year eleven so he didn't have to get a job in North End – the town's walled off upper-class district. He'd tried his hand at a number of jobs until I asked him to join my foraging team a couple of years ago. After one day out in the ruins with Michal, Leigh, and me, he claimed he'd found his life's calling. Not because of the job, but because of the various 'extra-curricular' activities we engaged in out there. Sadly, now that the Custodians were going to accompany us, we would have to curtail those activities.

"Go on, get in!" I hissed at David. He nodded and climbed into the back with Shorty and Leigh, while I jumped in and sat beside Michal in the front.

Michal looked down at me, clearly displeased about something. "You gotta be more careful, Ethan."

"Me?" I asked, not having the slightest inkling of what he was referring to.

"Yes, Ethan, you." He turned the key in the ignition and pumped the accelerator gently to get the engine started. The truck was pretty old and I doubted it had a single part that hadn't been replaced or refurbished at some point. "I'd wager my bottom dollar they're here 'cause they want to find out why our team brings in more metals than the others."

Our team was one of many that foraged in the ruins outside for non-corrosive metals – gold, platinum, copper, bronze and lead – that had survived the decades since the Apocalypse. We would take them back to the Recycling-Works where they would be sorted, melted down, and handed over to the factories.

"What do you mean?" I feigned ignorance.

"Them other three goons." He jerked his head back to indicate our workmates in the back seat. "They ain't too bright. They think you just know the best spots to look, but not me. I've seen you."

That sent icy tendrils of dread creeping back into my gut. "Seen me what?"

"You can drop your act with me, okay?" he said softly as he shifted the truck into gear and drove out of the Recycling-Works yard towards the town gates. "I've heard about people like you, and your secret's safe with me. Just don't keep hitting pay dirt every day from now on. Those Custodians aren't here to protect us from the Skel like they claim – or they'd have brought a Bushmaster instead of that G-Wagon."

He was right, and I knew it. The Custodians always rode in their Bushmaster Protected Mobility Vehicles when entering situations they perceived as potentially dangerous. That they came in an unarmoured G-Wagon today proved they were not expecting to encounter Skel as they claimed. That was just a smokescreen to cover their true intention – which was to find out which of us had my aberrant, mutant ability, which I used to locate the metals we were looking for. Personally, I thought of the ability as a gift, something everyone could benefit from it.

What was wrong with me? How had I convinced myself I could get away with bringing back a load of non-corrosive metals every time? Never once coming back empty-handed. We told the boss we just knew where to look and were extraordinarily lucky. But that kind of naivety really showed just how out of touch I was with reality – or was it typical thinking for teenagers, thinking we could get away with anything? The Custodians were relentless in hunting down those with genetic mutations. Ninety-nine percent were detected before birth and resulted in a terminated pregnancy. Anyone who survived with mutations like mine were taken away and never seen again.

These ruminations triggered one of my strongest childhood memories. I was five years old, making my own way to school, feeling proud of myself for my independence. I wasn't really alone, I was following some of the other boys who lived near my flat. I hummed merrily to myself, thinking of the long day ahead when unfamiliar arms grabbed me and pulled me into the shadows. I looked up into the face of an elderly Chinese man. He knelt down and forced me to meet his gaze.

"You must hide your ability, child," he said. "Hide it from everyone, even your family. Do not trust anyone! If the Custodians find out you have it, they will haul you away to the Genetics Laboratory to be dissected like a frog. You understand me, child? Like a frog!"

And then he walked off, leaving me shaking in fear – of him and of what he had said. Even by that age, I knew I was different, and I most definitely did not want to die like that! How the man knew I had the mutation, I still don't know.

"So where are we heading today, Boss?" Michal asked, snapping me out of my reverie.

"Back to where we went yesterday. There's still plenty of copper we can strip out there." Normally there was not much to find in the way of useful metals that close to the CBD – Melbourne's Central Business District. That whole area had been stripped virtually clean by foragers over the decades. However, yesterday I struck pay dirt when I found an old apartment block that still had copper pipes rather than the plastic ones used in later years.

"Hey Jones?" Leigh piped up.

"Yeah, what?" I twisted the rear-view mirror so I could catch a look at him as I answered. Leigh was a wiry built individual with spiked auburn hair. He was twenty, like myself. He was a typical school dropout – not too bright and full of lip. We had to watch him near authority figures to keep him in line before he got himself into too much trouble. When Trajan asked me to form my own foraging team two years ago, he insisted I include his nephew, Leigh. He'd promised his sister he'd give him a job. I had seen Leigh at school, of course, but hadn't had much to do with him back then. Still, he was an okay bloke, and I was glad to have him on my team.

"Why do you reckon the Custodians are gonna accompany us on our trips from now on?" he asked.

"To keep us safe from Skel attacks. At least, that's their excuse," I replied.

"Oh come on, Skel? I'd bet my bottom dollar they're here to make sure we 'behave' out there. They just want to rob us of the only freedom we've got left!" Shorty retorted angrily.

Shorty was our youngest member – a recent school dropout. With long white-blonde hair, he was a head shorter than me, but was as nimble as a monkey. He could climb anything and get through virtually any gap or hole. He was also quite the comedian, which was surprising really, when you considered his parents. His father was an automotive factory worker who never stopped cussing. Every time I saw him at Shorty's place, he was slumped in a chair in front of the TV with a stubbie in one hand a smoke in the other. He had a habit of launching into endless tirades about things that got on his goat. And everything got on his goat. Shorty's mother wasn't much better. To say she was a little rough around the edges would be the understatement of the century.

"They probably think we're doing drugs or having wild sex parties out there," Leigh suggested.

"I wish!" Shorty declared a little too enthusiastically.

"Which one?" David laughed.

"Both, of course." Leigh grinned.

"And where do you suppose they think we're finding the drugs and women?" Shorty asked.

"You'd be surprised," David answered from where he sat watching out the window. "Not long before you joined us, Shorty, we found a whole stack of tins packed with drugs in airtight bags."

"Fat lot of good that haul did us, Jones made us burn the lot," Leigh said.

"He what?" Shorty stared at me as though there was something seriously amiss with my head.

"That was for your own good!" I insisted, remembering the horrified expression on Leigh's face when I gave the order – and then stayed to make sure he followed it.

"But...but if you'd sold it you'd have been set for life! You know, I've got some contacts..." Shorty began. He was definitely on the same page as Leigh.

"Selling drugs is an automatic death sentence!" I shot back at him. "And don't get me started on how they can totally mess up your life."

"Custodians are a confounded waste of space, can't they find something useful to do with their lives apart from ruining ours?" Leigh moaned. "Hey Jones, let's introduce 'em to some real Skel today. Bet they soil themselves and go runnin' home to mummy."

"Yeah, that's the ticket! Do it, Jones, do it!" Shorty bounced in his seat.

"As attractive as that sounds, I wouldn't wish Skel on anyone, not even Custodians. We are supposed to be on the same side, remember?"

"Yeah, but do they know that?" David asked.

"Pipe it down guys, the gates are ahead," Michal announced as the massive metal gates loomed before us. A twelve-foot high, outwardly curving concrete wall, topped with spikes and barbed wire, ran the perimeter of the entire town. There were only three exits, each with two tall metal gates that rarely opened. The only people permitted to leave the town were foragers and Custodians, and the latter rarely did so. There were also man-high secret exits with concrete doors that became flush with the walls when shut. I saw the Custodians using one when I was snooping with my binoculars one night.

We stopped at the gates so Michal could show the guards our papers. They examined them carefully and then strolled down to talk with the Custodian squad following us. Using the rear-view mirror, I watched them talk with Sergeant King for a few minutes, before they returned our papers to us. The gates swung slowly open on well-oiled hinges and Michal finally drove out of Newhome with the Custodians' G-Wagon close behind. We crossed the 250-metre wide no-man's land that surrounded Newhome. All of the buildings surrounding the town were demolished so that no one could approach without being seen from the guard towers on the walls.

Heading to Victoria Street, we entered North Melbourne's eerily quiet and empty streets. Slowly decaying buildings were in the process of being overgrown by shrubs, creepers, trees and wild grass. Wrecks of rusting vehicles littered the roads as well, but not in great numbers. Most of the city folk who survived the bomb fled to the country after the water, gas and electricity cut out. Sadly, most of them died of starvation, malnutrition and disease. The country towns that had not been bombed were unable to cope with the influx of over two million people.

The buildings in this part of the city were relatively intact, though for the most part their windows had been either blown out by the bomb, or smashed by vandals or foragers. The nuke that hit Melbourne a century ago must have had the wrong co-ordinates, because it came down in the southeastern suburbs, leaving the city's Central Business District mostly untouched. I could see it now, dominating the skyline ahead of us, a motley assortment of skyscrapers of varying heights and designs. We'd only ventured in there a few times, for many of the buildings looked structurally unsafe. Not to mention there were 'things' in there. Things I hesitated to call people – they made the Skel seem friendly. Besides, there were still plenty of resources to scrounge up from the suburbs.

As we drove I pondered what Shorty said; that the Custodians were with us to curb the only freedom we had left. I wondered if he was right. Perhaps Michal and I were being paranoid. Yet if he was right, that meant I had spent years downplaying my intellect and abilities in school so I could flunk out and get a job as a forager – all for naught. Only foragers were allowed out of Newhome on a regular basis, and I needed that freedom. Foraging was the only time I felt free and alive. It was only out here that I could use my special abilities without the danger of getting caught. Alas, thanks to the Custodians, that was no longer the case.

Perhaps it was time to re-examine my original plan of going AWOL during one of these foraging outings, never to return. However, the situation that caused me to shelve the plan in the first place was still in effect – my kid sister was ill and I was the only one in our family willing to buck the system to help her. I was convinced her health would continue to decline if I didn't keep slipping nutritious lunches to her when the others weren't looking. Well, that's what I kept telling myself. The fact was she didn't eat much of what I brought her. She didn't eat much of anything, period.

Chapter Two

With our truck in the lead, we eventually reached Victoria Street and headed east through a ghost city of eerily silent shops, hotels, and office blocks. We finally entered Carlton, where we found the ten story apartment building we raided yesterday. Michal drove around the rusting shell of a semi-trailer and turned into and parked in an extremely picturesque side street. Trees flourished down its length, casting it into shade. Sparrows fluttered about the ground and twittered in the branches, while crows cawed from rooftops. It was one of the most peaceful and tranquil spots we had encountered, though sadly, it was in appearance only. Skel could turn up anywhere in the ruins of Melbourne.

The G-Wagon pulled up beside our truck. Sergeant King and two of his goons climbed out, leaving the driver inside the vehicle. As they glanced about nervously at the trees and high-rise buildings that crowded around us, their typical arrogance was absent. In fact, they weren't just uncomfortable, but nervous as well, and that gave me a great deal of pleasure. This trip was quite probably their first time outside the town.

"What next, Jones?" the sergeant demanded.

I picked up a crowbar and pointed at the ten-story apartment block to our right. "We worked the first two floors yesterday, so we'll be hitting the third and fourth today."

"Right."

"Will you be coming in with us?" I asked, and then as an afterthought added, "Hopefully we won't run across any Skel today."

King's eyes widened ever so slightly. "Ah, no, it is imperative that we remain out here to guard the vehicles."

Guard the vehicles? What a convenient excuse to stay outside where they felt safer – so much for their claims that they were here to protect us. Their choice to remain outside actually revealed their true intention, which was to determine which one of us was the mutant. I presumed there was a monitoring device in the G-Wagon that would squawk like a stuck pig if I used my ability.

Pondering the Custodians attempts to catch me out reminded me of the first time I saw them apprehend a mutant. It was my second day in first grade. I was in Class A with twenty-nine boys – Class B had thirty. I heard the Custodians standing outside the classroom, arguing amongst themselves. One asked why they couldn't just drag every kid in the school down to the hospital to have an MRI scan and physical examination to check for mutations. Another replied that there would be widespread protests from the parents if they took 700 plus boys to the hospital without parental consent.

A moment later, they entered the classroom and told our teacher not to mind them because they were just running a routine test. I noticed they were carrying some kind of audio device, but all the same, I was taken completely by surprise when they switched it on and a painfully loud ultrasonic noise stabbed through my head. All I wanted to do was press my fingers into my ears and scream in agony, but I recalled the Chinese gentleman's instructions to hide my ability. So I bit the inside of my cheek until I bled to distract me from the pain.

Little Scotty White wasn't so quick, though. As soon as the ultrasonic sound blasted out, he screamed and doubled over, pressing his hands over his ears. The rest of the kids looked at him in surprise. They hadn't heard the sound, of course. After that, the Custodians switched off the device, grabbed Scotty, and marched him out of the room.

We never saw him again.

Letting my mind return to the present, I found myself resenting these blasted Custodians and their endless attempts to uncover mutants like poor Scotty and myself.

Well, they could go take a long walk off a short pier. I was not going to play into their hands by using my ability today. On the other hand, knowing I couldn't use it left me feeling naked and exposed. If the Custodians hadn't been here, I would have already scoped out the immediate area for any Skel waiting in ambush. I looked up at the ominously dark apartment building that reached up to blot out the overcast sky, and at the trees and bushes that ran wild throughout the street – all perfect Skel hiding spots. I shivered. Today we'd have to do it the hard way.

"You ready, Ethan?" Michal asked as he hefted a sledgehammer over his shoulder.

"Coming." I turned to say one last thing to our valiant Custodian leader. "Oh, Sergeant, try not to stand too close to the building, because we'll be tossing all the copper we find straight out the window, and we don't want a stray piece striking one of you guys on the head."

King glared at me, aware I was both warning and mocking him. "Point taken." He sneered.

I hurried after the others, who were already tramping into the darkened foyer of the apartment building. Bringing up the rear, I walked carefully over a floor covered with shattered glass and caked with windblown dirt. I hesitated a moment for my eyes to adjust. I could see weak light coming in through the windows, but the far end of the foyer, elevator shaft and stairwell were shrouded in darkness.

Shorty moved to the fore and switched on his powerful torch, casting its beam over the room. I reached out a hand to stay him and then clicked my tongue on the roof of my mouth. I'd never used flash sonar, more commonly known as echolocation, in such a mundane manner outside Newhome before. However, with the Custodians waiting outside, I wasn't gonna do it the way I normally did as they could have an ultrasonic detector in the G-Wagon.

"Whatever are you doing, Jones?" Leigh asked.

"Shh, I can't hear nothing if you keep yabbering," I snapped, and went on clicking.

"Hear what?"

By listening to the echoes of my tongue-clicks with my abnormally sensitive hearing, I quickly ascertained there were no Skel in the room; however, a metallic object that had not been there yesterday was near the elevators. I grabbed Shorty's hand and moved the torch beam over to the object I'd detected. It was concealed by a dirty, torn rag, but the thin metal wire than ran from the object to the other side of the room twinkled in the torchlight.

David took a few steps forward, his face alight with excitement. "A Skel booby trap?"

"That's my guess." I resisted the urge to flee the room as fast as I could. I hated Skel booby traps.

"That means Skel are here – we gotta go!" Leigh said in panic as he backed towards the door.

"Not necessarily. It just means they could be in the general vicinity," I said.

"That bomb wasn't there yesterday, which means they saw us and put it there on the off chance we'd be back. And here we are, so let's go!" Leigh wailed. Sometimes he really got on my nerves, always whinging and carrying on. Sometimes I wondered if he had some of Shorty's father's DNA in him.

"I reckon they'll be laying low with those armed Custodians out there," Michal mused.

"David, is it easy to disarm? Or should we just step over the tripwire?" I asked.

"I ain't stepping over no wire," Leigh declared.

"It looks simple enough – keep the torch on it, will you Shorty?" David picked his way slowly over to the rag-covered bomb.

"And we're just gonna stand here while he pokes at it?" Leigh's voice rose an octave higher.

"Relax Leigh." David laughed. "There's nothing to worry about with this one."

"That's what you said with that spring-loaded spear gun..." Leigh said as he backed quickly towards the doorway.

The Skel were ingenious with their booby traps. Once we'd blundered right into one when we were about to move a threadbare sofa aside that was blocking our access to a house. I'd detected the booby trapped spring-loaded spear gun and told everyone to freeze while I studied the trap and tried to work out which members of our party were in danger, and how to get them out of it. At that point, David rushed in and assured us there was nothing to worry about – he'd have the booby trap disabled in a jiffy. Instead, he accidentally set it off. My quick reflexes saved Leigh from getting skewered by the spear gun, but it still grazed his leg on the way past. Twelve stitches later...

"Done!" David announced. In that impossibly small amount of time he had removed the trip wire, pulled the bomb apart and even removed its detonator.

"You're a miracle worker, Mister Chen!" I said as I stepped forward and clapped him on the back. "I knew there was a reason we brought you along."

"Ha ha."

I took the detonator from him and stuffed it in my pocket. Never knew when something like that might come in handy. "Right, up we go!" I announced as I strode without hesitation towards the stairwell.

Leigh was beside me in a moment. "Just keep doing that clicking thing, okay, Jones? I'd rather not get blown up today."

"Just today?" I asked as I pushed open the door to the stairwell and let Shorty take the lead, his torch panning left and right. "Okay guys, ninja mode." I had spent many hours teaching the guys how to move silently through any environment. It was something I worked on throughout my school years – trying to walk so quietly that I couldn't hear my own footsteps – a task that had proven impossible due to my extremely sensitive hearing, but it was great training all the same.

Shorty led the way up the stairs while I followed, clicking at random intervals in the silence of our passage. To our relief, no more booby traps awaited us.

We exited the stairwell on the third floor and entered a long corridor with apartment doors on either side. Those on the right overlooked the side street where the truck and G-wagon were parked. I checked out the first two rooms with tongue-clicks to see if there were any more Skel surprises. Finding none, we set to work.

Shorty, David and Leigh took the first apartment, while Michal and I took the second. The door was already hanging off its hinges, so getting in was a cinch. The foyer, lounge and dining rooms were combined into one large open space. Muted sunlight filtered in through aluminium window frames devoid of glass. And as to be expected, the place was an absolute mess. Plaster panels were hanging from the walls and ceilings, exposing rotting wooden beams. Threadbare sofas that revealed more of their rusting skeletal frames than their original forms were tipped over; and dirt and leaves covered everything.

Michal switched on a battery-powered lamp, led us to the bathroom, and put the lamp on the floor. We set to removing what was left of the plastic and plaster walls with a sledgehammer and crowbar, and then got stuck into the copper plumbing. After a century of neglect, there was no point trying to separate the pipes from their couplings, nuts and unions. Instead, we cut them with a hacksaw, or in Michal's case, smashed them apart with his sledgehammer – brute strength had a subtlety all of its own.

As we worked, I reflected on the unlikely friendship that had blossomed between Michal and me. When he graduated from primary school and started attending high school, Michal was so messed up that I went out of my way to avoid him. That was in spite of my being his senior by one year. On his first day, Michal beat the daylights out of several year niners. It became quickly apparent that he was not only taller than all the other boys, but stronger and more vicious too. We all learned to steer clear of him during recess or lunchbreak. He'd thump just about anyone for even looking at him.

Turned out there was a reason for his violent behaviour – his home life was hell, something I found out after we become close friends by some miracle. Some days he'd come to school with a limp, others he'd struggle doing the woodwork class because one of his arms was too badly bruised to hold the saw. And then there was the time he favoured his ribs for six weeks, causing me to conclude that several had been fractured.

Michal never let on where he got these injuries, but when I considered his refusal to discuss his home life and his insistence that we never visit him at home, the pieces of the puzzle fell into place. When I tentatively broached my suspicions with him one day, he surprised me by admitting what I suspected – his father was a violent alcoholic. He frequently came home drunk and beat up

Michal or his mother. He never touched the younger sister and brother though – probably because Michal always kept them away from his father when he was in one of his alcohol-fuelled rages. He chose to present himself as a target to save his younger siblings the same treatment.

I tried to talk Michal into reporting his father to the authorities, but as fathers in Newhome were considered authority figures second only to the Custodians, he wouldn't hear of it. So I tried to help him in any way I could: a supportive word here, an encouraging word there, and more practically, I'd sneak bandages and healing ointments from home to dress his bruises and fractures.

When he left school at seventeen, Michal was so big that his father stopped hitting him when he was drunk. From then on, his attacks took the form of verbal rather than physical abuse. That was an improvement, but abuse is still abuse.

An hour of strenuous activity passed and Michal and I finally had all the copper on the floor. We scooped it up and headed over to the lounge room windows. Looking down, I saw Sergeant King and two Custodians standing beside the G-Wagon. The other private was still in the vehicle. A smile creased my lips as I imagined myself 'accidentally' tossing the pipes so far out the window that they hit the sergeant on the head.

"You thinking what I think you're thinking?" Michal asked, the corners of his mouth twisting into a smile.

"Absolutely, and you know, it just may be worth dying for," I laughed, before I turned and shouted to the Custodians below. "Incoming!"

And then we tossed the pipes out the window.

This was one part of the job that always gave me immense pleasure – if not a headache as well. The noise made by that many copper pipes when they hit the ground from a third story drop was rather substantial. And even though they had been warned, the Custodians still jumped.

The next job was to strip the copper out of the toilet, but even as I contemplated doing so, a painfully loud bang shattered the still morning air.

The Custodians had heard the sound too, as they had unslung their Austeyr assault-rifles and were looking apprehensively towards Victoria Street.

Michal looked worried.

"Come on, let's check it out," I said as I darted from the apartment. Having heard the explosion as well, our three teammates joined us and we hurried down the corridor together.

I sent a quick look at the others as we ran. "You guys finished stripping out that bathroom yet?"

"Well..." David answered sheepishly.

"Shorty..." I growled.

"Hey, why do you always blame me?" Shorty complained with mock indignation.

"If the boot fits..."

"Yeah, yeah," he mumbled.

We reached the last apartment and barged in, picking our way quickly across the ruined lounge room. Glancing cautiously out the window that overlooked Victoria Street, I was shocked to see two large black cars under attack by Skel. The cars had been heading west towards Newhome and had run straight into an ambush. The lead vehicle had triggered a bomb that blew off its front end and killed the driver and passenger.

The second vehicle had been more fortunate, having escaped the bomb's effects. Its driver and front-seat passenger were using their open car doors as cover while they fired their handguns whenever they thought they spotted a Skel.

Their situation, however, was a hopeless one. Skel armed with crossbows were furtively approaching the car on both sides of the road, using a rusting bus and two derelict cars as cover.

"We've got to help them or they'll be overrun in minutes," I said as I sprinted out of the apartment.

The others raced after me with Leigh at the back and grumbling as usual. "What's with the 'we,' Jones, this ain't got nothing to do with us. Let's get out of here! I ain't never seen that many Skel in one place before!"

"Can we vote on it?" Shorty asked as we practically flew down the stairs and out of the building to meet Sergeant King.

"Sergeant," I said between gasps for breath, "Skel have ambushed two cars a hundred metres up the road. We've got to help them."

"We've got to do no such thing, Jones," the sergeant barked back, clearly offended I had the gall to tell him what to do. "Saddle up people, we're out of here."

Chapter Three

I reached out a hand to stay the sergeant. "Sir, those cars – those people – are heading for Newhome. Surely it's our responsibility to find out where they're from and what they want."

"Jones, this is a foraging operation, not a combat mission. I'll call for reinforcements, but for now, we've got to go. This is not our fight."

"That'll be too late!" I stressed, fully aware that we didn't even have time to stand there arguing. "Sergeant, the guys and I have fought and killed Skel before. This isn't new to us. And," I hesitated, knowing that I was treading on dangerous ground, "we're gonna help them whether you come or not."

Without waiting for King's response, I rushed over to our truck and motioned for my team to join me. "Kit up mates. Looks like we're doing this one on our own."

"Jones..." began Leigh, his eyes wild.

"Shut it," I snapped as we unlocked and opened a large storage box between the truck's cab and bed. We quickly retrieved our five Japanese Hankyu half-bows and quivers full of sharpened arrows that could penetrate Skel bone armour. I found the five-foot-long bows hidden in the basement of a dilapidated Japanese embassy. We also found the full-sized Daikyu seven-foot bows, but the half-bows were more suited for short range use. We strung the bows with practiced ease and tossed the quivers over our backs.

King's eyes were practically popping out of his head. "Civilians are forbidden to possess weapons of any kind! Now hand them over! Get in your truck, and follow us. That's an order!"

The crack of gunfire could still be heard in the distance. We were going have to hurry or there would be no one to save. "Sergeant, it's a different world out here and requires different rules to survive." I turned to my team. "Come on guys. When we get to Victoria Street – Michal, David, Leigh, you go left, Shorty and I'll go right."

We had taken no more than a few steps when King called out again.

"Okay! You've made your point. We'll rescue your blasted visitors. But when we get back home, there'll be a reckoning over this, Jones."

Having almost reached the corner, I turned back to face King. "Sergeant, my lads and I are going enter the buildings on either side of the road and then pop out behind the Skel and give 'em a taste of their own medicine. I strongly suggest you follow us."

The sergeant looked at the decrepit, decaying buildings and shook his head. "Hand-to-hand combat with Skel in dark buildings is not what we signed up for. You want to risk going into the buildings, go ahead, but it's straight down the road for us." With that, the sergeant called the driver out of the G-Wagon and ordered his men to form up beside him.

Now that the driver was out of the G-Wagon, I gave him, the sergeant and the other two, a quick visual going over to make sure none of them were holding portable ultrasonic detectors. I breathed a sigh of relief when I saw that they were not. That meant I could finally use my flash sonar to its full potential. The tables had just turned on the Skel.

Skel are uncivilized savages who live in nomadic tribes. They ambush their victims, and they excel at it, so attacking them frontally was suicide. However, every time my foraging team had gone up against them, we overcame them most successfully by ambushing them.

The lads and I raced over to the corner apartment building and observed the scene unfolding on Victoria Street. Not much appeared to have changed; several Skel were still trying to get the drop on the two men from the second car. Those men would surely be out of ammunition soon and then it would be over.

Keeping my back to the Custodians running up behind us, I shouted several times with my voice pitched above the audio range of what dogs could hear. Anyone watching me would have heard nothing and assumed I was yawning rather violently. That I could create and use ultrasonic echolocation in the same way that bats did was my abnormality. The Custodians said such abnormalities were nuclear-radiation caused mutations of the human genome that would pollute and destroy humanity if not ruthlessly exterminated.

My brain processed the returning ultrasonic echoes as something I could actually see. It also allowed me to see in the dark, in shadows, and even through some materials. I could see someone's heart beating in their chest if I was close enough. The 'sight' created by the ultrasonic echoes was not in colour – it had a surreal effect to it, kind of like a skeletal outline. One major advantage was that it allowed me to see hidden enemy before they even knew I was there. The louder I shouted, the further and more detailed I could see.

Now that I was much more aware of our surroundings, I was ready to act. "Michal, see the corner building that overlooks the cars? There are two Skel with crossbows hiding behind the third window from the right, on the second floor. You three take them out and then provide covering fire for the rest of us."

"Got it," he whispered back. Having one trustworthy person who knew about my gift might not be not so bad after all.

There were another four Skel creeping up on the second car. Shorty and I would slip around behind them and strike them from the rear.

Six more Skel were hiding amongst the ruined bus and cars, popping up now and then to fire their crossbows at the car's defenders. As they were directly in front of the Custodians line of approach, I decided to let them deal with it.

"Okay, let's go!"

Michal, Leigh and David crept silently down the left side of the street, crouching low so as not to be seen as they headed for the corner building's doorway.

Shorty and I bolted across the road and into the abandoned shop on the opposite side. We dashed around rotten wooden benches and over rusting metal chairs strewn about the floor, all the while treading carefully so that we made as little sound as possible. We ran through a kitchen stripped clean of anything even remotely usable by vandals and foragers. From there we ran out a side door into an enclosed courtyard.

We pushed open the rotting wooden door of the adjacent single story brick building and rushed inside, hurrying through several rooms until we reached the foyer. The front door and all of the windows were gone, giving us a fairly good view of the street. In fact, a Skel was using the doorframe as cover from the Custodians, who were advancing up the road, firing short bursts from their assault-rifles.

The sight of the Skel standing there, waiting for his opportunity to murder innocent people, filled me with revulsion and anger.

I used hand signals to tell Shorty to take out the Skel to the left of the doorway outside. I would deal with the two to the right. But first we needed to eliminate the one in the doorway.

I withdrew an arrow, fitted it to the bowstring and raised both arms just above my head. As I lowered my arms, my left arm extended to its full length while my right hand drew the arrow back to my ear. I let go and the modified arrow flew straight and true, striking the Skel in the back and penetrating his hardened bone armour, lodging in his heart. The man collapsed to the ground like a marionette with its strings cut.

"Come on, let's go!" Shorty hissed, his bow drawn and ready.

I notched another arrow and nodded. Shorty sprang lithely through the doorway and turned left to despatch the Skel hiding just a few metres away. I ran out after him, but turned to the right, expecting to see the backs of the two Skel who were advancing on the second black car.

However, the closest one must have noticed his fellow collapse. He had turned around and his crossbow was aimed at my head. I didn't have time to shoot, so I dodged to the right and thrust my bow inside the crossbow's mechanism and twisted up so the weapon was no longer pointing at me.

The Skel shouted a string of expletives and threw his body weight forward as he tried to untangle his weapon from mine. As I struggled to overcome him, I remembered why I loathed fighting these psychotic savages so much. His eyes, which were visible through his garish human-skull helmet, were wide open and bloodshot. His few remaining teeth were black and yellow; his breath stank, and he reeked of open sores, decay and filth. The stench made me gag. His entire body, with the exception of his neck, was protected by hardened human bones. A rib cage protected his chest, a pelvis bone covered his stomach, and smaller bones connected with wire covered any gaps. Even his arms and legs were similarly protected.

I tried to kick his protected his groin. He noticed and countered my kick, driving his armoured leg into my shin, denting it deeply. The pain was so overwhelmingly intense that I couldn't breathe and my vision began to fade as I staggered back, favouring my injured leg.

The Skel yanked his crossbow backward, separating it from my bow. He arched it towards me, but before he could shoot, an arrow swished past my ear and embedded in the Skel's left shoulder. The shock of the impact almost caused him to drop his weapon. I sent a mental 'thank you!' to Shorty for saving my life.

Having regained my breath, I threw my bow at the Skel's head and tore the crossbow from his hands. I rammed it stock first into his skull-like helmet until I heard the bone armour crack and shatter. Blood flowed, and the Skel finally collapsed. It would be some time before he regained consciousness - if at all.

Glancing about apprehensively, I used my flash sonar. I saw that the two men hiding behind the car doors were now lying on the road with crossbow bolts in their chests. The 4WD had two more passengers, and they were hiding between the front and back seats. I watched the third Skel reach the car, fling open the rear-passenger door, and aim his crossbow at the two people inside.

Luckily, the crossbow I had appropriated was still loaded, so I raised the weapon, aimed, and pulled the trigger. The bolt hit the Skel's neck and he went down, his bone armour clattering noisily against the hard ground. He fired his crossbow as he fell, but the bolt flew over the car.

With the Skel no longer an issue – for me at least, I paused to survey the battle. Michal, David and Leigh had overcome the Skel in the building across the road and were preparing to provide covering fire. The Custodians had not fared as well against the Skel. Two were down, slain by crossbows or rusty iron clubs. King and his last man were desperately trying to fend off the last two Skel, who were hacking away at them with animal ferocity. The Custodians must have run out of ammunition as they were now using their guns as clubs.

A massive Skel smashed King's gun out of his hands with such force that the sergeant was knocked over. The Skel lifted his spiked club to finish him off, but five arrows hit him in the back in quick succession, courtesy of Michal, Leigh and David. Four arrows stuck in his bone armour without causing injury, but the fifth penetrated his armour and hit his spine. He keeled over with a scream of rage. Shorty fired several arrows at the last Skel, leaving him looking like a pincushion. The nomad finally went down when one of the arrows struck his exposed neck.

All Skel accounted for, I tossed down the crossbow, retrieved my bow and hurried to the second black car. It was the biggest four-wheel-drive I'd seen, even larger than the Custodian G-Wagon. We didn't have many cars in Newhome, and certainly none like this one. I wondered where these people were from. I was distraught that we hadn't been able to save them all, but relieved we'd managed to save the two who were still hiding in the car.

Chapter Four

I limped over to the car and stepped slowly past the open rear passenger door so I wouldn't appear as a threat. Crouching on the floor between the front and back car seats was a middle-aged Asian man with cropped black hair. He wore a black suit and exuded an air of authority, despite his current predicament. I hazarded a guess that he wasn't Chinese.

I realised he was studying my face as closely as I was studying his. Perhaps he was unsure of our intentions. "And where are you from, young man?" He asked with an accent so peculiar that it took me a moment to work out exactly what he said. In fact, some words I could not quite understand at all.

"I – we – are from Newhome, Sir. You're lucky that we just happened to be in the area today."

His face lit up with hope and he reached out to take my hands. "From Newhome? That is most fortunate!"

"So you were on your way there? That's what I thought. I'm so sorry we couldn't get here soon enough to save your companions," I said as I helped him step down out of the car. His hands were shaking, but I was not surprised considering how close he'd just come to getting skewered by a Skel.

The man bowed. "Please forgive me, but I do not speak English. I am from Hamamachi."

I stared at him in confusion regarding his claim that he couldn't speak English. Apart from his weirdly disturbing accent, he was doing just fine so far. "Oh, you're from the Japanese colony over near Inverloch," I said. From what I knew, the colony was established around the same time as Newhome, by a Japanese whaling fleet that had been working the South Pacific Ocean when the bombs rained down. Rather than return to Japan, which was said to have been completely destroyed, the fleet made landfall near Inverloch and established a colony there.

I handed the Japanese man over to Shorty, and then turned to help the remaining passenger out of the car. And then I froze, dumbfounded. Sitting on the floor between the seats was a teenage girl: seventeen-years-old at a guess, and everything about her blew my mind. Over a black top and a pink-and-blue lace skirt she wore a faded light-blue jacket with black zebra stripes. Her knee-high black boots nearly covered torn pink leggings, and around her neck was a black dog's collar, from which hung a silver bell and a pair of golden rings.

Her black hair barely reached her jaw and curled in to frame her face, while her dark pink bangs reached below her eyebrows. Two much longer locks of pink hair cascaded over her shoulders. The nose ring was another unexpected touch.

However, it was her dark brown eyes that caught my attention – they were completely encircled by thick, black eyeliner, and were studying me intently.

I don't know how long I stood there staring at her, and her me, but she finally flashed me a shy yet encouraging smile as she reached out a small, delicate hand. "I'm Nanako."

"Nice to meet you, Nanako – I'm Ethan," I replied hesitantly as I helped her down. *Nice to meet you?* I berated myself. She had just watched Skel murder four of her companions and had been seconds away from meeting the same fate, and that was all I could think to say?

I didn't realise just how petite she was until she stood beside me – the top of her head only just reached my chin. I stood there, holding her small hand, too confused by her strange appearance to form any coherent thoughts, – let alone speak.

"Thank you for coming to our rescue, Ethan. I was terrified those Skel were gonna..." her voice trailed off. I noticed she spoke with the same, peculiar intonation as her companion, but I was able to understand her a bit better.

"It's okay, it's all over now."

"Did you shoot the Skel that was about to kill Councillor Okada?" she asked.

"Yes, that was me. You speak English very well, by the way."

She tilted her head slightly to one side, and this time spoke with a broad Australian accent. "I wasn't speaking in English."

"You weren't? Then what language were you speaking?"

"Japanese." She eyed me curiously.

I looked at her, astonished. How on earth could I understand Japanese?

"Jones, get over here!" bellowed Sergeant King, interrupting any further attempt at conversation. "Bring the girl. I need her to translate what this guy is trying to tell me."

The sergeant was attempting to talk to the Japanese gentleman, Councillor Okada. Judging by the look on his face, he wasn't getting anywhere. Nanako and I hurried over to them. Well, she hurried, I hobbled. Sergeant King had a huge, bloody gash along his arm. The other surviving Custodian was busy trying to bandage the wound, but King was making it difficult for him by refusing to stand still.

"You're limping, Ethan, are you hurt?" Nanako asked with genuine concern as we joined the others.

"I'm fine, it's just a bruise," I assured her, surprised she had noticed.

Nanako nodded, and then began to translate what her companion was saying to Sergeant King.

Councillor Okada and Nanako were representatives from Hamamachi, and were on their way to Newhome in the hope of initiating trade between our two towns. They had brought with them a sampling of the goods they produced; primarily electronic items like microwave ovens, personal computers, mobile phones and cameras. He also expressed his very deep gratitude that we arrived in the nick of time to save them from the Skel.

The weird thing about listening to Councillor Okada speaking and Nanako translating was that I understood much of what he said before she translated it. And yet somehow, I could barely determine the difference between the two languages, apart from the peculiar accent. Was this was another attribute of my mutation? That I could discern the meaning of any spoken language, even though I had not learned it? Surely that could not be so, but what other explanation was there?

It was a hypothesis I could not test easily. No language other than English was permitted in Newhome since the Custodians had banned multiculturalism. Not multiethnicity, mind you, as Newhome boasted a number of different ethnic groups: the good old Anglo-Saxon 'Aussies' like me, Koreans, Chinese, Vietnamese, Greeks, Italians, Indians, Turkish, and others. However, it was forbidden for the ethnic groups to follow or practise their own culture and customs. The concept was drummed into our heads at school:

> Multiculturalism leads to division
> Division leads to conflict
> Conflict leads to violence
> Violence leads to war
> War leads to extinction

That war lead to extinction was a lesson not lost on the survivors of World War Three, in which the human race was virtually annihilated. All the same, each ethnic group in Newhome rebelled against the banning of multiculturalism in their own way, primarily by only marrying people of their own race. Hence generations after the Apocalypse, the different races were still distinct. For all we knew, the ethnic groups in Newhome could be the last of their race in the world.

When I was in grade two, I asked the teacher what caused the war and which nations were involved. He gave me a vague answer that it was a result of every ethnic group in the world attempting to assert their independence to the extent that every nation became involved. When I asked him which nation or nations had nuked Australia, he told me to stop asking divisive questions or he'd send me to the principal's office. I got the impression that he didn't actually know the answer. Or perhaps he did, but could not reveal the knowledge because people from that nation lived in Newhome. Should that knowledge get out, there could be revenge attacks against the innocent descendants of those responsible for nuking Australia.

To this day, I still don't know the answers to those questions. After becoming a forager, I read countless contraband newspapers, magazines, and books that I found in the ruins. Although I found many articles reporting the global war against fanatical terrorist groups arising throughout the world, I found nothing at all on the nuclear war that practically destroyed the human race. That led me to conclude that the nuclear attack that triggered the war, and the other nations' retaliation, had occurred so suddenly that it left no time for journalists to write newspaper or magazine articles about it. That Melbourne had been left without electricity was no doubt a factor as well. You can't print a newspaper if you can't power up your printing press or digital printers.

"Right!" Sergeant King declared once he had garnered the needed information from Councillor Okada, bringing me back to the present. "We must return to Newhome immediately, otherwise more of those abominations may find us. We will take the bodies of my men and the Japanese escorts back with us. I'm not leaving them for those vultures."

"Michal, fetch the truck. Leigh, help him get all the bodies in the back," I said, agreeing with the need to rush.

"We have to bring the trade samples from the wrecked car too." Nanako pointed to the Japanese car that had triggered the roadside bomb.

"No probs, we'll see to that!" Michal shouted back as he ran back to retrieve our truck.

"And we must destroy this car. We cannot leave it for them," Councillor Okada said as he helped Nanako lift items out of the destroyed car's boot.

"Sergeant King, Councillor Okada says we must destroy this vehicle," Nanako translated.

I pulled the detonator from my pocket and threw it to David. "Reckon you can manage that if you retrieve the Skel bomb you disarmed back there, David?"

"On it!" he shouted and ran off after Michal.

Sergeant King sent the private off to bring back the G-Wagon. Then he, Shorty and I helped Councillor Okada and Nanako – who was surprisingly strong for her diminutive size – unload the samples from the lead car.

"You wounded, Jones?" King asked when he noticed my limp.

"Just a bruise, Sir." Actually, a dented bone and a bruise. It still hurt like blazes.

"You boys handled those Skel like professionals, Jones," King said as we worked.

"Thank you, Sir," I answered cautiously.

"It wasn't a compliment, Jones – makes me wonder what you boys have been doing out here."

"Sir? Surely the amount of metals we bring back answers that question." I tried to rein in my irritation at his veiled accusation. What did he think we were doing, planning a revolution?

"Which is three times more than any other team does."

"In that case, Sergeant, perhaps you need to ask the other teams what they have been doing out here?" I shot back as fear and trepidation took a hold of me again. He was still searching for which one of us was a mutant.

He glared at me. "Got an answer for everything, haven't you, Jones?"

"We're just doing our job, Sir."

King made to leave, but turned back. "Put your weapons in the back of the G-Wagon."

I suddenly felt very vulnerable. How could we forage safely without them? "You're taking them from us, Sir?"

"Let's put it this way – if the other Custodians find them in your truck when we get back, you'll be in a world of hurt just for having them, and so will I for letting you use them."

"Understood, Sir," I acquiesced to his demand. We would part with our precious bows and arrows.

Michal reversed the truck down the road until it drew level with the wrecked 4WD. We loaded the trade samples in the back, and then reverently placed the bodies in there too, covering them with tarpaulins we brought with us. Once that was done, David crawled beneath the wrecked Japanese 4WD and rigged the Skel homemade bomb and detonator to its petrol tank, setting the timer to five minutes. We were lucky the Japanese still used petrol, it made destroying the car a lot easier. All Newhome vehicles were solar powered.

One minute later, our three-vehicle convoy headed off to Newhome. Sergeant King led the way driving the G-Wagon himself. Next came the Japanese car and its two passengers, driven by the Custodian private. We brought up the rear with our weather-beaten truck and its cargo of trade samples and our slain comrades. The copper we stripped from the apartment building lay forgotten in the street.

We hadn't gone far when David's bomb went off, assaulting our ears with a massive bang as a huge, angry fireball soared into the sky behind us. I guess there wasn't much left of the car now.

"Man, did we kick some or what!" Shorty exclaimed excitedly. We had fought Skel four times over the past two years, but never a dozen like today.

"That's 'cause we rock," Leigh added, his face also flushed with excitement – quite in contrast to his pre-combat expression.

"You did good, guys," I said. However, the bodies in the back of the truck drove home an unpleasant thought – if the Japanese had not come when they did, the Skel would have attacked us instead. Since I wasn't using my flash sonar, that would be our bodies in the back of the truck. On the other hand, the fact that the Skel had set up an ambush, complete with bombs directly in the Japanese convoy's path worried at the edges of my mind. Something wasn't right.

I brought my left leg to my chest and gingerly explored my shin. The dent in the bone was quite noticeable and even now, it still throbbed with pain. Associated with the injury were memories of the Skel who had caused it, sending shudders of revulsion through me.

Looking to the Japanese car in front of us, I was surprised to see the girl turn and glance at us – well, not at us but at me. Her brown eyes locked with mine for an instant. An expression I could not decipher fled quickly across her round face before she turned away.

Suddenly a crystal-clear image flashed in my mind. An image of several pairs of slippers, shoes and high-heeled black boots, arranged neatly in rows across a polished wooden floor. I was hit by an overwhelming feeling that this exact situation, right down to its smallest detail, had occurred previously. I instantly rebelled against this – for I knew that was not impossible. As I tried to wade through the implications of what I had just experienced, a sharp metallic taste filled my mouth, followed immediately by a sensation of falling from a great height.

I grabbed the truck's dashboard to steady myself, but almost as soon as it began, the sensation ceased. Intense pain exploded through my stomach, and then vanished. As if that wasn't enough, the unnerving episode concluded with every nerve ending in my body spiking with adrenaline. It felt like thousands of ants had bitten me.

The entire occurrence, from image to adrenaline spike, had taken perhaps a few seconds, but the after effect was weird. I felt as if I'd woken from a very deep and exhausting sleep.

"You okay, Ethan?"

I looked at Michal, who was glancing at me as he drove.

"I...uh, I'm just tired, I guess," I replied. I mean, what else could I say — I had absolutely no idea what just happened. It defied all logic. The vision made no sense, for I had never seen that polished floor, shoes, boots or slippers. Was my mind reacting to the most stressful day of my life? Or, and I shuddered to consider this disturbing possibility, was it a premonition of some sort?

Whatever it was, I never, ever wanted to experience it again.

Chapter Five

"Hey, check it out, that girl keeps glancing at us," said Leigh as our three-vehicle convoy reached the end of Victoria Street and turned right to head north up Dryburgh Street.

"Did you see her clothes? She looks like a doll!" Shorty exclaimed.

"And her hair? What's with the pink?" Leigh laughed.

"Hey, don't knock her, mate. I wish Newhome girls were permitted to dress like that," David said.

"Can you imagine the Custodians reaction? They'd go psycho," Leigh agreed.

"Hey! You reckon all the girls are like her where she comes from? What's the place called?" Shorty asked.

"Hamamachi," I replied.

"Right – 'cause if they are, next chance I get I'm going AWOL and heading straight there. And I ain't never coming back!" Shorty vowed.

"She's not looking at us," Michal said after a moment. "She's looking at Jones."

That brought a chorus of ribbing and jokes from the three in the back seat. I looked at Michal and sighed, but truth be told, the corners of my mouth had turned up ever so slightly. My life would be rather dull without those three clowns to liven it up. The 'Dour Duo,' that's what they called Michal and me. I guess that summed us up pretty well. I hadn't always been so glum, though.

I'm pretty sure I had a more positive outlook on life before that ceiling fell on my head just after I turned eighteen. I have no memory of the event, just a gaping hole in my mind that covers pretty much my whole eighteenth year. My father told me the injury caused shocking epileptic seizures as well as chronic amnesia. All I remember is how I felt when I woke from the operation that healed me of those afflictions – disorientated, confused, and empty. It was like my life was only a shell of what it had been before.

I glanced at the 4WD in front of us again and concluded that Michal was right. Nanako was only glancing at me. Moreover, on occasion it was more like a long stare, causing me no small amount of discomfort.

I had seen very few girls in my life. Just my sisters and glimpses of those attending the Solidarity Festivals held several of times a year.

Thanks to the male-dominant, oppressive society the Founders created when they established our town a hundred years ago, girls were not permitted to attend school. Rather, they stayed home to learn practical skills from their mothers such as needlework, food preparation, and house cleaning. For that reason, I didn't know how to respond to Nanako's attention, and I was the one who broke eye contact.

Why was she looking at me anyway? Was it because I saved her life? Perhaps she thought I was an accomplished soldier? If that was the case, she would soon learn the truth – I was nothing but a school dropout and lowly forager.

As Dryburgh Street merged into Macauley Road, I ran my fingers along the scars on the left side of my head. My hair covered them now, but when I got my next buzz-cut, they would be visible for the whole world to see.

When we reached the town's eastern gates, some rather astonished Custodians spoke at length with Sergeant King before giving the vehicles a once over. Satisfied, they opened the gates and let us through.

King led us through streets lined with ominous row after row of grey ten-story blocks of flats; past the commercial district with its market stalls, green grocers, hardware and department stores and clothing shops. These were frequented by everyone except the North Enders.

We drove past a massive billboard on the side of the road. Below the slogan *'Play Your Role in Creating a Better Tomorrow'* was a picture depicting a group of contented men – factory workers, farmers, teachers and students. Beside them, equally contented women and girls were portrayed in the home, cooking, sewing, and cleaning.

I wondered what our Japanese guests thought of the billboard, and of the others like it we drove past on our way through the town. That the Japanese sent a female translator along with Councillor Okada could indicate that their society is not as male-dominated as ours.

After that we passed the greenhouse enclosed market gardens and finally reached the imposing walls of North End. This was where our world ended and the VIPs' world began — a world that could have been mine had I chosen to live in it. However, as far as I was concerned, a well-to-do prison was still a prison.

North End occupied the land north of what had once been the Flemington Racecourse. The austere, grey-concrete walled factories of the industrial sector had been built over the top of the racecourse itself.

Our convoy stopped before North End's gates. King got out to talk to the officer in charge and then sauntered over to our truck. "Hop out boys, we'll take it from here."

"What do we do now?" I asked King as we clambered out of the truck, seething with anger at the impertinence of the stuck-up North Enders. They wouldn't even let us drive our own truck in there!

King rewarded us with a forced smile. "You get the rest of the day off."

"Our pay better not get docked because of this," I grumbled louder than I should have.

The sergeant looked me in the eye and raised his eyebrows. "Is that right?"

I knew I should have backed down, but I was sick and tired of kowtowing to the Custodians. "You've got our truck, Sir. We can't go back to work."

"Tell you what, since you're so concerned about it, I'll give your boss a call later and fill him in."

I did not know if he meant it or not, but I gave him the benefit of the doubt. "Thank you, Sergeant."

"Right then. You lot are dismissed. But don't worry, I'll have your truck back to the yard by day's end, so it's work as usual tomorrow. Now, Jones, a word with you," King said.

My teammates backed off, leaving me standing alone with King. I tried to meet his gaze, but instantly regretted it. Now I was gonna pay for today's list of misdemeanours.

"Not only did your team have weapons – which by itself can get you a three year prison sentence – but you disobeyed my direct orders today and put my squad and your team at risk," King growled in my face. "Give me one reason not to lock you up right now, Jones."

I had gotten away with blue murder today and I knew it, but one wrong word now could put me away for years. "My sincerest apologies, Sergeant, but had we left when you said, Councillor Okada and his translator would have been killed. We wouldn't have known about Hamamachi's attempt to trade with us. As soon as I saw their big black cars, I knew something important was going down."

"The results never justify the means, Jones."

"We did save your life, Sir," I added somewhat hesitantly.

"Which was only placed in jeopardy by your disobedience and recklessness!"

"As I said, I'm sorry, Sir."

"Just make sure you never pull a stunt like that again, you hear me?"

"I won't, Sir."

"You'd better not. Now get out of my sight." Having said his piece, King strode away to join his fellow Custodians.

I watched him go, mystified by his inexplicable behaviour. A Custodian would never let off someone who had committed such blatant misdemeanours with nothing more than a verbal dressing down.

I rejoined my work mates and Michal grabbed my arm and pulled me to him. "What's wrong with you today, Ethan? You wanna get locked up or something? Why King hasn't already done so, I don't understand."

"I just couldn't let the Skel kill those Japanese," I argued.

"I'm not talking about that," Michal said. "I'm talking about you giving lip to King."

"Hey, don't cramp his style." Leigh laughed as he slapped me on the back. "He gave that Custodian what's what, he did."

"Be more careful, okay?" Michal said as he shoved Leigh back with a hand on his face.

I nodded, and the five of us turned to make our way home. As we walked away, I looked back one last time to see if the Japanese girl would glance at me again. To my surprise, she was watching me, concern etched on her face. I wondered if I should wave or something, since I'd probably never see her again. Not knowing what to do, I returned her stare until she was out of sight.

"Hey, let's head back to my pad and watch the box and play cards," Leigh suggested. Like me, he had worked long enough to be able to rent a two-room flat. No one owned property in Newhome – it was all rented from the town council.

The others all replied in the affirmative to Leigh's invitation, but having the rest of the day off afforded me an opportunity to do something I was rarely able to do – and that was to see my twelve-year-old sister during the daytime.

* * *

An hour later, I was behind the block of flats in which my parents lived. I had a small bag on my back. I checked carefully for Custodian patrols. If they caught me scaling up the back of the building and creeping into a woman's bedroom, I would be in a world of trouble. No male was ever permitted in a woman's bedroom, except her husband, and then only on nights when he…well, where my parents were concerned, that wasn't a thought I was gonna entertain.

Seeing no Custodians, I began the ascent to my family's third-floor flat. Using balcony floors and railings, I could climb quite quickly, hauling myself up from one floor to the next. Of course, if anyone looked out their back window at that moment they would see me. The same applied to the inhabitants in the next block of flats, since the buildings were built close to one another.

I reached the third story and clambered over the railing covered with doonas – my mother always hung them out to air them. I threaded my way through the clothes horses covered with drying garments.

I slipped into the women's bedroom, since the door was never locked, and quietly closed it behind me. Waiting for my eyes to adjust to the darkness, I could hear Mother and Elder Sister moving about in the kitchen, and the shallow breaths of Younger Sister, who was in bed. Her name was Meredith, but as a sign of endearment, family members did not use each other's names, but their kinship classifications. The Founders gave us this system, saying it would draw families closer together and prevent division. I never thought twice about it until I started reading books when foraging. Now I realise it may be a custom peculiar to our town.

"Got the day off, have you?" Younger Sister asked.

My eyes had adjusted enough to see her now. I went and sat on the edge of her bed, which was the one closest to the windows. Elder Sister's bed was next to hers, and Mother's beside the door. With two tallboy chests of drawers against the wall opposite the beds, there really was little space left in the room.

A plate with a couple of golden crumpets sat virtually untouched on her bedside table – the remains of her breakfast. "Yep, our truck's in for repairs, and we can't do much without it." Which was close enough to the truth.

"You'll have to put it in for repairs more often." She smiled.

"Sounds like a plan." I laughed as I leaned forward to examine the sores at the corners of her mouth. They were definitely worse than the last time I saw her. She was paler as well. I opened the backpack and handed her a tube of antiseptic cream. "Rub this into your sores three times a day."

"Okay," she replied somewhat dubiously.

I dug into the backpack again and took out two plastic containers and some mandarins. "I got you some lunch." Younger Sister looked at the grilled chicken, tofu, bread, and fresh veggies, and shook her head. "Oh no, I can't eat it, Older Brother. You spend too much of your money buying me these lunches!"

"Yes you can, and no I don't." I smiled. I opened the containers and laid them out for her, handing her the plastic fork.

"But chicken is so expensive."

As all of our food was grown in Newhome, we rarely had meat. The only 'animals' raised here for food were chicken – raised by the thousands in the poultry shed. All the same, it was expensive.

Younger Sister stabbed a piece of diced chicken breast, nibbled at it, and then put it back.

"What's wrong? Isn't it nice?" I asked, frustration and helplessness adding to the fear that rose up within me every time she refused to eat.

"It's nice, but I'm just not hungry," she said softly, refusing to meet my gaze.

I looked at the nutritious food I had laid before her and despaired. "Younger Sister, for your health – please eat."

She took a small bite of carrot and returned the rest to the container. Next was a bite of bread, after which she lay back against the bedhead.

"You can't stop there, you've barely touched it." I tried but failed to knock the frantic edge off my voice.

"I'll have some later," she said, which probably meant she wouldn't eat it at all. And that created a problem. If Mother found out I was bringing her food she would not be impressed. On the other hand, she had never eaten much of the food I brought her, and Mother had not mentioned it yet.

I took her hand in mine and brushed my thumb over her upward curving nails. I decided to talk about something other than her refusal to eat, which was driving me insane. "You been reading those books and magazines I got you?" Sometimes I found contraband books when I foraged for metals, and would smuggle them to her to read.

"Oh yes – and I just loved that teenage girl's magazine. When I can find the energy, I sit in front of the mirror and practice the braids and plaits the girls in the magazine are wearing." She paused and then pouted as she continued. "I can't believe the world used to be so full of life, Older Brother – people free to go where they liked, able to own so many things – even their own apartments, and wear such bright and colourful clothes, and having the most remarkable adventures!"

"It was a different world back then, that's for sure," I agreed as I stood. A different world, but not a better one, if you consider where it got us. "I better go before Mother or Elder Sister comes in and catches me here."

"Please, don't go yet," she pleaded.

I never could say no to her – her sickly life was so lacking I'd do anything to cheer her up – so I sat back on the bed. We chatted softly about the books she had read, and of the things that I found when I went foraging. Finally, I really had to go. I lifted her chin until her brown eyes met mine. "Please, for me, eat the lunch I brought you?"

She looked down at the barely touched food. "I'll try."

Powerless to help her, and driven to distraction by it, I caressed her pale cheek with the back of my fingers. Then I slipped out of the bedroom, over the balcony, and climbed down to ground level.

Mother rang me earlier this morning and insisted I have dinner with the family tonight. Perhaps that would give me the opportunity to talk to Father about my younger sister's health, which had clearly deteriorated since the last time I saw her. She needed to see a doctor.

Chapter Six

That evening I sat with my father in the family dining room at a table that could seat six, but due to our town's custom of women waiting on the men while they ate, my mother and older sister, Ruth, stood at the doorway where they would remain until summoned.

The somewhat subservient role of women in our town was one of many customs given us by the Founders. During the Solidarity Festivals, the Chancellor and councillors drummed into our heads the value of our unique culture. They explained how the Founders had created a completely new society, built from the ground up. A society that would not foster misunderstanding, anger and resentment. A harmonious society rather than one characterised by division, conflict and violence. Because of this, our town would not make the same mistakes our ancestors made – mistakes that lead to war and eventually, worldwide obliteration.

I refused to believe any of that nonsense. Surely it was the fear of the Custodians and the magistrates' harsh sentences that kept the town's population in line. It had nothing to do with treating the womenfolk as second-class citizens.

I went back to examining my parent's flat.

The combined dining/lounge room was rectangular, stretching the full width of the flat, with monotonous, unadorned duck-egg blue walls. The lounge, which was to the right of the front door, had beige sofas and a 42" flat-screen TV. The dining room, to the left of the door, contained the dining table and a large wooden hutch full of Mother's precious collection of china cups, bowls and plates.

I finished a bowl of lentil soup and got stuck into a slice of homemade whole-grain bread topped with melted tasty soy cheese. Glancing at my father, I wondered what frame of mind he was in today. People said I took after him in appearance, with his square jaw, high cheekbones, and full head of thick auburn hair. We were even the same height, though my figure had yet to fill out. Thankfully, that's where our similarities ended. He adhered religiously to Newhome's customs and traditions, and with Tunnel-vision devoted himself to the councillors who ran the city. He also had little patience and no time for those who did not share his opinions. As I disagreed with him on practically everything, we didn't get on. My deepest fear was that I might turn out like him one day.

"Son, I heard we had some visitors from another town today," Father said gruffly between bites.

"Yeah, two people from the Japanese colony over near Inverloch. My foraging team and Custodian escort found them and brought them here," I replied.

I thought he would be at least a little impressed by my claim to fame, but his expression as he actually met my gaze was not a complimentary one.

"You stay away from them, you hear?"

I could not be bothered getting into another "I'm-over-eighteen-now-Father" argument, as we normally did after he ordered me to do something I considered unreasonable. I settled for, "Don't worry, the Custodians took them straight to North End."

"Good," he grunted as he served himself another dish of vegetable casserole.

I figured now was as good a time as any to broach the subject of my sister. "Ah, Father, Younger Sister is not looking so good these days – I think she needs to see a doctor."

"Younger Daughter just needs to snap out of it and pull herself together," he said to me. He aimed the next comment at Mother, standing deferentially at the doorway. "She's just lazy; it's as simple as that."

"Have you seen her lately, Father? The sores on her mouth, her white skin and shallow breathing, and finger nails growing upward? There is something wrong with her."

"Ethan, you're young and naive. Those sores are caused by lying in bed all day for month after month. Mother needs to stop mollycoddling her and show her some tough love. Otherwise, no one's ever going to want to marry her and I'll be stuck with her for life – a leech sucking up my money forever. Besides, we can't afford a doctor."

I glanced at Mother, whose eyes were glazing over with tears, while I trembled with rage at the callous insults directed at his own daughter! I wish I could put him through what she goes through for just one day. He'd change his tune soon enough.

"Why can't you afford it, where does all your money go?" I demanded.

Mother's eyes widened in shock and she shook her head ever so slightly, warning me away from this conversation. Unfortunately, it was too late. Father pushed his plate away and turned to face me, trembling with barely controlled rage. "Where does all my money go? You really want to know, do you, Son? Okay then, every spare cent I earn, after the food and rent, goes to pay back a fifteen year loan I had to take out."

"Take out – take out on what?" I was too angry to heed Mother's warning – she was still shaking her head.

"On you!" my father shouted. "For your operation! Remember the brain surgery you needed after that ceiling fell on your head two years ago!"

Suddenly I felt like the world's biggest fool. I'd accused him of wasting his money, only to find out he was spending it all on me. "I...I didn't know. Father, why didn't you tell me?"

"I did what had to be done, what's to tell?" he huffed.

My shoulders slumped in resignation, but I tried one last half-hearted attempt to help my sister. "In that case, let me help pay off the loan, or at least pay for her visit to a doctor."

That, apparently, was the worst thing I could have said. "I do not need your financial aid like I am some...some charity case!" he bellowed.

Head bowed in defeat, I tucked into my dinner until half was left, and then gave my mother a meaningful glance. The women of a household always served the best food to the males and ate less costly foods and any leftovers themselves. So when I had dinner with my family, I always left half my dinner on the plate so that my mother and sisters could divide it amongst themselves later.

That done, I bade them farewell.

My father's anger would simmer for the rest of the evening, but tomorrow he'd act as though the whole conversation had never happened.

I couldn't turn my emotions on and off like that, so I walked away torn by powerful, conflicting emotions. I was angry with my father for being so obstinate, for refusing to acknowledge my sister's health problems. His arrogance and pride was robbing her of a normal life. On the other hand, I felt so guilty for believing Father didn't care for me. I could see now that he did. The proof was the massive loan to finance the operation that healed me of the epilepsy caused by the head injury.

That my father cared for me sent my mind spinning, causing me to re-evaluate my opinion of him. I'd concluded years ago that he didn't care for me. I mean, throughout my life he never really did anything with me. When he wasn't at work, he'd come home and lose himself in a newspaper or the television. When I reached my adolescent years and shed my fear of him, we began to argue about nearly everything. When I flunked the year eleven exams and had to leave school, he flew into such a rage that he came within an inch of tearing my head off – literally. He didn't know I'd failed deliberately, so had jumped to the conclusion that it was a result of slothfulness and that galled him all the more. If I'd told him the truth, he would have hit me, I'm sure of it.

One of the greatest causes of contention between us was my choice of vocation. Father had lofty ideas for what I could do, and took offense at my choice of such a demeaning and dangerous job. Once we argued so vigorously that a neighbour banged on our door to complain. That was one of the most humiliating moments of my life, and an eye opener. I realised I could not keep living like this – arguing with my father one minute and put down by my older sister the next, so the day I turned twenty I rented a flat.

My father didn't like that, either. Took it like a personal attack accused me of abandoning the family. Getting married was the only justifiable reason for a child to leave their family, he had shouted in my face. All that did was convince me I'd made the right choice.

When I got home after a short walk, I climbed the apartment block's ten flights of stairs up to the building's flat roof, using the exercise to clear my mind and rid my body of tension.

It was refreshingly cool up on the roof and comfortably shrouded in near-darkness. The only light sources were the light above the stairwell exit and the stars.

I collected the disassembled parts of my contraband binoculars, which I had hidden in three different places on the roof, and fitted them back together. One advantage of my vocation was that I could find almost anything in the city ruins.

I sat down on the long side of the roof that faced north-west and dangled my legs over the edge. (There was no guardrail.) I used the binoculars to zoom in on North End – sometimes I looked over the city walls at Melbourne's darkened ruins, but spying on North End was more fun. It was like another world in there, with larger and better-furnished apartments. There were immaculately kept, multicolour brick footpaths instead of crumbling and cracked ones like ours, and jungle gyms built like castles in the school yards. There were cinemas with facades lit up with sparkling lights; nightclubs where you didn't have to line up to gain access; and, to top it all off, no curfew. There were multistorey buildings devoted to scientific, genetic and engineering research and development, and the council offices themselves were magnificently opulent. Men and teenage boys wandered the paved streets as they chatted and headed to nightclubs to play cards, billiards, bowling, and drink.

The clubs were all-male affairs, of course – no woman was permitted on the streets after dark, not even with a chaperone. The Founders created this rule, saying it was for our protection. That by keeping women at home after dark kept them safe from males who may be struggling with temptation. It also protected the males by removing the source of temptation. Yeah, right. I often thought of my mother and sisters, stuck at home, while we guys went out and hit the restaurants and clubs. Didn't seem fair to me.

I often wondered what my life would be like had I chosen to live in North End instead of out here. My life as it was, wasn't a particularly happy or fulfilling one. There was a deep, aching hole in me that gnawed endlessly at my mind and emotions, threatening to pull me into a miry pit from which there was no escape. I hadn't always been like that. Before the injury and operation, I was more positive and resilient. I was sure of it.

The only time I felt at peace was when I was out there, rooting through the ruins looking for metals, and – ahem, doing all the other extracurricular activities we engaged in once we'd filled our truck. We had archery competitions, practised stealth techniques by playing hide and seek, and explored old buildings. Once we even found an amazing stash of guns. That was fun. There's an old billboard out there that will never be the same. We also unearthed and read old books and magazines that had not perished over the decades.

As I continued to search aimlessly through North End, I almost dropped my precious binoculars when I spotted the Japanese girl, Nanako, sitting on the flat rooftop of a North End apartment block. She was sitting with her back against the stairwell exit, cradling her knees to her chest. I zoomed in closer and gasped when I saw she was crying, her black eyeliner running down her cheeks.

Was her sorrow due to having endured such a terrible day – ambushed by barbaric Skel and seeing four of her people slaughtered? That was probably the case, though as I examined her I thought I recognised something of my own despondency in her forlorn expression. I wondered if she was weighed down by an impossibly heavy burden. I wished there was something I could do to lift her spirits, to help her carry whatever it was that weighed her spirits down.

My reflections were interrupted when I heard several pairs of feet scurrying up the stairwell behind me, followed by the door banging open.

"Ha! Told you he'd be here." Shorty laughed as he emerged. Then he began doing cartwheels around the roof, as was his habit. (A roof, that is ten stories up and has no guardrail.) Leigh, David, and Michal emerged next, each smiling broadly when they saw me.

Okay, I admit it, there was one other time I forgot about the emptiness that haunted me, and that was when I was with these four goofballs. "Hey guys, what happened, got sick of cards?" I stood and went over to join them.

"Not the same without you, mate," Leigh said as he thumped me on the back.

"And," David added as he took off his backpack, "it's not windy tonight, so I suggested that we – wait for it – have another paper plane war!"

"And there's nothing like seeing them Custodians picking up the planes in the morning and scratching their beefy heads, trying to work out where they came from," Shorty laughed after he cart wheeled over to us.

"Hey Jones, if the Custodians catch you with those." Leigh gestured at my binoculars. "You're gonna be in trouble with a capital 'T,' mate."

"Hey, can I have a go?" Shorty smiled deviously.

"Why? What do you want to look at?" I asked, suspicious.

"You can see into people's apartments, yeah?"

"I guess so."

"Into women's bedrooms," he continued in a most conspiratorial manner.

"Probably." I tried hard to remain serious.

"Then hand 'em over, Jones me boy," Shorty said as he held out a small hand.

"Ain't no way you're using my binoculars to be a Peeping Tom," I said. However, there was another reason, too; I didn't want him to see Nanako crying.

"A peeping who?"

"It's an expression. It means...oh, never mind," I said.

"Please," Shorty begged.

"There's a reason these things are banned," I pointed out, looking down at his over eager face.

"Yeah, and that's to stop us spying on North End and seeing what we're missing," said David, flicking his head to the north.

"I won't do that, honest," Shorty said sincerely.

"I've no doubt that's the real reason, David," I said. He'd hit the nail on the head. "But Shorty, seriously, would you want people spying on your mother and sister in their bedroom?"

"Ewww, of course not. Look, I promise I won't spy on anyone, I'll observe them for purely educational purposes."

"I. Ain't. Letting. You. Use. 'Em."

"You're no fun," he pouted.

David held up a sheet of blank paper and shook it. "Guys, focus. Paper plane time!"

"I'm in, hand over a sheet," Michal said.

We mobbed David and grabbed sheets of paper, moved back to the stairwell exit so we could see, and set to work with frenetic zeal. Several minutes later, we stood in a line one step back from the edge of the roof.

"Putting a stone in the nose of your plane is cheating, Shorty," David said.

"Hey, what? Why, that would be dishonest, David. I give you my word there is no stone in my plane."

I leaned forward and clicked my tongue a couple of times. "Will you look at that, David, Shorty's telling the truth – he didn't put a stone in his plane."

"You see."

"He put in a piece of metal," I said.

Shorty looked up at me. "I don't like that clicking thing you do, Jones."

"We throw on the count of three!" David announced. "One. Two. Three. Throw!"

Five paper planes flew off the roof. Shorty's lead-nose plane flew straight and true, flying maybe twenty metres before it hit the road down below. Leigh's landscape-orientated plane was blown straight up by the slight updraft from the front of the building and disappeared behind us. Mine corkscrewed in a northerly direction, while Michal's long, narrow plane almost gave Shorty's a run for its money. However, the plane that got our attention was David's – tiny red and green lights at its wing tips blinked on and off as it sailed into the night.

"David, how did you...?" Michal stammered, voicing what we were all thinking.

"Trade secret."

"David, it's a piece of flat paper! How did you get lights in it?" Shorty demanded, upset his winning throw had been upstaged.

"Round two!" was David's come back.

We made paper planes of all shapes and sizes and tossed them off the roof for another fifteen minutes, littering the ground below with them, but then called it quits. If a Custodian night patrol was to spot us on the roof, we'd find ourselves in a spot of bother.

"There's something I've been meaning to discuss with you, Ethan," Michal said after we'd plonked ourselves down beside the stairwell exit.

"Okay, shoot."

"If you're ever gonna do what I think you're planning to do, you gotta tell us before you do it," he said.

"Can I have that in English please?"

"What Michal's trying to say, Jones," David explained, "is that if you're planning on doing a runner one day, you gotta give us advance warning so we can come with you if we want to."

"We talking about going jogging or something?" Shorty whispered to Leigh.

"No, dufus, they're asking Jones to let us know if he's gonna make a run for it when we're out foraging one day," Leigh explained.

"As much as I'd like to do a runner, it's not on my current list of things to do," I replied.

"Why ever not? What's here that makes you wanna stay?" David demanded.

"My kid sister."

"She still sick?" Michal asked.

"Yeah."

"What's that got to do with you?" Leigh asked.

"He buys her food – good food – and other stuff she needs," Michal answered for me.

"Why can't your mother do that?" Shorty asked.

"She can't afford it."

"That sucks."

"I know."

"All the same, you gotta tell us if you're gonna change your mind, okay?" David said. "You've got a knack for spotting Skel ambushes, so if we were to make a run for it together, I reckon we'd make it."

"What about the Custodians, you forgettin' they're with us every day now? Trying to make a run for it won't be so easy now," Leigh reminded us.

"We could lose them with our eyes closed," David said.

"And with our hands tied behind our backs," Shorty added, giving David a high-five.

I held up my hands. "I hear what you're saying, so yeah, if I'm ever gonna do a runner, I'll let you know first. Just don't hold your breath, okay? It's not gonna happen anytime soon."

"Aw man, that sucks. I was getting all excited for a moment there," Shorty pouted.

We kept chatting for a while and then I bade the others good night and sent them back downstairs, mostly because I had to disassemble the binoculars and hide the pieces, but also because I wanted to check on the Japanese girl.

She was still there, sitting with her back against the stairwell exit. She had put on a pair of very odd-looking goggles – they were opaque and had a button on the side, which she kept pressing from time to time. I must confess I was perplexed. I'd never seen anything even remotely similar to them.

I was about to call it quits when for a second time that day a vision-strength image burst into my mind. This time of a narrow walking track in the bush I'd never seen before. Gum trees grew on both sides, and the track was overgrown with ferns, wild grass, sticks and leaves. Once again, a powerful feeling of déjà vu persuaded me that this experience – of seeing this image while standing on the roof, had happened before. Bewildered, I tried to reason that it couldn't possibly be true, but then came the metallic taste followed by the sensation of falling. And like this morning, the strange attack concluded with intense stomach pain and every nerve ending in my body spiked with adrenaline.

I half sat, half collapsed onto the roof, breathing heavily as I waited for the after effects of the horrific experience to fade away. What was happening to me?

I had been in the bush on foraging trips in the past, but never on a bushwalking track. Was this a premonition of the future, about an event that was going to happen?

I lingered on the roof for another hour until, exhausted and sleepy, I stumbled down the eight flights of stairs to my flat. I could have used the elevator, but that would've meant breaking my vow to never use it. Stairs were an excellent medium for staying in shape.

Chapter Seven

The next morning I was surprised when I strolled into the Recycling-Works yard and saw our truck was back. Looking unaffected by its trip into North End as well. As I walked over to join my workmates, I ran my eyes along the battered body. Memories of yesterday's encounters with the Skel and the Japanese ran through my mind. I hoped today would be a bit less exciting.

There was no sign of Sergeant King and his Custodians. In fact, we might even be sent a different squad since King lost half his men yesterday.

As if summoned by my thoughts, a Custodian Bushmaster Protected Mobility Vehicle roared down the street and backed slowly into the yard, parking parallel with our truck. The Bushmaster looked like a box on wheels, but from what I heard, it was bulletproof, impervious to mines, and coated with fire retardant paint. It was also very, very old – all our Bushmasters pre-dated the Apocalypse. Just about every part of them had been reconditioned or replaced at some stage over the years.

"Looks like they're expecting Skel today," Michal said dryly.

"Yeah, got a bit of a shock yesterday, they did." Shorty laughed.

"Two of them also got a bit dead." I reminded them.

The Bushmaster's rear door swung open on well-oiled hinges – and wouldn't you know it – out stepped Sergeant King, ready and willing to face the Skel again. My respect for the guy went up a notch.

Trajan, the boss, rushed outside to talk to King, no doubt thanking him for his squad's wonderful effort in saving my team yesterday. I wonder what he'd say if he found out it was the other way around.

Hearing light footsteps in the street outside piqued my interest. I turned around and froze in shock when Nanako walked into the yard with Councillor Okada trailing behind her. She held a small, black box wrapped in a checked-pattern handkerchief.

Upon spying me, her petite, round face lit up with joy and she hurried over to me. She bowed briefly and held out her hands. "I made this for you."

I looked down at the beautiful lacquered wooden lunchbox and had no idea what to do. Just seeing her, a single girl, out here in the streets of Newhome – albeit with a chaperone – was a concept so unfamiliar that my mind whirled in confusion.

"For me?" was all I could think to say.

"It's obento." She nodded to encourage me to accept the home-cooked lunch.

Michal gave me a gentle shove, whispering, "Go on, accept it, you drongo."

I stumbled forward a step and took the beautiful lunchbox, trying not to stammer. "This is wonderful. Thank you, Nanako."

Sergeant King chose that moment to interrupt, casting a questioning glance at Nanako and Councillor Okada. "Okay boys, the day's not getting any younger. Saddle up and move out!"

He could have at least greeted them, the unsociable sod.

We clambered into the truck and as Michal drove, Nanako walked to the gate with Councillor Okada. She stood there quietly, watching us drive off. I flashed her a warm smile and waved, clutching her unexpected gift with my other hand. She bowed, and held it until we were out of sight.

As we headed for the town gates, I wondered what had prompted her to give me such a gift. Did she feel indebted to me for saving her life yesterday? If that was the case, I had to tell her that she didn't owe me anything. It had been my honour to save her from the Skel.

It took us multiple stops and almost the whole morning to find a source of non-corrosive metals to strip out. There was no way we were gonna return to the Victoria Street apartments, and I couldn't risk using my flash sonar again. We eventually found a virtual gold mine in a street of ransacked one-story houses. They still had their external gas hot water systems.

The Custodians gave the work site a quick once over when we arrived and then retired to the Bushmaster, where one of them operated the roof mounted machine gun at all times.

After we had removed and disassembled several hot water systems to cannibalise the parts we wanted, my watch chimed one o'clock.

My workmates and I ripped off our gloves, wiped our hands clean with antibacterial hand wipes, and climbed onto the truck's bonnet or roof to eat, just as we did every day.

Sitting cross-legged on the bonnet, I carefully removed the handkerchief from the lacquered lunchbox, aware that my workmates looked on with baited breath. I lifted the lid and gasped. The partitioned tray was filled with a whole host of painstakingly prepared delicacies, the likes of which I had never seen. There were tomato slices with sculptured rabbit ears, slices of carrot carved into flowers, and marinated chicken pieces. There were slices of bread curled about beans, tendrils of fried fish, and even rolls of scrambled egg. Beneath this tray was another, this one filled with fruits and vegetables, each imaginatively presented.

"Well, do we share?" I asked.

"Get real," Michal laughed, "She made it for you, Ethan. We ain't gonna touch it."

"Hey, speak for yourself," Shorty complained.

"Yeah, I think I'd sign up for some of that," David agreed.

Michal glared at the others and they quickly backed down.

"I think she likes you." Shorty ribbed me with a knowing smile.

"Don't be ridiculous."

"Well, come on, if you ain't gonna share it, taste it and tell us what it's like," David demanded impatiently.

And so began the most delightful culinary experience of my life. "It tastes even better than it looks!" I exclaimed with my mouth full.

As I ate, I imagined a young, petite Japanese girl getting up early, buying fresh food from the market, and slaving away in her kitchen as she prepared the meal. And this is the bit that blew me away – she did it for me! I also thought of her walking all the way to the Recycling-Works to deliver it by hand. She must have asked someone where I worked, including when I started my shift. I was deeply moved by her gesture – and with the strict segregation of males and females in our society, I wondered if this was the first time something like this had happened in Newhome.

Shorty said Nanako liked me, but how could that be possible when we had just met and spoken only a few words to each other?

Having consumed the obento to the very last morsel, I packed up the lunchbox and made mental plans to drop it off at North End's gates this evening with instructions to return it. Nanako had clearly brought it with her from Hamamachi and as it looked quite valuable, she would want it back.

"Ethan, I've been thinking about yesterday, and something bothers me," Michal said when we finished eating.

"Go on."

"Excluding yesterday, we've fought Skel, what, four times in two years? Three of those times were in the middle or outer eastern suburbs, and there's never been more than three or four of them. So, have there been other occasions where you've 'detected' Skel and steered us away from them?"

Michal was on the ball all right. The times we fought Skel was when they tried to jump us while we were in the act of stripping out a place. "Yes, on several occasions. And to pre-empt your next question, it was normally in the outer eastern suburbs."

Michal met my gaze. "So why were there twelve yesterday, and practically on Newhome's doorstep?"

"I've been pondering the same thing. I hope it was just a one off, but life is never that simple, is it?"

Glancing at the other three sitting on the truck's cab, Michal indicated Leigh, who was staring into space with a dreamy expression.

"What's up, Leigh?" I called out. "Never seen you this quiet before – can't find something to grumble about?"

"Leigh's been doing something lately that he shouldn't be," David answered somewhat testily.

"Like what?" I asked, curious. Whatever Leigh was doing, David was green with envy.

"You don't want to know, Jones," Shorty said with a giant smirk, before adding in a whisper, "but he's not a model citizen these days."

"Please don't do anything stupid, Leigh," I implored.

"Too late for that!" Shorty laughed.

"Keep your voices down, you drongos!" Leigh hissed.

I grabbed his forearm and made eye contact. "I don't know what this is about, Leigh, and I don't want to, but whatever you're doing, cut it out before it's too late. You hear me?"

"Whatever!" he snapped back.

I don't think my message got through to him, so I gave up and jumped down to stretch. "Let's get back to it, guys. We don't want the Custodians keeping tabs on the length of our lunch breaks."

Chapter Eight

I got to work a bit earlier the following morning as I was secretly hoping Nanako would bring me lunch again. Not because of the meal, but because I wanted to see her. She was the first thought on my mind when I woke, and I couldn't deny my interest in her.

These desires, however, confused me. What was I hoping to achieve by seeing her again? She would return to Hamamachi with Councillor Okada soon and that would be the end of it.

I had read about romance in novels I found in the ruins of Melbourne, but it hadn't ever occurred to me that I might experience it myself. All marriages in Newhome were arranged by the children's fathers and were typically devoid of romantic love.

My teammates were already in the Recycling-Works yard, lounging against the truck as they waited for me. Sergeant King and his squad were there too, talking quietly amongst themselves, their box-shaped Bushmaster parked near our truck.

"Hey Jones, you wet the bed or something?" Shorty teased.

"What?"

"You've never been here before nine o'clock before," Leigh said.

"First time for everything," I laughed as I joined them. However, I wasn't really listening. I was straining my ears in the hope of hearing Nanako's small footsteps.

And then I heard them, coming down the street as she and Councillor Okada approached the Recycling-Works. A moment later, they stepped into the yard, the obento lunchbox cradled carefully in her arms.

I stepped towards her, eagerly anticipating the chance to speak with her again. I had taken only a few steps when a Custodian G-Wagon roared down the street and with a screech of brakes, came to a halt in the yard. Three Custodians leaped out, readied their semi-automatic rifles, and headed straight for us.

Nanako and Councillor Okada stepped quickly back into the shadows of the gate. I moved back towards my teammates, my face white with terror. Surely this was it – I had been found out.

"We are looking for a Leigh Williams," announced the Custodian commander – a tall, wiry corporal, practically snarling in our faces.

I was so sure they were here for me that it took a moment for their words to sink in. "Sorry, did you say Leigh Williams. For what reason, Sir?" I asked, hoping against hope that Leigh had not done something exceptionally stupid.

The corporal gave me a withering look and barked, "Is he here?"

To my relief, Sergeant King chose that moment to join us. "Can I help you, Corporal?"

"Sir, I have a warrant for the arrest of one Leigh Williams, for allegations of serious sexual misconduct," replied the corporal as he returned the salute.

"Let's see it then," King demanded.

The corporal handed it over and waited impatiently, aware that King was of higher rank, but empowered by the warrant to carry out his task without obstruction.

"All seems in order," King announced after giving the warrant a quick once through. "Mr. Williams, you will surrender yourself to Corporal Thompson."

Eyes wide with fear, Leigh stepped haltingly towards the corporal, glancing back at me as he went. I didn't know what he thought I could do, but I couldn't believe he was stupid enough to sleep with a woman outside of wedlock. Especially considering the draconian punishments that applied to those who did.

"Wait a minute. There must be some mistake, Sir," I said far too aggressively as I stepped forward.

The corporal and his men aimed their assault-rifles at me, thumbing off the safeties. "Step back, Civilian!" The corporal thundered.

I locked eyes with the officious corporal and refused to budge. Leigh was my friend and one of my team – a valuable member and we needed him! I was going to press the issue when strong hands grabbed me and slammed me back against the truck's bonnet.

"What the..." I snarled, but stopped when I saw that it was Michal who had grabbed me.

"Don't be a drongo, Ethan, they were about to pop you!" he whispered.

"But Leigh!"

"Has been an absolute moron," he replied softly.

"You mean he's really done what they've accused him of?" I whispered back, shocked. I watched as the Custodians snapped cuffs on Leigh and marched him to their G-Wagon.

"Remember what David and Leigh ribbed him about yesterday?"

"Yeah, so?"

"Well, Leigh and his neighbour's daughter – well, someone must have ratted 'em out."

"Oh good grief!" I groaned, as the G-Wagon reversed and drove out of sight. I immediately ran over to Sergeant King, who was returning to the Bushmaster as though nothing had happened. "Sergeant King!"

The brawny Custodian stopped, but didn't turn around. "What is it, Jones?"

"What'll happen to Leigh?"

He turned and appraised me with clear disapproval. "You know, Jones, I'm beginning to think you've got a death wish."

"Sir?"

"The little stunt you pulled back there? And attacking the Skel two days ago? You'd better ramp it back, boy, or we'll be scraping you off the road before you know it."

"But Sir, isn't there anything you can do about Leigh?" I pressed, ignoring his accusation that I was reckless.

"Mr. Williams will face the magistrate today along with the woman he has been accused of engaging in sexual misconduct with. If sufficient evidence is presented to prove their guilt, they will be sentenced according to the law," King explained, annoyed that I would not let the matter drop. "Now enough of this. To work. And that is an order."

I fumed at King's cold indifference to the matter, but more than that, I was terrified for Leigh. The typical sentence for sexual conduct outside marriage was the death penalty. At least for the woman: if the man was lucky, he may have his sentence transmuted to some lesser punishment. This was another example of discrimination against women in our totalitarian, male-dominated society.

Dispirited and concerned for our friend, we clambered into the truck and drove off towards the gates with the Bushmaster right behind us. However, as we did so, a thought thrust past the fearful and angry thoughts consuming my mind – Nanako!

I turned in my seat just in time to see her step out of the gate's long shadow, disappointment etched on her face. In her hands was the obento lunch she had gone to such lengths to prepare and deliver.

I had a frantic impulse to tell Michal to stop the truck so I could quickly receive her gift. However, with the Custodians behind us plus King's displeasure that we were running late, I resisted the urge. I slumped back into my seat, leaving Nanako behind.

That I had let her down so dreadfully weighed heavily on my heart, and the memory of her sad face as she watched us drive away tore a hole right through me.

What followed was one of the most unpleasant days I could recall. All day I fretted endlessly over Leigh and his girlfriend's fate. Had they seen the magistrate? Was there sufficient evidence to convict them? Would the magistrate punish them to the fullest extent of the law, or would he show compassion?

Furthermore, I couldn't stop wondering what Nanako was thinking and feeling. How early had she risen this morning to buy the food to make the lunch? How long had she spent preparing it, adding personal touches like rabbit ears on the tomato and apple slices? Only to see me get so caught up in the morning's trauma that I completely forgot about her. I recalled how dejected she had been when she cried alone on the roof two nights ago. I feared my actions today only added to her misery.

To make matters worse, another of those strange turns visited me as we worked. This time I saw a beaten-up ute parked in a derelict factory courtyard overgrown with wild blackberry bushes. And just like before, although it felt as though I had seen this place before, I knew I had not. It seemed these bizarre turns were here to stay, and as they were accompanied by a massive adrenaline spike, I dubbed them 'spike attacks' for want of a better name.

* * *

The workday finally came to an end and we drove back to Newhome in silence. Michal parked the truck with a screech of worn breaks and the four of us rushed into the Recycling-Works, signed off in the logbook, and hurried to find the boss.

He was in his office, a poorly lit room on the second floor with dirty, virtually opaque windows that overlooked the scrap metal yard. He pushed back his chair and stood when we knocked at his door. "Come in, boys."

We filed in, taking care not to knock over the piles of logbooks, scrap metal records, connotes and delivery receipts that crowded the floor in ungainly piles.

"You've come to find out about Leigh, I suppose?" He ran his hand slowly through his balding hair.

"Yes Sir," I replied, a sinking feeling in my gut, "Did he see the magistrate today?"

"I'm afraid so."

"And?" Shorty prompted, concern etched over his normally jovial face.

"I'm afraid the magistrate found Leigh and a Miss Amelia Lin guilty of unlawful sexual conduct, and, ah, both were sentenced to death."

"What?" we all shouted in horror.

The boss held up his hands. "Wait! Leigh's sentence was reduced to six years hard labour in a prison factory."

I think I almost fainted with relief at this news; Leigh was going to be alright! Yet at the same time, we wouldn't be able to see him for six long years. Our foraging team would also be one member short.

"What about the girl, Boss?" Michal asked softly.

The boss avoided our eyes. "I'm sorry, she was executed by lethal injection at midday."

"How old was she?" I whispered.

"Eighteen."

Outrage drove back the funk that had taken hold of me today. "What kind of society do we live in that executes eighteen year old girls for falling prey to temptation?"

"Be careful, Ethan, verbalising such thoughts could be considered treason," the boss cautioned me.

"But Sir, how can they possibly justify such a sentence? It's barbaric!"

Trajan sank slowly onto his chair, still not meeting my gaze. He finally answered my question. "You know what their answer will be, Ethan. 'Justice must not only be done, it must also be seen to be done. Otherwise the very fabric of society would unravel and revert to anarchy.'"

"But they render that argument invalid by reducing Leigh's sentence but not the girl's. Why didn't the magistrate reduce her sentence too?" I reckoned I knew the answer to my question, and it made my blood boil. Thanks to the Founders establishing a male-only workforce, men were indispensable. Women, being only homemakers, were not. What rubbish! Women played an equally important role in society and were just as indispensable. Why couldn't they see that? What made me even angrier was that the Chancellor and councillors could have overridden this absurd practice, but they enforced it.

The boss sighed and looked up. "Listen to me, Ethan – all of you. I know you are angry and disappointed with today's proceedings, and you'll find a sympathetic ear with me. However, as even the walls have ears, I think it best we drop this now and keep our mouths shut. The last thing I need is for the rest of you to end up in prison on the charge of treason. Do you understand?"

It took a moment to get my anger under control, but the boss spoke the truth and I knew it. I hated the system, but there was nothing I could do about it. And he was right, to even criticise it would see me in a prison factory alongside Leigh. Though at least I would get to see him sooner than six years.

Our spirits crushed, my teammates and I wandered back down the stairs and into the yard.

"I'm gonna go to the Foragers Club to get sloshed," Shorty said dejectedly as he looked up at us. "Who's coming?"

"Okay," David agreed, though with some reluctance. He looked like he would rather be by himself.

I grabbed Shorty's arm. "There's got to be a better way of dealing with this than getting drunk. Why don't we go for a long walk or something?"

"I'll pass on the walk," Shorty shot back. "Look, why don't you come with us for a change, Jones?"

"Sorry guys, I'm heading home," I said. I could think of a million better things to do than destroying brain cells and waking in some random location, sick as a dog.

"I'll keep an eye on 'em," Michal said.

"Thanks mate." I appreciated Michal's maturity, which always shone through at times like this.

I got back to my small apartment half-an-hour later. I showered and was donning clean clothes when my phone rang. I watched it ring for some time, willing the person on the other end to give up and leave me in peace. But it just kept on ringing so I answered it. "Ethan speaking."

"Good evening, Son. You must come over at once," my father said in a tone that brokered no argument.

"Look, Father, I've had a really bad day and I need a quiet night."

"Out of the question," he snapped. "Special guests are joining us for dinner, and your presence is required. Be here in ten minutes."

"Special guests? Father, really, I'm in no condition to be socialising."

"The young woman I have chosen for your wife, and her family, are joining us for dinner. I figured you would like to meet her before the big day."

I think my reply came out as a strangled squeak. Traditionally, all brides in Newhome were chosen by the bridegrooms' father. I knew this day would come, but I certainly did not expect it to come today. I told Father on numerous occasions that I had no desire to marry before I was thirty. "Very well, see you soon."

I hung up the phone and stood there, dumbfounded. I really, really didn't want to do this today. The legal marriageable age in Newhome was eighteen, and though most girls got married close to that age, the men did not. They normally married between the ages of twenty and thirty. So why was my father in such a rush?

It was a short walk to my parents flat, as their apartment block was directly behind mine. As I walked, I realised my mind was not pondering the girl my father had chosen for me to marry. Rather, it was fixed on a mysterious Japanese girl I feared I had inadvertently snubbed, and on the fate of my friend who was to spend the next six years in prison.

Chapter Nine

When I entered my parent's home, for a moment I thought I had entered the wrong flat. Sitting at the dinner table on the far side of the room was Sergeant King, albeit in civilian clothes. Seated at the head of the table beside him was a man who was obviously his father since they shared the same large, muscular frame and facial features. On the senior King's left sat two women who had their backs to me – one with greying hair and the other brown.

My initial reaction to this scene was one of stunned confusion, but upon observing my father and younger sister sitting at the opposite end of the dinner table – which had been extended to seat ten – my world collapsed about me. The only logical conclusion I could reach from this unlikely scene was that the girl my father had chosen to be my wife was Sergeant King's sister!

With a flash of revelation, I realised why King had let me off with just a verbal warning today. He couldn't have come home and told his father that he had locked up his sister's husband-to-be, now could he?

"Come in, Ethan," Father said as he rose to his feet to welcome me.

The others stood and my father introduced everyone. The sergeant's father, Aiden King, shook my hand with a vise-like grip that almost crushed mine. Sergeant King himself – Liam – studied me with a rather disturbing intensity as his handshake crushed the few bones in my hand that had survived his father's grip. I could not even begin to imagine what thoughts were going through his head right now, as surely I was the last person in Newhome he wanted as a brother-in-law. Mrs King, who glanced at me briefly as she gently shook my hand, was nearly as tall as I.

My bride to be, Sienna, was introduced last, and although in her mid teens, had already reached her mother's height. She had a strikingly beautiful face – thankfully with her mother's looks – long brown hair, and a slim figure, which like mine, had not yet filled out.

The introductions over, I sat on my father's right, opposite Younger Sister, while my mother and older sister brought in the pumpkin soup entrees in fine-China soup bowls.

As we sipped slowly on pumpkin soup made as only my mother could make it, Mr. King Senior began his attack. "Your father has told me much about you, Ethan, but I would like to hear from you too. Tell me, what do you consider to be the most important things in life?"

I shot my father a piercing glare – he had obviously been communicating with Aiden King for some time, so what was with the mere ten-minute warning he gave me? Did he think I would have gone AWOL if he had given me advance warning? If I were honest with myself, that's probably exactly what I would have done.

"Family," I replied. "Family is the most important thing, with friends coming a close second. And not to use them or take advantage of them, but to give generously as well as receive. To put their needs and concerns equal or above my own."

"A respectable answer," Aiden replied, though I got the clear impression it wasn't the one he sought. "You are on a metals foraging team, correct?"

"That's right, Sir. That's been my vocation since leaving school."

"I believe it is in that capacity that you have met my son," Mr. King Senior replied.

"That's correct, Sir. Sergeant – I mean – Liam, is in command of the Custodian squad assigned to protect my foraging team."

"It's lieutenant now, actually. Liam's valour against the Skel who ambushed those two cars from Hamamachi earned him a promotion and a service medal," he boasted.

"Is that right?" I glanced over at Liam, who met my gaze squarely, almost daring me to contradict his father. I wondered what story he had given his superiors when he made his report. Of course, I couldn't exactly be angry or resentful for his lies and commendation. Those lies were the very thing that saved my teammates and I from receiving a prison sentence for having illegal weapons. And for ignoring his direct orders.

Completely missing the sarcasm in my voice, King Senior continued proudly. "My son's goal is to achieve the rank of major so that he and his wife can live in North

End. After that he will continue his ascent through the ranks until he becomes a general."

King had a wife? I found that thought rather unsettling. I hope the poor woman was as tough as nails. Imagine waking up next to him every morning?

"What are your plans for the future, Son?"

I ain't your son, I wanted to snap back, but aware of my father's iron gaze fixed upon me, I answered civilly. "Just the dreams of teenager, Sir," I answered vaguely, since I couldn't exactly tell him about my plans for the future. I only wanted to help my younger sister regain her health and then run away during a foraging trip and never return. Dreams I would have to forsake if I married Sienna King.

A swift kick under the table from my father informed me that I had given the wrong answer, so I tried harder. "Honestly, I guess my plans are to get married, have kids, and raise them to be responsible, productive citizens."

King Senior was frowning, as was Liam. Still the wrong answer. What did they want me to say?

"Come on, Son, don't be modest. Foraging is obviously a stepping-stone you are using towards your future career. Tell us what it is."

I could shoot my father for not letting me prepare for this, for how could I possibly answer that question without lying? I decided to veer the conversation off on a tangent. "Well Sir, as you probably guessed, foragers have a whole host of job opportunities available to them, especially in the manufacturing industry. Before I go into all that, may I ask Sienna some questions?"

"Very well," King Senior said, although he was clearly annoyed by my blatant attempt at dodging his questions.

"Thank you, Sir," I said, and turned to Sienna. "What do you expect from a husband, Sienna?" I asked, too lost to think of anything else to say. The truth was that Sienna was not the kind of girl to cause interesting questions to spring effortlessly to mind. On the other hand, I couldn't help but think of all the questions I could ask Nanako. How long would she stay in Newhome? How old was she? Where had she learned to cook and where did she pick up her broad Aussie accent? Moreover, I wanted to know why she was interested in me and why she was crying on the roof that night.

"Sienna is looking for a reliable, dependable husband with a..." her father began.

I held up my hand, rudely cutting him off. "If you don't mind, Sir, can Sienna answer the question please?"

King Senior glared, but nodded his consent all the same. And this time I ignored the painful kick I received from my father. I wondered how many bruises my leg would sport by the evening's end.

Sienna spoke haltingly at first and then with more confidence as she went on. "My goal – my dream, is to live in North End. What I want in a husband – in you – is for you to work your way to the top of your profession as quickly as you can, change to a more challenging vocation, work your way to the top as before, and keep doing this until a door opens for you to get a job in North End."

Was this to be my future? To marry into the King family to a beautiful yet manipulative and controlling wife, whose only purpose in marriage was to use it – to use me – as her ticket into North End? North End, the very place I had been avoiding my whole life?

I could already tell I would never be good enough for her, and for the first time I resented the custom of father's choosing their sons' wives. I didn't want this.

I wondered how things were done in Hamamachi. Would Nanako's father choose her husband? I wished my father had arranged for Nanako to be my wife instead of Sienna. Unfortunately, such thoughts were vain imaginings, and I knew it.

"Is everything alright, Ethan?"

I realised I had zoned out while Sienna was speaking to me, staring blankly into space as she droned on. Great, what did this mean for our marriage to come? "My apologies, I've had a pretty stressful day." Thoughts of Leigh, shocked and terrified, filled my mind, along with the image of Nanako's despondent face when I drove away without receiving her homemade obento lunch.

Sienna nodded in understanding, and then glanced at my father and her brother before continuing. "When your father contacted us with this marriage proposal, he said you have great intelligence and potential and that there is nothing you could not do if you set your mind to it. My brother, having met you, is of the same opinion."

I didn't see that compliment coming. Had I done the impossible and impressed Lieutenant King on the day we rescued the Japanese? I sent a fleeting look in his direction, which he returned with an unfathomable expression. I found it hard to believe that after his put downs and derisive looks, he was willing to have me as a member of his family.

At this point my mother and older sister brought in the main course – roast chicken with oven baked turnips, potato and carrots, and garnished with a side salad. She had spared no expense to impress the King family.

After the meal, my father and Mr. King Senior conversed at length, with some input from Liam. I found it difficult to focus on what they were saying and did not get involved unless spoken to directly.

The King family bade us farewell, and then my father and I accompanied them to the door. It was decided our families would dine together again tomorrow night, to finalise the wedding plans. Now that Sienna was eighteen, Mr. King Senior wanted her to marry within two months.

Chapter Ten

I got to work early again the next morning after spending a restless night worrying that Nanako wouldn't bring me lunch today. I stood beside our truck with Michal, Shorty and David as we waited for King and his Custodian squad to arrive.

A horrible feeling of unease worked through me, beginning in my mind and spreading into my stomach, where it remained. It would evaporate instantly if I could but hear Nanako's footsteps in the street outside, but regardless of how attentively I listened, she did not come.

The Recycling-Works glass doors swung open and a barrel-chested man strode purposely towards us. His head was shaven and he wore a forager's get-up.

"Who's he when he's at home?" Shorty asked suspiciously.

The man, who topped me by at least ten years, stopped when he reached us. "Okay guys, gather around."

"Who are you?" I demanded. With the Custodians joining our foraging trips, Leigh's arrest, and the shock announcement that I was about to get married, I was not in the mood for any more surprises.

"I'm your new team leader. The name's Cooper, but you can call me Boss," he announced in a no-nonsense voice.

So much for no more surprises.

"Excuse me?" Shorty snapped angrily.

Cooper stared down at Shorty and answered him curtly. "Concern has been raised over the reckless behaviour of your previous team leader, and due to my extensive experience in said role, I have been assigned to replace him."

"I'm standing right here!" I shot at him, wondering who on earth had decided to lumber us with him, when I recalled Sergeant King accusing me of those very same words. So this was his doing. Perhaps he was afraid he was about to lose his future brother-in-law and his sister's ticket into North End.

"Good for you," he snapped.

"Forget it, Cooper," Shorty said, deliberately drawing out his name. "We've got a team leader and he's done alright by us. You can go back to whoever gave you your marching orders, and tell 'em to stick 'em up…"

Michal might have been tall, but he was fast too. His hand clamped over Shorty's mouth before he could finish. "Shorty's got a point, Cooper," he said in a more polite tone, "what we need is another worker to replace Leigh, not a new leader. Who gave you your orders?"

"Sergeant King," he replied.

My suspicions were correct. This insult felt like the last straw that broke the proverbial camel's back. All of our freedoms while foraging were gone now. Not only were Custodians following us everywhere, ensuring we no longer got up to extracurricular activities, now this stooge was gonna be with us every moment of every work day too.

The thought also occurred to me that as King had appointed him, Cooper might be a Custodian informant.

"So, we're all good now?" Cooper asked condescendingly.

"Super," David replied as he glanced at me, hoping I could do something to get rid of this clown.

"Right then, here's the way I do things," he began. "Rule number one, and this is hard and fast – we are a foraging team, not a Custodian squad – we do not engage Skel in combat for any reason. If you see a Skel, sound the alarm and retreat. Rule number two, my word is law. If I say something, you do it straight away, and without fussing. Rule number three, we are out there to collect metals, and nothing else. If I so much as catch one of you guys even peeking at anything else, I'll bust your chops."

The Custodian Bushmaster chose that moment to arrive, backing carefully into the yard until it was next to our truck. As Cooper rushed off to speak to King, I motioned for the guys to come closer. "As long as this Cooper guy is with us, don't ask me to do tongue-clicks to find things, okay?"

"Why?" David asked.

"If the Custodians hear about it, they may suspect Ethan is something other than what he is," Michal explained.

"But blind people can do it," David pointed out.

"I know," I replied, "but I'm not blind, so just don't mention it, okay?"

"So what the blazes are we gonna do to spot Skel booby traps?" Shorty demanded.

"We'll just have to be careful, like usual." I didn't tell him that before the Custodians joined us, I bounced ultrasonic shouts off our surroundings to check for traps. Now we were really gonna be in the dark.

King approached us with Cooper in tow. "I hear you boys have met your new team leader."

We shifted about in agitation, but no one said anything. I made eye contact with my future brother-in-law and wanted to protest, to scream blue murder, but I knew it wouldn't achieve anything so I kept my mouth shut.

"Right then, let's get this show on the road," King said once it was clear that we were going to take the leadership change lying down.

"I'll drive. Who's got the keys?" Cooper asked. Michal handed them over.

I could have said something, but was too focused on what I was hoping to hear – Nanako's footsteps. What if she came while we were driving off? I did not want it to look like I was snubbing her efforts a second time.

"Jones, get your butt in gear!" Cooper bellowed.

I glanced at my watch and my hopes floundered on the rocks of despair when I saw it was five past nine. She wasn't coming. I must have hurt her feelings yesterday and extinguished her interest in me. I knew nothing could have come of it, but I wanted to talk to her, even if only briefly. Deflated, I walked to the truck and sat beside Cooper. *Thanks so much, Michal for sitting in the back and forcing me to sit next to the doofus.* I stared daggers at Michal in the rear view mirror, and he rewarded me with the barest hint of a smile.

Cooper drove to a street in Carlton with a crumbling, weed-overgrown footpath and an asphalt road that was cracked and pitted. The houses in this street were quite old and of brick construction, so were still structurally intact. Though much of the woodwork had rotted away long ago, and all the windows were smashed or blown in.

"Right boys," Cooper said after we climbed out of the truck. "The Recycling-Works says we're running low on lead, so kit up and we'll strip these houses bare."

I glanced at King, who was standing outside the Bushmaster, which was parked beside the truck. He was watching me keenly, wondering how I would react to my demotion. "We've already done this street, Cooper." I said.

"Is that right, Jones? In that case, follow me and I'll show you all the spots you missed." His tone was patronising.

"We didn't miss anything," I assured him flatly.

He patted me on the shoulder. "Ah, the arrogance of youth. Now follow me. After I've shown you the places to find lead, we'll split up and tackle the houses in two teams."

Cooper unhooked a ladder from the truck, placed it against the nearest house, and addressed us as though we were fresh out of school. "You'll find lead sheeting used as flashing around the sides of the chimneys and electrical wire connections." He clambered to the top of the ladder, and then stopped, surprised. "Oh, those spots have been stripped."

After that, he led us throughout the house, looking for lead sheeting in the cornices, around the bases of down pipes, in the conductor heads and window frames, and so on, until he had exhausted every possible source of lead – and didn't find a single scrap.

"Told you we didn't miss anything," I said.

Cooper glared at me. "You know Jones; foraging teams have worked these suburbs for a hundred years, so how do I know that you're the ones who stripped this house?"

My teammates, who had been gloating at our victory, glanced unsurely at one another. How were we going to prove we'd done it?

I so wanted to smash my fist into Cooper's cocky, know-it-all expression, but I somehow – barely – managed to resist the urge. "Take a look inside the roof above the laundry manhole," I replied. "You'll find some things we found but left behind, you know, since Newhome citizens aren't allowed to touch them."

Cooper grabbed the stepladder and stomped back into the house. He returned a moment later with three rifles wrapped in plastic. "You're supposed to return all firearms to the Recycling-Works so they can be given to the Custodians, something I'm sure you are aware of."

"Proves we're the ones who stripped the house, doesn't it?" I ignored his comment completely.

Cooper stuck his face an inch from mine. "I don't like you, Jones." With that, he stomped off to present the rifles to the Custodians.

My teammates and I gave each other inconspicuous high-fives.

"Score one for our team, Jones," laughed Shorty.

After that, we drove around our assigned sector of Melbourne striking out time and again. After eating our lunches in the truck – apparently, you don't need an actual lunch break if you don't do any physical work – Cooper found an old restaurant with thin lead sheets used to waterproof the floor.

My teammates would not speak to Cooper as we worked, except to answer direct questions, and they always called him 'Cooper,' not 'Boss,' which annoyed him to no end. To rub salt in the wound, they called me 'Boss' instead. My friends were the best. For myself, I was so deep in the doldrums because Nanako didn't show up this morning that I barely spoke a word.

When I got home that evening, I had a quick shower and dressed in my neatest casuals. I had to be at my parent's flat soon to finalise the details of my pending marriage.

The thought of marrying a girl like Sienna King gave me the shudders. To be honest, I knew that few marriages in Newhome involved loving relationships, but all the same, I had always hoped to respect and get on with my wife. I couldn't see that ever happening with her.

A knock on my door snapped me out of my reverie. Thinking the guys had dropped over for a visit, I pulled the door open and my heart stopped.

Standing in front of me was Nanako, wearing long pink and black striped socks that reached to her thighs and an oversized men's blue and black flannelette shirt, which she wore as a dress. And she was holding two plastic bags full of fresh food.

Chapter Eleven

Peering up at me from beneath her pink bangs, Nanako held up the bags and smiled warmly. "Hi Ethan, I've come over to cook dinner for you tonight."

I don't know how long I stood there staring at her, working my way through the conflicting thoughts her words sent zooming through my mind. Foremost was the liberating relief that came from realising I had not hurt her feelings yesterday morning. Second was the sheer delight that I finally had an opportunity to spend time with her. This was followed by panic because I was due at my parents' house shortly. There was no way I could fit dinner with Nanako and with my parents into the one evening. Then of course was the gut wrenching fear associated with the knowledge that it was not permitted for a single guy to be alone anywhere or at any time with a woman who was not a member of his family.

I realised I had to send her away, but as I stood there looking down into her hope filled face as she waited for me to let her in, I knew I couldn't disappoint her again.

"That sounds wonderful – please, come in." I said as I stepped back to let her in. As she walked past me, I noticed Councillor Okada standing a couple of doors down, either playing the part of chaperone, or watching to make sure she arrived safely at her destination, if not both. I wondered if I should ask him to come in too, but he bowed politely and walked away before I had the chance.

Nanako dumped the bags on my miniscule kitchen bench – the kitchen was beside the front door. She started digging through the drawers and cupboards beneath the stove and bench.

The view of her of slender thighs exposed between her over-knees striped socks and the shirt was so mesmerising it took a great deal of effort to find my voice. "Sorry, I don't have much stuff."

"Oh, that's fine, I'll make do," she said cheerfully as she pulled out two dented saucepans and a battered wooden chopping board that I bought second hand at the market.

"I have to make a phone call," I said as I reluctantly tore my gaze from her thighs back up to her beautiful face.

"Oh – I haven't interrupted your plans for this evening, have I?" she asked while chopping carrots with a speed I didn't think was possible. I would have chopped my fingers off if I tried that.

"Oh no, it's just some minor thing I can reschedule for another night," I assured her. *Yeah, just a minor thing like working out my wedding date.* "I'll be right back."

My flat was narrow but long, extending from one side of the building to the other. Opposite the kitchen was the enclosed bathroom with shower, basin and toilet. Next was the dining room with the dining table and an old ratty two-seat sofa that faced the TV. The dining room morphed into the bedroom, which was occupied solely by my double bed. Next to the bed was the rear window and back door that lead to the balcony.

I grabbed the phone from the shelf beside to the bed and rang my father. This was not gonna go well.

"Jones residence," my father answered.

"Hello Father. Look, I'm sorry, but something very important's come up and I can't make it tonight."

"Do not be absurd, Ethan. The King's are already here and your mother and sister are about to serve the meal. Get over here right now," he ordered brusquely.

My head burned red hot from the pressure of the fix I had gotten myself into. I knew the correct thing to do was to obey him, but when I glanced at Nanako studiously preparing our dinner, I knew I would have to defy father for the first time. "Father, I am otherwise detained and it's not something I can get out of."

"What are you talking about, Son? Are you suddenly bereft of your senses? You knew the King's were coming tonight to finalise the wedding's details. How can you be otherwise detained?"

"I'm sorry, Father, but as I said, I'm literally unable to come. Please pass my apologies to the King's as well."

"Wait a moment." He snapped, and he must have placed his hand over the receiver, because I heard nothing for a couple of minutes, and then, "Son? I have passed on your message to the Kings, and they are most displeased, as they should be. However, after much apologising, they have agreed to return tomorrow night."

I let out a huge sigh of relief, as I thought he was going to insist that I come over until I caved in. "Right, thank you. I will be there. As I said, I'm sorry."

My father slammed the phone down before I finished talking, causing me to wince. I was gonna get a major dressing down tomorrow night. Something to look forward to.

My face was boiling hot and my conscience felt as though it had been pierced by a red-hot poker, but I returned to the kitchen and leaned against the fridge to chat with Nanako as she prepared dinner.

"Is everything okay?" she asked.

"It's all sorted," I assured her as I watched her pop small balls of fish meat into a saucepan bubbling with boiling oil. "Doesn't Councillor Okada need you to translate for him tonight?" I asked.

"I told him I wanted the night off," she said as she started peeling potatoes.

"And he let you?"

"Of course," she replied, as though the answer should have been obvious.

"Do you mind if I ask how you can speak English so well, but he doesn't?"

"I went to primary school in Inverloch," she said. "My parents thought it would be good if I could speak both languages."

"They were right. Imagine the trouble you and I would have trying to communicate if you only spoke Japanese," I laughed.

"I don't know." She smiled. "You understand Japanese well enough."

"Yeah, and that's kind of weird."

"Why's that?"

"Because I never learned it."

"Really? Then why do you think you understand it?" She studied my face carefully.

"Can't say, to be honest." Which was true, I really couldn't tell her it may be because of my abnormal abilities. I decided to change the subject. "Hey, how did you know where I live?"

"Councillor Okada asked an official for your address. He said he wanted to drop by and say thank you."

"I see."

"That was okay, wasn't it?" she asked, suddenly concerned.

"Of course." I gave her an encouraging smile. "Hey, do you have any brothers or sisters?"

"One of each," she replied. "My brother is ten, and my sister eight."

I waited for her to return the question, but when she didn't, I volunteered the information anyway. "I have two sisters, one twenty and the other twelve."

She nodded as she continued cutting vegetables.

"What are you cooking?" I asked, my interest piqued by the appetising smells filling the flat.

"Oden," she replied. "It's a Japanese winter dish. I was lucky to find some of the ingredients in North End and most of the others in the markets. I had to make my own fish cakes, though. We normally eat rice with the dish, but we'll have to make do with bread rolls since Newhome doesn't grow rice."

"I see. Hey, you're an amazing cook, you know. The obento you made was the best lunch I've ever had."

"Oh no, you are too kind – my cooking is nothing special."

"You're too modest," I laughed. "Where'd you learn to cook?"

"I've had a lot of practice."

Suddenly, I could contain my curiosity no longer. "Nanako, if you don't mind my asking – how old are you?"

Her dark brown eyes peered out from beneath her fringe. "I'll be twenty-one in a couple of weeks."

I was dumbfounded. She was years older than she looked and older than me as well. "You sure hide your age well. I figured you were seventeen at the most. In fact, you're a couple of months older than I am. I turn twenty-one at the end of February."

"Then we are virtually the same age," she said, rewarding me with another of her winning smiles.

"Yeah, amazing hey?" I laughed, before asking, "What do you do in Hamamachi, are you, you know, the town's translator or something?"

She shook her head, "Oh no, there are quite a few of us that speak English. Actually, I'm a forager like you."

"You're kidding! Where do you do your foraging?" Maybe they came to Melbourne sometimes, and if so, perhaps we could bump into each other from time to time.

"Mostly abandoned country towns, but I've been to Melbourne's eastern suburbs too, looking for anything old tech – mobile phones, computers, tablets, and books, of course."

"Books from outside Newhome are banned here," I said sadly.

"Why?"

"Apparently, they can plant subversive ideas in our minds. All the same, it doesn't stop me reading them when I'm out foraging," I admitted slyly.

"How long have you been foraging, Ethan?"

"Two years."

"What did you do before that?" She began adding number of ingredients into the larger saucepan – boiled eggs, potatoes, carrots, white noodles, her hand-made fishcakes, and a vegetable I hadn't seen before, kind of like a large white radish. She must have bought it in North End because I'd never seen it in our markets.

"It's a long story," I answered.

"I don't mind long stories."

I didn't want to go there, but as she wouldn't let the matter drop, I didn't have much choice. "Honestly, I don't remember. After I left school at seventeen, I started foraging, but a few months later, I suffered a head injury that caused me to have amnesia and very bad epileptic seizures. All I remember is waking up in a hospital after the operation that stopped the seizures. My memory of that year never returned."

"When was the operation?"

"December 2120."

"And you don't remember anything about that year? About what you did before the accident or your time in hospital?" she asked.

"Not a thing."

"Have you tried triggering the missing memories, like going back to the hospital?"

"I've been back a few times for checkups, but it didn't spark any memories. I don't think there's anything left to remember, the accident did too much damage."

We made idle chatter until the meal was ready. As she cooked, my gaze continually strayed to the tantalizing glimpse of her exposed thighs. I tried to fight the impulse, but try as I might, I failed miserably. I was afraid she might catch me ogling her legs and then I'd just die of embarrassment. Fortunately, if she noticed, she said nothing, but acted as though my behaviour was nothing out of the ordinary.

I must admit I was rather confused when she set two places at my small dining table instead of one. Two bowls, two cups, and two plates stacked with bread rolls. She indicated that I should sit and after sitting opposite me, served the oden into both of our bowls. This was a most pleasant surprise. She was gonna eat with me rather than of waiting on me and eating later, as did Newhome's women. She handed me two wooden sticks.

"You want me to eat with chopsticks?" I asked.

"Yes, please," she replied. There was a twinkle in her eye.

"But I've never used them before."

"You'll do just fine."

I picked up the chopsticks and dug into the oden, while she did the same. To my astonishment, I could use the chopsticks quite proficiently.

The oden's ingredients had been cooked in a soy-flavoured soup, giving them a wonderful flavour, including the potatoes and boiled eggs.

As I watched Nanako noisily slurping down noodles, I gave her a heartfelt smile, which she immediately returned, her eyes sparkling merrily. I was immediately struck by the growing attraction I felt for her, which both confused and surprised me, since we'd known each other for such a short time. If someone had told me a week ago that this was going to happen, I wouldn't have believed it.

Another thought popped unbidden to my mind. I imagined I married Nanako instead of Sienna. That we ate together like this every day, and that I might have a future filled with joy rather than endless frustration.

I picked up a large piece of radish, which had changed from opaque white to translucent brown. As I did, another 'spike attack' tore ruthlessly through me. Not wanting to concern Nanako, I tried to hide it by concentrating on eating until it passed. The image that accompanied this attack was of a bathroom mirror and a cluttered basin, including two toothbrushes, soaps, shampoo and conditioner, washing-cloths, and cotton balls. I was convinced I had experienced this exact moment before – eating oden with Nanako while seeing this vision, but my rational mind dismissed this as mere nonsense. *What's going on in my head?*

My next scheduled check-up with the hospital neurologist was in two days, so I figured I should tell him about these turns. Just in case.

"You okay, Ethan? You look pale all of a sudden."

"Just tired, I guess." I smiled, hoping she hadn't noticed the attack.

She studied me intently, as though trying to see into my mind. I did not want to mention the strange turns that defied all logic so I asked the second question I had been dying to ask her. "When are you and Councillor Okada returning to Hamamachi?" I dreaded she might answer that she would return tomorrow. She had brought such light into my gloomy, dark life and I didn't want her to go.

"Your town council is preparing a selection of items that Newhome manufactures and wishes to offer in trade with Hamamachi. As soon as they are ready, your Custodians will escort the samples and Councillor Okada back to Hamamachi."

"But what about you? Aren't you going with them?" I asked, thinking she had left her name out by accident.

"No, I'm not going back."

"What, why not?"

"Because there's something here I want," she said, a smile tugging at the corners of her slightly upturned mouth.

I wracked my mind, trying to think what she was referring to. "Oh, and what is this thing you want?"

She giggled. "Oh Ethan, you're a smart guy, but sometimes you aren't too bright."

I thought there was a compliment in there somewhere, and a massive hint of what she wanted, but try as I might, the answer eluded me. "You're not gonna tell me what it is?"

"Nope, you'll have to work it out by yourself."

"Well, whatever it is, I'm glad it's keeping you here," I said.

"And why's that?" She leaned forward, her gaze suddenly intense.

I blushed, turning bright red in the process, no doubt. "So you can keep making me these marvellous meals." Which of course, was not the reason at all. I wanted to tell her it was because I wanted to keep seeing her – sharing meals with her, talking to her, and daydreaming about the impossible.

"Is that right?" she smirked. "In that case, I'll make you udon tomorrow night – you'll love it."

"Can we make it the day after? I have to go out tomorrow night," I said as I served myself another potato and fish ball.

"Really – where are you going?"

I squirmed in my seat and looked at my hands as I replied. "My father's chosen my bride and our families are meeting at six tomorrow night to finalise the wedding date."

Nanako choked and sprayed a mouthful of water over the table, her eyes wide with horror and dismay. "Who is this girl?"

I could only glance at her as I replied miserably. "Remember Sergeant King, the leader of the Custodians who helped rescue you on Monday? It's his younger sister. I met her last night for the first time."

"Do you…love her?" Her voice waivered as her eyes bore holes through mine.

"No, of course not," I replied without hesitation. "All she cares about is using the marriage to help her get into North End. My father told her father I am capable of accomplishing anything."

"Then tell your father you won't marry her," she said.

"I can't," I replied sadly. "All marriages in Newhome are arranged by the fathers. The children have no say in the matter."

"That's crazy," she said, and then after a long pause, "When do you think the marriage will take place?"

"Probably within the next two months."

At that news, her face paled quite considerably. "Where are you meeting with them tomorrow night?"

"At my parent's house."

She nodded and then rose to collect the dirty dishes. She took them to the sink and washed them, making no further attempt at conversation. I put the leftovers in a plastic container and left them on the bench to cool down.

After that, we adjourned to the sofa and although I tried to draw her into conversation, I soon gave up. If she responded at all, it was never more than a word or two.

Her reaction clearly had something to do with my impending marriage, but I could not understand why she took it so badly. We barely knew each other. I had assumed her interest was only to repay the debt she thought she owed me for saving her life, but with her cryptic comments tonight, I suspected that was not the case. And if it wasn't, then what was her purpose in pursuing me?

"I had best head back, it is getting late," she said as she retrieved what appeared to be a working Smartphone from her pocket.

I watched in childlike wonder as she activated it. "Councillor? Owatta. Hai hai, ja, mata."

"Your phone works/" I virtually squeaked when I found my voice.

"Certainly does."

"But, their batteries are all dead, the digital programming has perished, and there are no satellites to connect them to," I protested.

"That was the case, but we've learned how to repair them and make new batteries. We even found a suitable satellite that survived the Apocalypse."

"I'm impressed," I practically drooled. It occurred to me that if I had one of those phones I could talk to Nanako any time. I couldn't just come out and say that. It would be too forward. So I said, "Hey, if I had one too, could I talk to anyone?"

She nodded, though without enthusiasm. "Well, the only people you'd know with Smartphones are Councillor Okada and me."

"Then maybe I could ring you?"

There was a sharp rap at the door before she could answer. Councillor Okada had arrived. I don't know where he had been this evening, but it was obviously close by.

I hurried to open the door and returned the councillor's polite bow. As Nanako joined him, I studied her downcast face and wished there was something, anything, I could do to lift her spirits again. "Thank you for a wonderful evening and delicious meal, Nanako," I said.

She didn't reply, but rose to her toes and pecked a light kiss on my cheek. She turned and left with the councillor without a backward glance.

I glanced quickly about to see if any Custodians were around to see her leave my apartment, but was relieved that none were in sight.

After I closed the door, I slid to the floor and just sat there, at a loss. I touched the cheek she had kissed, and my emotions and thoughts swept into a storm of confusion. I hated to see her so sad. It tore me up inside, as did the fact that the night ended on such a negative note.

I hadn't even confirmed if she was still coming over the evening after next.

Chapter Twelve

"Breathe! Come on, Ethan, breathe!" a nurse shouted as he slapped my face.

My chest heaved as I sucked in a deep breath.

"That's it, keep going," he encouraged.

I tried to focus on the nurse, to work out where I was, but everything felt off. I'd never been blind drunk, but I reckon this was what it felt like. My thoughts were sluggish, I could barely move, I couldn't focus my eyes, and I couldn't speak. I was also vaguely aware that my head was swathed in bandages.

"Don't fight it. You're just feeling the effects of the general anaesthetic. It'll wear off soon enough. Just go back to sleep, eh?" the nurse said...

...and my body jolted as though struck, pulling me out of the dream. Morning sunlight streamed through the windows. I realised I was in my apartment, lying on the floor beside the front door. I wasn't in the hospital. That was just one of my recurring nightmares where I relived waking from the brain surgery I'd had when I was eighteen. I remember those days clearly, although I wish I couldn't.

The brain surgery had cured me of the epilepsy and cyclic amnesia. However, it also affected my minor and major motor skills, including speech. After my recovery, I spent day after day in rehabilitation with speech therapists and physiotherapists. It was agonisingly slow going and extremely frustrating.

I tore my mind away from the nightmare and memories of that most unpleasant time, and wondered how many hours I sat against the door last night before finally fallen asleep. I was stiff and sore, but not overly so as I often slept on the concrete rooftop of the building.

Still tormented by the troubled, miserable expression on Nanako's face last night, I had zero interest in food. I drank a glass of water and threw a couple of pieces of fruit and a bottle of water into my backpack. I didn't pack food for lunch as I figured I'd be in no mood to eat at lunchtime either.

That done, I left my flat and headed for work. It normally took fifteen minutes to walk there, but I stretched it out to half an hour so I wouldn't arrive early. I had no interest in talking to anyone today, especially not In-Your-Face-Cooper.

My walk was plagued with thoughts of Nanako, of how a perfect evening with a beautiful and mysterious girl turned sour when I told her I was getting married. That she reacted like this could mean she felt something for me, and was hurt by the news of my marriage. If so, such a strong reaction surprised me, for we had only known each other for a few days. Surely she could see that there was nowhere our relationship could go from here.

Could I be her reason for not leaving Newhome with Councillor Okada? It sounded so improbable, but when I considered all the evidence, I realised this had to be a possibility.

I was still lost in this mental quagmire when I saw Lieutenant King waiting for me at the Recycling-Works gates with a savage scowl on his face. This wasn't gonna be a good day.

"That was some stunt you pulled last night, Jones," he hissed when I reached him.

Still feeling somewhat distressed, I was in no mood to placate him. "My apologies, Lieutenant, but I was otherwise detained," I replied, the tone of my voice bordering on insolence.

"My father was most displeased. Don't pull any stupid stunts like that tonight, you hear me?"

"I will be there as arranged, Sir," I assured him.

"You'd better be. Now hop in your truck and let's go."

As I walked over to my teammates, Michal saw my dour expression and raised an eyebrow. I just shrugged in response. I wasn't going say anything in front of the others.

"Okay scavengers, pack them behinds into the truck!" Cooper ordered as he reached for the driver's door.

"We're foragers, not scavengers," Shorty protested.

"A kettle by any other name is still a kettle, Shorty. We go out into a dead, ruined city and scavenge amongst the decaying ruins for scrap metal. Calling us 'foragers' is just some drongo's attempt to make us think more highly of ourselves than we ought. Now, let's go."

On a normal day, I would have taken issue with Cooper's scornful comments, but I didn't have the heart for it. I climbed in next to him and we set off for the town gates, the Bushmaster roaring after us.

There was no sign of Nanako, just as I expected.

Once out of town, Cooper drove us east, following exactly the same route he took yesterday. We drove slowly down Dryburgh Street and then towards the CBD itself. We went past rusted out cars and trucks, through shrubbery and wild grasses that flourished in every crack in the roads and sidewalks, until we reached the restaurant we had worked on yesterday.

Cooper backed the truck up to the concrete steps and we clambered out and put on our utility belts. The Custodians parked the Bushmaster in the middle of the street, one private popping out the roof hatch to operate the machine gun, while King and another private exited the vehicle by its rear door. They glanced about the street once, announced their thorough investigation was complete, and gave us the go head to begin work.

"David, you're upstairs with me," Cooper snapped, "You other three finish tearing out the lead sheeting from the kitchen floor."

With Michal wielding his sledgehammer and Shorty and I our crowbars, we traipsed up the concrete steps and into the shell of the restaurant's foyer. All the windows were gone and the wooden frame of the customer-service counter had rotted away, leaving the plastic top lying on the floor amidst a carpet of leaves, twigs, dirt, and plaster that had peeled from what was left of the ceiling. We threaded our way across the dining room, which was an even greater mess than the foyer. The wooden tables had rotted quite badly – most of their legs had collapsed, and the chairs had fared no better. Chunks of plaster had fallen on everything, and the place stank of mildew and mould.

Switching on his torch, Shorty led us to the large kitchen out the back, where we paused and surveyed our previous day's handiwork. After moving the ovens and benches we could shift, we had ripped up most of the disgustingly filthy linoleum floor tiles so we could pull out the grimy, thin lead sheets beneath. Lead sheeting was a common waterproofing system in commercial kitchens. Several kilos of lead were rolled up, but we were only part of the way through.

I grabbed Shorty's torch and panned it back and forth as I considered which section of the floor to tackle first, when an uneasy feeling rose in my gut. "Hold up, guys," I said quietly, examining our surroundings with more than casual interest now. If I wasn't mistaken, the room had been tampered with ever so slightly. "I don't recall seeing the freezer door open yesterday, and I'm sure we put those rolls of lead in front of it, not beside it."

Michal hefted his sledgehammer and we approached the walk-in freezer as quietly as we could. Suddenly Cooper started screaming "Skel!" at the top of his voice, followed by the sound of his heavy boots thumping on the floorboards above.

At the exact same instant, the walk-in freezer door swung open and a horrifying, skeletal apparition burst into the room, made all the more terrifying by the flickering torchlight and the cow horns protruding from the sides of the skull-helmet. The Skel looked like a demon from the depths of hell. He was also one of the biggest I had ever seen. He charged us while yelling obscenities and brandishing a converted axe. Shorty and Michal fell back in shock, but I noticed he was timing his swing to hit Michal, not me. So I did the last thing the Skel expected. I ducked inside his swing and thrust my crowbar at his throat. Unfortunately, his beefy arms got in the way and threw off my aim, causing the blow to glance off his skull-protected face.

The good news was that my attack had given Michal time to recover his balance, step forward and deliver a mighty swing of his sledgehammer to the Skel's head. The human skull he wore as a helmet exploded and he went down with a massive thud.

However, before we could breathe a sigh of relief, the door at the back of the kitchen smashed open, allowing brilliant sunlight – and two more Skel – into the room.

"Run!" I shouted.

Shorty and Michal didn't need any convincing and sprinted out of the kitchen while I brought up the rear. The Skel, one small and one large, gave pursuit – two more nightmarish ghouls to haunt my dreams for the rest of my life.

As I darted into the dining room, a crossbow bolt missed my head by inches and imbedded itself into the far wall. I glanced back and cried out when I saw that the smaller Skel was only a step behind, hands reaching out to grab me. I threw myself to the right as I twisted to the left and brought down the crowbar. It connected with my pursuer's right arm, breaking the bone armour and possibly their arm as well.

To my surprise, a woman yelped in pain and uttered a stream of four letter words that would have made me blush had I not been in such dire circumstances – the smaller Skel was female!

Refusing to let this astonishing revelation distract me, I regained my balance and rammed her with my shoulder, sending her reeling into a half-collapsed table. I would have followed this with another crowbar strike, but decided against that particular plan of action when the larger Skel barged out of the kitchen.

I turned and raced after Shorty and Michal, glancing back on occasion to make sure he wasn't gaining on me.

My teammates and I sprinted out of the darkened restaurant and into the sunlit street. At the same time, the Custodian operating the Bushmaster's roof-mounted machine gun opened fire upon a target on the far side of the street.

King rushed over to us, gun at the ready, "Forget the truck – get in the Bushmaster!"

"Keep your eyes open," I shouted to Shorty and Michal as we ran around the truck to reach the Custodian's vehicle, "they've got us surrounded!"

Hearing a machine gun fire a short burst behind us, I glanced back and sighed with relief when I saw that King had gunned down the Skel who had pursued us in the restaurant.

We hurried to the back of the Bushmaster, where a Custodian held the door open with one hand while keeping his Austeyr assault-rifle ready with the other. Shorty and Michal clambered in and sat down next to Cooper, who was sitting at the front behind the driver's position.

"Where's David?" I demanded as I put one foot into the Bushmaster and safety.

Cooper refused to meet my gaze, "I don't know, one minute he was behind me, the next he wasn't."

"You left him behind?" I asked incredulously, not believing what I was hearing.

Cooper glanced at me, guilt and fear etched on his face.

I think I hesitated for all of a second, and then the enormity of what he was saying exploded in my mind. The Skel had David! My teammate and friend had been caught by those abominations, who were even now no doubt carting him away to a fate far, far worse than death.

Chapter Thirteen

I backed away from the Bushmaster and accosted King, who had just come up behind me. "What are you doing, Jones, get in the vehicle!" he shouted.

"They've got David!"

"That's unfortunate, now get in."

"We have to save him!"

King glanced quickly about, taking in the buildings, wrecked vehicles, shrubs and weeds that surrounded us, and shook his head. "We have no idea where they've taken him, and it's far too dangerous to go rooting around trying to find out. We have to get out of here."

As if to emphasize his point, a crossbow bolt hit the Bushmaster's door right beside King's head with a loud bang. The Custodian manning the roof-mounted machine gun returned fire in the general direction the bolt had come from. Bullets shattered bricks beside a second story window in the building across the road.

Without thinking, I struck a pressure point on King's right forearm with a knife-hand blow, ripped the Austeyr assault-rifle from his hands, and darted back towards the restaurant. I couched the gun against my shoulder as I ran, and noticed that King had set the gun on fully automatic fire. That was no good, as I could empty the thirty-round magazine in seconds. I flicked the automatic lockout back to the exposed position so that the gun would fire in semi-automatic mode. I don't know how I knew all this, but as soon as the gun was in my hands, I knew what to do, almost like instinct.

I glanced about as I ran, letting rip with ultrasonic shout after shout, the flash sonar enhancing my vision so I could 'see' into every shadow and darkened room, and through every shrub and bush. If the Custodians were somehow monitoring the sound frequencies and spotted me using flash sonar and it cost me my life, then so be it. I had to save David. Period.

I figured the Skel would have taken him out of the restaurant through the kitchen, so I would have to find a way to get behind the restaurant. However, before I could do that I had to do something about what the flash sonar had revealed – the entire area was crawling with Skel. Many of the buildings around us had Skel crossbowmen hiding in them, using shadows to remain concealed. Three more of the degenerate nomads, armed with Molotov cocktails, were scurrying towards the Bushmaster from the other side of the road, using wrecked cars, shrubs and wild grass as cover.

And to top it all off, two hundred meters back down the road we had used to get here, several Skel were setting up bombs to immobilise or destroy our vehicles if we retreated back the way we came.

As much as I wanted to go straight to David's rescue, those three with the Molotovs had to be dealt with first. Instead of continuing towards the restaurant, I ran across the road, ducking two bolts fired at me from second story windows. When I got behind the wrecked cars, I ran quietly back towards the Bushmaster and the three Skel stalking it. I found them as they were preparing to lob their horrific weapons – the Custodian operating the Bushmaster's machine gun had no idea they were there and that he was about to be doused with burning petrol. I opened up on the three skeleton-encased warriors before they could throw, and put them down with three shots to the back of their unarmoured necks. That done, I ran back to the restaurant, where I was almost shot by the Custodian, who thought I was a Skel. He jerked the machine gun away at the last second, sending a stream of bullets whizzing past my head.

My flash sonar detected two Skel hiding in the restaurant's darkened foyer. Rather than take them on frontally, I entered the fast food joint next door. I dashed past a smashed service-counter and then popped silently through a gaping hole in the wall that lead into the restaurant's dining room – right behind the Skel. Two more shots and they were down. One dropped soundlessly, but the other held his neck and screamed as he thrashed about on the floor.

My line of retreat now secure, I went back into the fast food joint through the hole in the wall and hurried through its narrow kitchen, then into the empty room behind it. But when I tried to push open the aluminium back door, I found it was stuck. I turned to the window beside the door and quietly shifted aside the window frame's head jamb, which had collapsed. After checking there were no Skel on the other side, I slithered through the gap.

The back of the fast food shop was a jungle of trees, bushes, and weeds jostling to get the most exposure to sunlight. I paused, quietened my breathing, and focused on what I could hear. I immediately heard several gruff Skel voices coming from the restaurant's back yard beside me. Three were discussing setting up a trap to ambush whoever was pursuing them. They had heard my gunshots, and the fourth appeared to be reporting their situation, though to whom I had no idea.

I threaded my way through the trees, bushes and weeds until I reached what was left of the chain-link fence that marked the back of the property. I forced my way through and entered the backyard of another building. I ran to my left and scaled a crumbling brick wall so that I was now directly behind the restaurant's rusty chain-link fence and backyard.

I could see four Skel – and – David!

The Skel closest to me was holding him upright with his left arm, using him as a human shield, while his right hand held a knife near his throat. Another Skel was over near the restaurant's back door to the right, and the other two were on my left, hiding in the bushes. The good news was that they all had their backs to me, as I had expected.

I had to disable the Skel holding David first, so I climbed slowly and quietly up a tree over-hanging the fence and braced myself in its lower limbs. I steadied the assault-rifle against a branch, took aim, and then fired a shot through the Skel's right wrist and then his throat. The nomad bellowed in pain and dropped both the knife and David, and then collapsed. Next, I put a shot through the neck of the Skel over near the restaurant's back door, and then jumped from the tree.

The other two chose that moment to burst from where they were hiding. I put down the closest skeleton-armoured brute first, but the second one fired his crossbow at the same time that I fired a shot through his throat.

The bolt struck me just below the left collarbone with the force of a sledgehammer, sending me staggering back to collide with a pile of rotting wooden pallets, where I slid slowly to the ground. Seeing the bolt sticking out of my chest felt surreal, but the truth sank in – I'd been shot! I wanted to surrender to the waves of pain washing through me and fall unconscious, but remembering that David was at my feet helped keep me focused.

I reached a hand out to his neck, and was relieved to find a healthy pulse. Hopefully they had only knocked him out, because I could not see any wounds on his person.

I also spotted a shiny black, palm-sized plastic object next to the Skel who had been holding David, so I grabbed it and popped it into my pocket.

I could hear more Skel approaching all around, but even closer were two pairs of footsteps rushing towards me through the restaurant's kitchen – footsteps that I instantly recognised. They belonged to King and Michal.

Knowing that help was nigh, I tried to stand, but the movement caused agonising pain to tear through my body thanks to the bolt in my shoulder.

Everything went black.

* * *

"Jones, wake up!"

I jerked awake to see King's ugly face two inches from mine. To say he was angry would have been an understatement – he was ropeable. I looked around frantically for a moment, wondering where I was. Then it came flooding back. I rescued David but had been shot in the process. The four Skel I had despatched lay sprawled about me, but Lieutenant King and Michal found me at last. Michal was picking up David and slinging him carefully over his shoulder in a fireman's lift.

"David...?" I asked.

"He'll live, but we've got to get back before more Skel find us," King snapped as he grabbed my right arm and hauled me roughly to my feet. Pain exploded through me and I almost blacked yet. "I'm sorry, did that hurt?" he mocked.

Looking at my shoulder, I saw that he had removed the bolt and placed a sterile gauze pad over the wound, and bound up the shoulder with bandages. "Press here – I don't want you flaking on us on the way back, 'cause then I'd have to carry your sorry backside."

With Michal leading the way back through the restaurant towards the Bushmaster and our comrades, it took all my strength to put one foot in front of the other. That was with King practically dragging me along with him. He was armed with a pistol; his re-appropriated assault-rifle was slung over his back.

As we left the dark kitchen, we heard the voices of several Skel who had entered behind us.

"Faster!" King snarled.

Somehow, we made it through the restaurant and safely back to the street, but had to give our faithful truck a wide berth as angry flames devoured it.

"Cover us!" King shouted to the Custodian operating the machine gun on top of the Bushmaster. The private fired over the top of the burning truck – and just in time too – a group of Skel were charging out of the building behind us. The hail of bullets soon had them scampering for cover.

With Shorty helping from inside the vehicle, Michal carried David carefully through the Bushmaster's rear door.

After that, Shorty reached out and helped me onto a seat. "Thanks for saving David, Jones, you're a legend."

I gave Shorty a weak smile.

King climbed into the vehicle, slammed and locked the door behind us.

The Custodian manning the machine gun suddenly dropped back inside the vehicle moaning in pain. There was a crossbow bolt embedded in his shoulder. A Custodian private grabbed a med kit, carefully removed the bolt, and bound up the wound.

King bellowed at the driver, "Go, go!"

Remembering the roadside bombs the Skel had placed on the route we had come, I grabbed King's arm feebly. "Don't go back the way we came, keep going east and then circle back using a different route."

"Belay that order!" King shouted to the driver. And then to me, "Why Jones?"

"This was a meticulously laid trap, King. You think they're not expecting us to flee back the way we came?"

He glared at me for a moment, and then told the driver to do what I suggested. The Bushmaster's idling engine roared to life and it quickly picked up speed as it surged eastwards down the street.

I suddenly remembered what had transpired to bring about this debacle – Cooper, our new team leader, had fled the Skel with no thought to David's safety. The coward was still sitting there behind the driver, shaking with fear. My self-control snapped and I lunged at him, striking him weakly in the face with a bloody fist. I couldn't get another blow in because I doubled over in pain and collapsed on the narrow floor.

Sending a look of pure venom in Cooper's direction, Shorty helped me up and guided me back into my seat.

After treating his wounded comrade, the Custodian with the med kit went to check on David.

"How is he – he gonna be alright?" asked Michal, who was sitting next to David and keeping him in his seat.

"Looks like just a concussion but we can't do anything more for him here. We need to get him checked out at the hospital."

I was relieved beyond measure to hear that my efforts to save David had not been in vain. He was going to be okay.

King moved from his seat at the back of the Bushmaster so that he could sit across from me. He sat there for several minutes, glaring at me as the vehicle drove at high speeds away from the ambush site, rocking and bumping us as it passed over broken asphalt and shrubbery.

He finally found his voice. "You're a damn fool Jones, not only did you almost get us all killed, but you assaulted me, a Custodian, and stole my weapon! You're looking at ten to fifteen in a hard labour factory."

Everyone was watching our exchange, both my teammates and the Custodians. They had all seen or heard me attack King, take his gun, and rush off alone to save David. Shorty and Michal looked on aghast when he mentioned the lengthy jail term.

I think my face went a shade paler as his words sank in. Ten to fifteen years in prison? All my hopes, all my dreams, my entire life as I knew it, was gone. Still, to save David from the Skel it was a price worth paying. "I'm really sorry, Sir, but I just couldn't let them take David."

King leaned closer. "So I noticed. And you know, Jones, I may not arrest you for what you did today."

I looked at him doubtfully. "I'm sorry, Sir?"

"You're an enigma, Jones – a puzzle that doesn't make any sense. For example, explain how you disarmed me with one strike – where did you – a forager – learn how to do that?"

"I don't know, Sir. When you, ah, hesitated to go after David, my instincts just took over."

"Cut the bull, Jones. You delivered a perfect knife-hand strike to a pressure point on my arm. Who taught you how to do that?"

I could see what was worrying him. Civilians were not permitted to learn the martial arts. "I'm serious, Lieutenant, I don't know how I knew that. It just…happened."

"That's garbage, Jones. And now on to the next question," King said as he leaned even closer. "When did you do an advanced gun handling course?"

"What do you mean?" I must admit that he had stumped me with that question.

"There are perhaps half-a-dozen Custodians who could handle an Austeyr assault-rifle with as much skill as you demonstrated back there."

I shook my head. "I just aimed and pulled the trigger."

"I said to cut the bull, Jones! You changed the gun to semi-automatic fire, couched it against your shoulder like a pro, and took down Skel with one shot kills. Even I can't do that."

"Lieutenant, seriously, I just grabbed the gun and used it. I've never done any form of gun handling course. I took up foraging as soon as I left school, and apart from the year I spent in the hospital after my accident, that's all I've ever done," I assured him.

"What accident?"

"A ceiling collapsed on me when I was foraging back in 2120, Sir."

"And you spent a whole year in the hospital for that?" he queried sceptically.

"Apparently, Sir."

"What do you mean 'apparently,' did it happen or not?"

"After the accident, I suffered from amnesia, Sir. I have no memories of that year."

King leaned even further forward. If he leaned any closer we'd be bashing our heads together every time the Bushmaster went over a bump. "Did it ever occur to you that you may have been a Custodian before your accident?"

"No Sir," I said, shocked by the suggestion – what a horrid thought! "My memories of leaving school and going straight into foraging are intact. It's the memories of the year after that are missing. Besides, what you suggest is impossible. Once a Custodian, always a Custodian, right?"

Which was quite possibly the worst thing to have said. Now King was probably back to suspecting I was part of some underground resistance movement, training its members to take on the Custodians. As if.

"Unless you bombed out during boot camp, or were discharged due to medical reasons – and with an injury like amnesia, you would have been," he answered as he leaned back in his seat, but he wasn't finished. He narrowed his eyes suspiciously. "As I said, something about you doesn't add up. When I get to the bottom of it I'll decide whether or not to arrest you for today's indiscretions."

Actually, the reason he wasn't arresting me right now was because of my pending marriage to his sister. What would his father say if he came home from work today and announced he had stuck his sister's ticket to North End in prison for ten to fifteen years?

Though to be honest, I had to admit I was just as surprised that I had instinctively known how to use King's gun, since I'd never touched one before. At least, I had no memories of ever having done so. What if his suspicions were well founded? What if I had joined the Custodians or had been part of some underground, paramilitary resistance group? Both thoughts sent shivers down my spine.

"Everyone, listen up," King said as he snapped his fingers to get our attention. "Regardless of what you think you saw happen today, Jones did the Lone Ranger thing and rushed off unarmed to try and save David. I went after him with Michal, I killed the four Skel who took David and wounded Jones, and then Michal and I brought them both back. Is that understood?"

As everyone responded in the affirmative, I wondered what rank King would be next time I saw him. The thought occurred to me that if he were to stick with me, I would catapult him to that esteemed rank he sought in next to no time.

Chapter Fourteen

When we got back to Newhome we found it a hive of activity. Custodian squads in Bushmasters and G-Wagons were patrolling the no-man's land that surrounded the town. This was because several other foraging teams — what was left of them, anyway — returned before us. They had all been ambushed by Skel too.

The town hospital looked like a field hospital in a war zone. Wounded Custodians and foragers filled the operating theatres, emergency department, and intensive care unit. Some suffered burns from Molotov cocktails and burning vehicles, others were shot with crossbows or hurt by booby-trap bombs. Others had broken bones or other injuries caused by Skel hand weapons. Doctors and nurses rushed back and forth with a frantic sense of purpose.

Our foraging team and Custodian squad were the 'lucky ones,' as most of the other foragers had been wounded, killed or captured, and the Custodians hadn't fared much better. Four more foraging teams had yet to report in. This was truly the darkest day in Newhome's recent history. The thought of some of our brave, faithful men captured by the Skel weighed heavily upon our hearts. —No one deserved to receive such an appalling fate – to be worked to death as a slave.

The technician who X-rayed my wound said I was lucky because the crossbow bolt hadn't done any serious damage. Somehow it did not penetrate as deeply as it should have. When I told him it had been fired at point blank range, he said he suspected that the crossbow string had lost much of its tension. For the first time, I was relieved the Skel did not maintain their weapons very well.

After that, they stitched up the wound, wrapped my chest in bandages, and gave me a blood transfusion.

After I was transferred to intensive care, I attempted to snatch some sleep, a difficult task due to the noise of visiting families and hospital staff. Just as I was drifting off, wouldn't you know it, Lieutenant King made a house call.

"Leave us," he snapped at Michal, who had been keeping me company.

Michal quickly retreated to join Shorty and David, who's his bed was at the other end of the room.

"Do you feel as bad as you look?" King asked gruffly as he stood stiffly before my bed.

"I've felt better, Sir."

"I suppose you've heard the Skel hit all our foraging teams today. Two teams haven't even come back, which means they must have taken out the Bushmasters as well. All the foraging trucks were lost."

"So I heard, Sir."

"Any ideas why the Skel have done this?"

"It could be in revenge for us wiping out their twelve-man party on Monday," I suggested.

"But that's not what you think, is it?"

"No, Sir."

"Don't pussyfoot with me, Jones, out with it."

"I think today's attacks, and last Monday's attack on the Japanese cars, are part of a greater plan against Newhome. Though what it is I have no idea," I answered carefully, expecting him to refute my suggestion.

His face, however, remained neutral. "Okay, Jones. Let's say I buy this theory of yours, but there's one big problem with it."

"How did a loose collection of nomadic tribes manage to coordinate such a carefully thought out plan to attack all of our foraging teams on the same morning – teams that were spread all around Melbourne," I asked.

"Exactly – any ideas how they did it?"

"This is how," I said as I opened my right hand to show him what I had been holding all that time. (Michal retrieved it from my trouser pocket earlier.)

King's face became almost as pale as mine as he reached down to take the Smartphone from my hand. "Where did you get this?"

"From one of the Skel, Sir."

"And you leave it till now to tell me?"

"Sorry, with the injury and all it slipped my mind, Sir."

"Fair enough. I'll be off now, I have to hand this in." He turned to leave.

"The conclusion you've reached isn't necessarily the correct one," I said quickly.

He turned back to me. "And what conclusion is that?"

"That Hamamachi is supplying Smartphones to the Skel."

King stared at me long and hard. "You know about Councillor Okada offering to trade Smartphones with us? That information is classified."

Classified because they intended to offer the imported phones only to North Enders and Custodians, no doubt.

"I noticed our Japanese visitors had working Smartphones when we rescued them," I said. I could not admit Nanako was alone with me at my place last night.

"Okay, how else do you explain the Skel having them?" he demanded, holding up the phone, which was identical to the one Nanako had.

"If Hamamachi is willing to trade them with us, they must be trading them with other Victorian towns too. And who knows, maybe someone else has worked out how to repair them."

King did not look at all convinced, but his face suddenly softened and he asked, "Will we see you tonight? Or do you have orders to remain in the hospital for a few days?"

"Forget doctor's orders," I assured him with far more gusto than I felt. "I will see you tonight."

"Oh, one last thing." The softness I had seen on his face a moment ago vanished.

"Yes, Lieutenant?"

He leaned closer. "I checked the log of Custodian recruits from late '19 to early 2120 – and your name isn't in it."

"I already told you I went straight into foraging, Sir."

"As far as you remember, right?"

I nodded.

"This amnesia excuse is only going to cover you so far, Jones. I'm going to keep digging till I get to the bottom of this, and if I discover that you learned gun handling skills illegally, I'm going to nail you to the wall!" He stormed off in a huff.

Michal rejoined me a few minutes after King left. "What did he want?"

"He wanted to know my thoughts about the Skel attacking our foraging parties today."

"You're kidding," he exclaimed, "King asked for your opinion?"

"I know, right? Last thing I ever thought he'd do, though true to form he mixed in a few threats too. Hey, is David awake yet?"

"He is, but he won't say anything, just stares into space."

I reached over and ripped the needle out of my left hand and pressed a tissue over the hole until it stopped bleeding.

"What are you doing?" Michal asked with concern.

"Help me get dressed, will you? I want to see David and find out what's up." I hoped he didn't have amnesia or something like that. There wasn't a day that went by that I didn't regret the gaping hole in my mind of eleven months I had no memory of living.

Michal stared at me for a moment as though I was out of my mind, but then came over and helped me out of bed. My clothes had been stuffed unceremoniously into a large brown bag and placed in a cupboard beside the bed. Michal helped me out of the hospital gown and I struggled to get dressed. Since the nurses had thrown away my blood soaked shirt, he gave me his jacket to wear. It was several sizes too big, but at least it was clean. Getting my left arm into the jacket was agonisingly painful, but I gritted my teeth and put up with it. Adversity was something to cope with and overcome, not pander to.

"I need a sling." I searched the cupboard beside my bed.

"Hang on, I'll be back," he said before disappearing into the swirling crowd of doctors, nurses, patients and family members. I hadn't contacted my family. I had enough on my mind without them fussing over me too.

Michal returned a moment later with a sling and helped me put it on.

"Thanks Michal, I really don't know what I'd do without you."

"Do more things yourself?" he suggested.

"Hey, under the circumstances, I don't think that's particularly fair." I pretended to be hurt.

Michal replied with the hint of a smile.

"Mr. Jones, what do you think you're doing?" a young nurse demanded as he approached us. He was male, like all nurses and hospital staff, except for those in the maternity ward.

"Checking out," I replied.

"You need to remain under supervision for at least twenty-four hours," he insisted.

"Look, I'll rest better at home, and you've got your hands full, right?"

Realising I could not be swayed, he held up his hands. "Fine, but let me at least give you your course of antibiotics."

I yielded to his request and waited while he went to fetch them. He returned a moment later with a bottle of pills and gave me instructions to take them twice a day with food.

That done, Michal and I went over to see David. He was lying down with his head wrapped in thick white bandages, staring straight ahead with a blank expression, just as Michal had told me.

Shorty was sitting cross-legged on the foot of the bed, but clambered off to greet me as we approached. "What are you doing walking around, Jones? You're whiter than a ghost."

"I've spent enough time in hospital beds," I replied, and then stepped over to David, overjoyed to see him safe. I panicked so badly when the Skel had taken him, terrified we'd lost him forever.

I lay a hand on his shoulder. "Hey mate, how you feeling?"

"Why'd you save me, Jones?" he asked while staring straight ahead.

"What kind of question is that?"

"I'm the one who told them," he replied, stricken with grief.

I glanced at Shorty and Michal, but they just shrugged their shoulders. "Told who what, David?"

"The Custodians, I'm the one who told 'em about Leigh sleeping with his neighbour."

Although I heard what he said, I simply could not process the words. "You what?"

"He's always flaunting the law and bragging about it. And then he starts going on and on about how he's sleeping with this Chinese girl next door, and I got so angry, and jealous too I guess. So I just went and told a Custodian about it. I didn't even think about the consequences."

"David, Leigh's in prison for six years and the girl is dead!" The shock from his confession sent my mind reeling.

Shorty, who was closer to Leigh than a brother, exploded into rage. "You absolute and utter moron, David! What is wrong with you? How could you do such a thing to your friend? How could you turn anyone, let alone Leigh, into the Custodians? They're the enemy! I hate you!" He suddenly bolted for the door with tears streaming down his cheeks.

I grabbed Michal's arm. "Follow him and make sure he doesn't do anything stupid!"

"On it."

Michal left and then it was just David and me. I felt completely alienated and alone, even in a room full of people. I sat down on the edge of his bed and let my mind wander, thinking of all the good times the five of us had together, laughing, crying, talking, exploring the ruins, playing cards, even crying on each other's shoulders. And now it had come to this.

After many minutes of reflection, I reached out and turned David's head so he met my gaze. "David, you're just gonna have to deal with what you did, and when Leigh finally gets out, you gotta fess up and ask how you can make amends, okay?"

There was no response, he didn't even blink.

"Look, you stuffed up, and you stuffed up real bad, but I got shot saving your life today pal, so don't you dare waste that, you got me?"

David's eyes finally focused, first on my face, and then on my arm in the sling. Understanding what I was saying, he nodded slowly.

"Promise me you won't waste it," I demanded.

"I promise, Jones," he whispered, and then, "Jones?"

"Yes?"

"Thank you, you know, for saving me."

"That's better." I gripped his hand.

When Michal returned an hour later, he found David asleep and me sitting in the chair next to him.

"Shorty's okay now, he just needs some time alone," he said.

I stood slowly from the chair, but had to grab the bed to steady myself. "Cool, thanks."

"And where do you think you're going?"

"Have to be at my parents by six."

"And you're gonna walk there?" Michal asked sceptically.

"Well, I'd rather take a bus but can't do that since Newhome doesn't have any."

"How about you sit back down for another half hour and after that I'll get you there in fifteen minutes."

I fixed Michal with a withering glare. "I'm not going by wheel chair."

"This is no time for misplaced pride, Ethan, but don't worry, I've got a better idea. Stay here, I'll be right back."

I gave him a mock salute as he sauntered off.

Chapter Fifteen

Michal delivered me to my parent's apartment by six, and as he promised, didn't hurt my pride by carting me through Newhome in a wheelchair. He dredged up a two-seat tandem bicycle from somewhere – I didn't ask – and he rode while I pretended to. He even fetched a clean set of clothes from my place. I honestly don't know what I did to earn a friend like him.

Walking up the three flights of steps to my parents' flat turned out to be the most exhausting leg of the journey.

"You're late," my father scolded me when he opened the door and let me in. He gave no indication of noticing my arm was in a sling. In typical form, his mind was fixated on one thing – marrying me off to Sienna King.

The King's had already arrived and were seated as they were two nights ago. My mother and older sister were standing by the kitchen doorway, waiting for me to arrive so they could serve the appetizer. Mother's eyes widened in genuine concern when she saw me. Despite having my army in a sling, I was also obviously very pale. In deference to the formal setting, she did not speak, but

I knew that once the King's left, she would fuss over me and bombard me with questions.

As Father returned to his seat, I greeted the King family formally. Then I lowered my aching body in the chair on my father's right, directly opposite Younger Sister. She was holding her hands to her mouth in shock at my appearance. I tried to flash her an encouraging smile, but I don't think I was very convincing.

"Liam's been telling us about the Skel attacks on our foraging teams this morning," Aiden King said when I turned to face him. "Sorry to hear you got caught up in that, Son. How are you feeling?"

"A bit worse for the wear, Sir," I replied. Actually, now that the painkillers had worn off I just wanted to lie down and die. Well, not literally. I glanced at Sienna, thinking she must be concerned that I'd been injured. However, she examined me with little more than casual interest. That horrible sinking feeling returned to my gut. I was to spend the rest of my life with this girl?

A knock at the door interrupted my train of thought. I watched as Father rose and went to see who it was.

"What are you doing here?" my father snapped quite rudely at the mystery visitor.

"I came with the councillor from Hamamachi as his translator," replied a familiar voice. My spirits rose when I realised it was Nanako, but my initial excitement was followed by confusion. What on earth was she doing here?

"No," I heard my father say as he tried again, "What are you doing at my home?"

"Oh, I'm looking for Ethan. Is he here?" Nanako asked, trying to see into the flat past my father's broad frame.

We'd parted company last night on a very negative note, and I spent the rest of last night, and all of today, down in the dumps because of it. So this was an opportunity I wasn't gonna waste. I rose from my chair and stepped to the left so she could see me.

Her eyes widened in alarm when she saw the sling, and then, to my amazement, she slipped lithely past my father and rushed over to me. "What happened, Ethan? Are you alright?"

"We got jumped by Skel while foraging today," I replied.

She laid her petite, bronzed hands lightly upon my bandaged arm. "And you were hurt?"

I was aware that both families were staring at us in a mixture of confusion and disdain – all but Lieutenant Liam wondered how I happened to know such a strange and no doubt unmarried young woman. And me? I didn't care one iota. I shut them out and gave her my whole attention. I pointed to my wound, "I, ah, got shot by a crossbow."

"You got shot?" she exclaimed, her eyes brimming with tears. "So why aren't you in the hospital?"

"They let me go," I said, which was kind of what happened.

"But aren't you in pain?"

"Well, just a tad." Pride stopping me from admitting the truth.

"Oh Ethan, this is no good, you could have been killed! Promise me you'll find a safer job."

I was surprised by the depth of concern she showed. She really cared for me.

"I'll think about it," I replied as I glanced at Lieutenant King. The fact was, with all the foraging trucks gone and the Skel besieging the town, there would be no foraging for some time.

Nanako gestured to my chair. "Here, you'd better sit down, you're so pale."

"Let me introduce you first. Everyone, this is Nanako. She's the translator who came from Hamamachi on Monday," I said, after which I introduced each member of the King and Jones families to her. She bowed politely to each in turn.

When I got to Liam, she said, "I am honoured to meet you again, Sergeant King."

"It's lieutenant now, actually," Liam replied, clearly uncomfortable with this situation. "And, thank you."

My father had not moved from the door, which he was still holding open, clearly hoping Nanako would leave.

I, however, wanted her to stay. "Does anyone mind if Nanako joins us for dinner tonight? She is an esteemed visitor to our town, after all."

King Senior and my father begrudgingly muttered their approval, resentful that I had forced the situation. I purposefully asked if she could join us because if they refused, they would have lost face.

I ushered Nanako to the seat beside Younger Sister so she would be opposite me. As soon as she sat down, Sienna and her mother grimaced as though she was something the cat had dragged in from the gutter. My opinion of Sienna slid down a dozen more notches.

I returned to my seat as Father closed the door and sat beside me. He kicked my shin under the table and glared at me. Then he nodded to my mother and sister, who disappeared into the kitchen. They returned a moment later with bowls of tomato soup.

"This is scrumptious, Mrs. Jones," Nanako said to my mother after she tasted it. "What ingredients did you use?"

Everyone gaped at Nanako in disbelief. She, a female, had spoken at the meal table without receiving permission to do so from one of the men. My mother looked to my father, unsure of what to do. Although clearly displeased at Nanako's lack of manners, he nodded his permission.

"It is an English recipe," my mother answered quietly, "It has tomatoes, butter, chicken stock, tarragon, basil, sour cream, salt and pepper."

"I recognised the basil, but tarragon? What a fantastic idea, it really adds to the taste," Nanako replied enthusiastically.

Mother smiled bashfully.

Nanako noticed Younger Sister stirring her soup and taking the occasional sip. "You're Meredith, aren't you?"

Younger Sister's eyes widened in alarm, and she looked to father for permission to reply.

"Go on," I encouraged her, cutting in before father had a chance to respond.

"Yes," she replied shyly.

"You're very pretty." Nanako smiled warmly.

Younger Sister looked embarrassed, but at the same time, I could tell that she was moved by the compliment.

Nanako studied her with knowledgeable eyes, and I guessed she could see Younger Sister was not well. She had tried to cover the sores at the corners of her mouth with makeup, but they were still visible.

When the soup was finished, Mother and Eldest Sister brought out heated dinner plates bedecked with roast chicken, potatoes, pumpkin, and beans.

The tomato soup was the first thing I had eaten all day, so I tucked into the roast dinner with gusto, grinning unabashedly at Nanako while I ate.

Glaring with disgust at my undignified display of affection for Nanako, Sienna King touched her father's arm deferentially, and he nodded, giving her permission to speak.

"Nanako, is that how all the *girls* in Hamamachi dress?" she asked with contempt.

Nanako glanced down at her attire. She was wearing the same clothes she had worn on Monday. The faded black and blue zebra stripped jacket, black top with blue and pink lace skirt, torn pink leggings and black boots. And as usual, the black choker with bell and two gold rings. "This was the fashion three years ago in Hamamachi. It comes into vogue from time to time in remembrance of our Japanese heritage.

"Are you trying to say that outfits like that are traditional Japanese fashion?" Sienna asked sceptically.

"More recent Japanese tradition, but yes. It's from Akihabara in Tokyo in the late twentieth century, where fashion was inspired by Japanese comics and motion-picture animations," Nanako explained.

"Is that right? And if you don't mind me asking, how come your parents allow a child like you to act as translator for Hamamachi's emissary? Shouldn't you be at home with your mother?"

My respect for Nanako increased even more when she refused to respond in similar fashion to Sienna's attack. "Oh no, I travel a lot, actually. You know, to other Victorian towns. I also serve one month a year in our Militia. I'll be twenty-one at the end of the month, by the way."

Sienna's eyes just about popped out of her head. She had believed Nanako to be her junior, not her senior by two years.

"What is this Militia you mention?" Liam asked.

"It's our security force," Nanako replied between bites, "You know, like your Custodians."

King looked at her doubtfully. "And you serve in that?"

"Yes."

"In what capacity?" he demanded. I got the impression this had suddenly become an interrogation.

"My platoon patrols the outer lying areas of the town to provide security against raiders or Skel who try to steal our supplies or abduct our people."

"But you're a girl," he protested rather too strongly.

"So what?" she shot back at him with such feeling that everyone present flinched. "All Hamamachi citizens aged seventeen to fifty-five, whether male or female, serve in the Militia one month each year."

"So you don't have any full time security forces?" Liam asked, surprised.

"Apart from the Rangers, only the senior Militia officers serve full time."

"Rangers?"

"They're an elite military unit that specializes in countering Skel incursions and retrieval of kidnapped citizens, stolen supplies and livestock – stuff like that."

"Interesting," Liam murmured, nodding thoughtfully. No more questions came so it seemed the impromptu 'interrogation' was over.

"Mrs. Jones," Nanako said to my mother as she waited on us by the kitchen door, "The roast chicken is just amazing. I love the way you've brought out the skin's flavour with herbs and spices. And I love these roast veggies too."

"Thank you," my mother replied, glancing at my father, hoping she had done the right thing by replying.

"Oh, by the way Ethan, did you enjoy the meal I cooked for our dinner at your place last night?" Nanako asked me innocently.

While I gagged on a mouthful of roast potato and sprayed it all over my plate, everyone else gaped in shock. In fact, you could have heard a pin drop as all four King's, not believing what they just heard, looked to me to hear my response.

My face was burning hot. I could not believe Nanako had just gone and blurted that out in front of everyone!

"Ah, yes, it was delightful, thank you." I finally managed.

This response was met with stunned silence too.

My father was the one to break the uncomfortable silence, speaking just loud enough for all to hear. "So when you rang yesterday, Son, and said 'something very important's come up,' this 'something very important' was having dinner with her?"

My eyes darted frantically between my father, Nanako, and Aiden King. I wanted to avoid my father's wrath, and did not want to insult the Kings. However, I also refused to insult Nanako's generous hospitality by playing down how much having dinner with her meant to me. "Yes, Father, that's correct."

Sienna and her mother gasped in shocked outrage, their hands flying to their mouths.

Aiden King pushed back his chair and rose slowly to his feet, his voice trembling with anger. "Is this how you raised your son, William, to completely disregard courtesy, respect and honour? To be so flippant of his responsibilities?"

My father stood, his mouth working silently like a fish out of water as he glared daggers at me. "I'm sorry, Aiden, I don't know what's come over him, he's never behaved in such a manner before." He practically whimpered.

"Well, I have never been so offended in my entire life!" Mr. King growled as he motioned his family to their feet. "Come Daughter, Wife, Elder Son. We are leaving."

Leaving their half-eaten meals behind, the King family strode with exaggerated self-importance towards the door.

I stood as well, knowing I should say something to salvage the situation, but I had no idea what that might be. In fact, I found I had no desire to do so and said nothing.

"Son, apologize at once!" Father ordered me.

I sent a fleeting look at Sienna's haughty posture as she headed for the door, and then at Nanako's caring, kind face, and I knew I could not. The thought of marrying Sienna had scared the daylights out of me, and so this situation, although it brought dishonour to my family and I, was an absolute windfall for me. I shook my head.

My father took a menacing step towards me, but froze when Aiden King yanked open the front door and turned to face him. "And in case you hadn't worked it out, William, the marriage is off."

I became aware of a menacing presence at my shoulder, and almost jumped when I saw Lieutenant King's face less than an inch from mine.

"Were you alone with that girl last night, Jones?" he asked far too quietly.

"Councillor Okada came with Nanako," I replied. An answer, which if interpreted literally, was the truth. If I had answered in the affirmative, King would have arrested us both on the spot.

"You'll pay for this insult to my family's honour, Jones, I'll see to it personally," he hissed before striding out of the flat and slamming the door behind him.

Chapter Sixteen

My father was quivering with rage. I had never seen him this angry before, and to be honest, I was scared. I had no idea what he was capable of.

"What have you done, Ethan?" he shouted as he took a step towards me. "All my efforts – weeks of negotiations and discussions – to find you a wife who could elevate your station, who could give you the motivation you need to make something of your life, and you throw it all away. And for what – to have dinner with her?" He pointed at Nanako, but did not even grace her with a glance.

Nanako stood and made her way unobtrusively around the far end of the table and came to stand beside me. I was thankful for her silent support, although she appeared as shaken by my father's naked aggression and hostility as I was.

"I know you meant well, Father, but why couldn't you have discussed it with me instead of springing Sienna King on me at the last possible moment? She knew all about me, but I was completely in the dark," I answered as strongly as I dared, which wasn't particularly strongly at all.

"What's that got to do with it?" he bellowed. "I met your mother on our wedding day! You should have considered yourself lucky I agreed to the King's request to let the two of you meet before the wedding. Now go this very minute to the King's residence and apologise for your insulting behaviour and beg their forgiveness."

I did not want to deal with this today, I was sore and tired and just wanted to go home and sleep. "Look, Father, please don't think I don't appreciate the effort you put into all of this, but I don't want to marry Sienna King."

"What you want has nothing to do with it, Son. To marry a girl above your station like Sienna is an opportunity you will never get again – especially once word gets around about what you've done. Now off you go."

I didn't move.

"I gave you an order, Son!" he yelled.

To defy my father on any issue, and especially on a major one like this, went against everything I had been taught, yet I still wouldn't move.

"Now, Ethan!" he shouted furiously.

"Sorry, Father, I just can't do it," I practically whispered.

He lunged towards me and pulled back his hand to strike me across the face, but little Nanako, a head shorter than either one of us, suddenly jumped in front of me and dared him to strike her instead.

Father stood there, blinking and shaking uncontrollably, wanting to strike her, but unable to bring himself to do so.

"Get out of my home, you confounded nuisance of a girl!" he finally managed to say, his voice shaking with rage.

"What are you going to do if I refuse, Mr Jones – call the Custodians and ask them to throw me out?" she shot back vehemently.

I looked down at Nanako in surprise. Where had that burst of emotion come from? One thing was for sure, though, she had backbone. Far more than I had.

Father glowered at her for a moment, and then abruptly stormed from the apartment, slamming the door behind him.

Exhausted from standing too long, and from a confrontation that was going to come back and bite me, I slumped back into my chair.

Nanako pulled out a chair and sat beside me this time. "Are you okay, Ethan?"

"Jury's out on that one," I replied.

My half-eaten roast dinner was before me, a victim of tonight's conflict.

Nanako picked up my fork and handed it to me. "Eat."

"Lost my appetite," I answered.

"Ethan, you need to get your strength back, so eat."

I stabbed a roast potato and lifted it to my mouth. "You too, little one," I said to Younger Sister, who was sitting there wide-eyed. She sheepishly began picking at her dinner.

My mother came over and sat across from us. "Son, of all the things to defy your father on, why did you have to choose this one?"

"I'm sorry Mother, but I won't marry that girl."

"Got too much of your father's stubbornness in you," she sighed in resignation, and turned to Nanako "Thank you, young lady."

"For what?" Nanako asked gently.

"For the kindness you've shown my son this evening. Which was far more than his own family did, I am ashamed to say." With tears in her eyes, she turned to me. "Are you in pain?"

I nodded. Mother flicked her head at my older sister, who disappeared into the kitchen and returned with painkillers and a glass of water, which she dumped unceremoniously in front of me. I got the impression she agreed with Father, as usual.

I swallowed the tablets and tried to eat a dinner that had lost its appeal.

"Son, you two had better not be here when he returns," my mother said once I had eaten all I could manage.

"Yeah, I know," I agreed. I had seen enough conflict for one day, first with the Skel, then King, and now this evening's episode. The thought of having to walk home, however, was a most unpleasant one.

"I'll get Councillor Okada to give you a lift to your apartment. It's too far to walk in your condition," Nanako declared as she pulled out her Smartphone.

"In his car?" I asked incredulously.

She nodded as Councillor Okada answered the phone.

Looked like I was going home in style.

Councillor Okada drove me home (more like drove me around the corner) in his incredible black 4WD, complete with a touch screen navigation computer in the dashboard, air conditioning, and a host of other features I couldn't even begin to guess at. We sure had nothing like this car in Newhome.

When we reached my flat, Councillor Okada bowed and made to leave, but I reached out a hand to stay him. "Councillor Okada, can you please come in, there's something I want to discuss with you."

Nanako was clearly disappointed we wouldn't be alone, but translated my request nonetheless.

Inside the flat, the councillor and I sat at the kitchen table while Nanako dragged over my large footrest and knelt on it.

This was my first opportunity to speak with Councillor Okada since they had arrived. When I met him in the ruins I thought he was middle aged, but I misjudged his age, just as with Nanako. His hair was flecked with grey, so I guessed he was probably at least fifty.

Nanako made us all a cup of tea, and after engaging in some pleasantries, I began to share with Councillor Okada what was on my mind. Nanako translated quietly in the background. "The reason I wanted to talk to you, Councillor, is that one of the Skel who attacked us today had a working Smartphone that looked just like Nanako's."

Nanako sprayed a mouthful of tea over the table in shock. Councillor Okada's reaction was a little more controlled. "How do you know it was working?" he asked in Japanese, and just like before, I somehow understood what he said.

"The screen was lit up and covered with icons," I replied. "I'm also pretty sure I heard him talking to someone with it."

"That's impossible," he declared adamantly.

"I brought it back with me."

"Where is it? I must see it at once," he demanded, clearly alarmed.

"Sorry, I gave it to Lieutenant King."

The councillor looked crestfallen. "I really wish you had let me see it first, Ethan. I need to know what satellite service it is connected to."

"You could ask Lieutenant King to let you see it?" I suggested.

"Out of the question," he replied, "that would reveal you have divulged this sensitive information to me, and that could land you in much trouble."

I nodded, touched by his consideration for my well being. "Do you trade the phones to other towns?"

"Of course, the Smartphones are our most desired commodity. Every town we trade with has purchased them."

"So the Skel must have stolen the phones from their victims," I deduced. "Unless you trade with the Skel too, but you wouldn't do that, would you?"

"Of course not. We shoot them on sight," he replied indignantly. "But to answer your suggestion; stealing the phones cannot be the solution. The phones need to be constantly recharged."

"And how is that done?"

"The recharger plugs into any electrical outlet," he said, his forehead creased in deep thought. "And the Skel cannot have access to electricity, due to their nomadic lifestyle."

"I think, Councillor Okada, that we have all massively underestimated the Skel. If they are recharging their stolen phones – and they must be – it means they have appropriated a source of electricity."

"If you are correct, Ethan, this bodes ill for all Victorian towns. When I return to Hamamachi, I will request that a Ranger team be sent out to investigate this matter." To Nanako he added, "What a tragedy our most experienced Skel counter incursion team was lost a couple of years ago."

"Lost, how?" I asked.

"Four members of the team were killed and the fifth gravely wounded," he councillor replied.

"By Skel?" I asked, suddenly afraid. If Skel had wiped out Hamamachi's veteran Skel hunting team, what chance did anyone have?

"No, they were ambushed and shot. By whom, we do not know," he answered.

At this point eyes grew too heavy to keep open, and my head bobbed towards my chest.

I hadn't even realised I had fallen asleep until Nanako shook my right shoulder ever so gently. "Into bed with you, mister, you can't even keep your eyes open." I don't know how long I had been asleep in the chair. It was almost dark now and there was no sign of Councillor Okada.

I stumbled over to my welcoming bed, where Nanako helped me take off the sling and my shirt. I climbed under the covers and lay down.

"You did that on purpose," I said drowsily as my eyes sought her out.

She knelt on the floor and propped her elbows on the bed beside the pillow. "Did what on purpose?"

"Told everyone I had dinner with you last night so you could sabotage the proposed marriage." I stared into her dark rimmed dark-brown eyes.

"Maybe," she said, smiling mischievously.

I wanted to reply, to say 'thank you,' but oblivion reached out and sucked me down into its depths. But her sweet, round face was the last thing I saw.

Chapter Seventeen

I woke around seven, as usual. The throbbing pain in my chest was a great way to start the day. My first thought was to look for Nanako, which was absurd – of course she wasn't still here. Nevertheless, I couldn't stop myself glancing around the flat to confirm it. She must have gone home with Councillor Okada last night before the curfew took effect.

Getting out of bed was an exercise in pain as well, since every muscle was as stiff as a board and ached too. Yesterday had not been a good day for my poor body. I finally managed to sit and hefted my legs over the side. My wound hurt so such that I wondered if I should have stayed in the hospital another day. If I'd done that, however, I would be still be on course to marry Sienna.

Relief surged through me as the truth liberated my mind – I was free of that dark, horrid future!

I also pondered the all-out Skel assault upon our foraging teams and Custodian protectors, and I became very troubled. What was going to happen now? They had destroyed all the foraging trucks and even two Bushmasters. And as long as the Skel remained out there, surrounding the town, we couldn't send out any more foragers.

I wondered if the Custodians would mount an offensive against the degenerate nomads, but surely such an attack would be suicidal. The Custodians had no experience with Skel ambushes. And if the Custodians were wiped out, what would stop the Skel breaking into Newhome and kidnapping and murdering its citizens until their black hearts were content? The town's future, and that of the surviving foragers, was shrouded in the swirling fog of uncertainty.

I had finished dressing when I heard three pairs of boots tramping towards my apartment and smiled in spite of myself. My teammates had come to visit.

"Hey guys, what's up?" I asked when I let them in.

"Well, you are," Shorty complained as he stepped past me. "Now I gotta pay Michal twenty bucks."

"Ha-ha, that'll teach you to make bets about Ethan's habits," Michal laughed as he followed him in. David brought up the rear, downcast, but his head no longer swathed in bandages.

"How you feeling, David?"

"Like my head's been hit by a sledgehammer, which is kind of accurate, I guess," he replied.

"And how are you, Mister Lone Ranger?" Shorty teased me as he headed for the fridge.

"I've felt better."

"Take a seat," Michal said as he shepherded me towards the dining table. "Breakfast is on us this morning."

I sat but sent a worried glance in their direction. "Not gonna give me food poisoning or something, are you?"

"Hey, it's us!" Shorty protested in mock indignation.

"That's what I'm afraid of." I laughed, and then wished I hadn't because of the pain that followed.

They somehow managed to throw together an edible breakfast for four, and grabbing a couple of plastic chairs from my balcony, the four of us crowded around my two-person dinner table. I observed that although Shorty was ignoring David, he was at least tolerating his presence, which was a start towards reconciliation.

"Hey Jones, did the Recycling-Works ring you last night?" Shorty asked while stuffing scrambled eggs in his mouth.

"Me? No."

"Well, all foraging has been suspended until we are advised otherwise. But it's not all doom and gloom. The good news is that we have to report to work as usual tomorrow morning and assist with recycling."

I cocked an eyebrow at Shorty. "Did I detect a slight trace of sarcasm there?"

"Absolutely not," he laughed. "But you don't need to worry just yet, Jones me boy, the boss said you can take off as long as you need to recover from your wound."

"Without pay, no doubt," I grumbled.

"Nothing in this world's free," David chimed in.

I sighed. "I'll lose the flat if I'm out of work too long, so I guess I'll have to turn up as soon as I've got the strength to walk there."

"Hey Ethan, seriously, where did you learn to use a gun like that?" Michal asked quietly. "I couldn't believe my eyes when we caught up to you yesterday. You were sitting next to David, covered in blood, and surrounded by dead Skel."

"As I told King, I just grabbed the gun and somehow instinctively knew how to use it. Kind of eerie, when I think of it."

"That's impossible, Jones," Shorty said emphatically, "And to be honest, I wouldn't believe Michal's tale if I hadn't seen you disarm King and run off with his gun."

"I thought you were dead," Michal confessed, his eyes boring holes through me. "You frightened the daylights out of me."

"Hey, it worked out in the end, thanks to you and King." I tried to reassure him.

Suddenly an image of a disassembled Austeyr assault-rifle flashed into my mind with crystal clarity. I had only enough time to register that experienced hands – my hands – were reassembling the gun. The rest of the 'spike attack' symptoms followed.

I tried to hide the attack by taking a sip of tea and pondered the image of myself assembling an assault-rifle, for I had never touched one before yesterday. That these images could be premonitions of my future was not a pleasant thought.

At any rate, my check-up with the neurologist was today, so I would run these 'spike attacks' past him and see what he thought. He'd probably stick me in the loony bin.

"Hey Jones, you're in pretty high spirits today, which is quite the surprise considering you got shot yesterday.

So what gives?" Shorty asked. "Did that Japanese chick make you another lunch?"

David squirmed uncomfortably in his seat. The situation probably reminded him of what he had just done to Leigh under similar circumstances.

"Something like that," I laughed, and then grimaced in pain.

Michal was staring at me intently. "David, Shorty, you two head off to work, I need to speak to Ethan."

"Don't mind me," Shorty grinned, not moving an inch. "Besides, we've still got plenty of time before we need to leave."

Michal glared at him with such intensity that he sprang from his chair, grabbed his bag, and left the flat with David.

"I dropped by last night just before curfew, planning to see if you were okay," Michal said slowly.

As I had been fast asleep then, I'm not sure where he was going with this, but I could guess. "Oh?"

"And I saw Nanako slip out of your flat by herself."

"She and Councillor Okada gave me a lift home after I had dinner with my parents, and they stayed for a while," I said.

Michal was clearly hurt by my answer. "This is me you're talking to, Ethan, not some gullible Custodian. Councillor Okada wasn't there. He arrived a moment later in his car and picked her up."

"Sorry mate. Look, they did drop me off and they did both come in, but I fell asleep at the dinner table. When I woke up, it was a couple of hours later and Councillor Okada was gone. Nanako told me to get in bed and…"

"Whoa, stop!" Michal panicked, holding up his hands.

"Oh, cut out the theatrics, Michal, I'm not Leigh." I rolled my eyes in exasperation. "She told me to get in bed and sleep, and that's what I did. Next thing I knew it was morning."

Michal seemed to buy my story, but he still wasn't happy. "Don't go doing anything stupid with that girl. She's such an innocent little thing and doesn't know Newhome's draconian laws. Could you live with yourself if she was executed because you went and did something foolish?"

"I won't," I insisted.

"If I saw her leaving your apartment by herself last night, the Custodians could have seen it too. Don't risk it again, man."

"I'll be more careful."

"You'd better be," Michal said, and sat back with his arms crossed.

I sighed in defeat. He was only looking out for me, and as usual, he was right. "Okay, I'll ask the councillor to stay with us next time he brings her over."

Michal relaxed somewhat. "Thank you."

"So, how are things at home?" I asked after a moment's silence.

"Same."

"Your efforts aren't in vain, you know," I said, trying to encourage him.

"How do you figure that?"

"When your brother and sister grow up, whose example do you think they're gonna follow? His, or yours?"

"Why'd they follow his example?" he asked, confused.

"Well, that's often what happens, isn't it? Kids with a violent, alcoholic father end up walking in his footsteps. And when asked why, they say, 'How else could I have turned out with a father like him?' But you're showing your brother and sister that they don't have to turn out like him. They can turn out like you instead."

Michal flashed me a brief smile. "Thanks, mate, I needed to hear that." He glanced at my clock, "Well, I'd better be off or I'll be late for work." And with that he ran out to catch up to the others.

I had an hour to kill before I had to leave for the hospital, so I set my alarm and lay down to rest. I would have to walk there, but would give myself extra time so I could go as slowly as I needed.

* * *

I don't know why the hospital gave you an 11.00am appointment and then made you wait two hours before you could actually see the doctor. Why not just tell me to come at 1.00pm?

When the nurse finally told me I could go in to the neurologist's consultation room, I was stiff and sore and just a tad annoyed.

The neurologist, Doctor Nguyen, an Asian man in his forties, waved me to a chair by the window. "And what have you been up to, young Ethan?" he asked when he saw the sling.

"I took a Skel crossbow bolt in the chest yesterday."

"You did? Then what are you doing walking around? Why aren't you still in casualty?"

"Don't take this personally, Doctor, but I've had enough of hospital beds to last a lifetime."

"Yes, I suppose you have," he answered thoughtfully. "So, how have you been these past six months. Still seizure free?"

"Yes, Sir," I replied, "however, I've been having these strange turns. They're probably nothing, though."

"Tell me about them."

So I gave him a detailed description of the 'spike attacks,' and by the time I finished, he looked quite concerned. "What you've just described is a temporal lobe seizure," he said.

That was the last thing I expected him to say, and the shock hit me like a king-hit to the head. What if I ended up incapacitated by seizures like before? What if the amnesia got worse? "Can they become grand mal seizures like the ones I used to get after my accident?"

"It's very unlikely, but a possibility nonetheless. Now, what I would normally do at this stage is send you off for MRI and EEG scans, however, that is not an option at the moment."

"Why not?" I asked, puzzled.

"The Custodians have made it mandatory that all CAT, MRI and EEG scans be shown to their hospital representative before they are discussed with the patients," he said, angry at this invasion of doctor-patient confidentiality.

"Why is that a problem?" I asked, although I already knew the answer. It was another way the Custodians were trying to root out the mutants who had slipped through the cracks.

Doctor Nguyen stood, quietly closed the door, and sat again. "I went to great lengths to hide your...what shall I call it? Unique ability, when you came here in November 2120. I also used a hand-picked team I could trust to observe patient confidentiality when we operated on you."

I think my eyes were just about popping out of my head. "You know?"

"Of course," he said quietly. "Your brain, ears and voice box are very noticeably different from the norm, and very remarkable, I might add."

"Doctor, I don't know what to say." I was almost overcome by emotion. All my life I had hidden my mutation, believing I would be reported should it be discovered. Yet this doctor and the team who had operated on me had kept my secret, and at great personal risk.

"You don't need to say anything, Son," he said warmly. "There are many in the medical profession who will do virtually anything to hide the batches of children who were biologically engineered back in the early 2100s. The ultrasound technician who scanned your mother when she was pregnant was obviously one."

"Sorry, did you just say 'biologically engineered?'" I asked, not believing what I just heard.

"That's right, why, what did you think caused you to be like this?"

"The Custodians say it is a mutation caused by nuclear radiation."

"Oh no," he reassured me with a smile, "nuclear radiation may cause birth defects, such as cleft palates, extra fingers or toes, but that's all pretty much in the past now."

"So this was done to me deliberately? By whom and with whose authority?" I demanded, feeling a rush of anger.

"For your own safety, Ethan, it is best you do not know the precise details of what happened. Suffice to say it was an unauthorised experiment done in secret by a geneticist, who regretfully took his own life and destroyed his work when he was discovered."

"Do the Custodians know this?"

"The senior ones do, most certainly."

"So why are they trying to kill us?"

"Honestly, Ethan, that is not necessarily the case. All I know is that when the Custodians find any of the biologically engineered children, they take them to a secret facility in North End and they are never seen again."

They could have been dissected in an attempt to see what made them tick, or they could be alive and imprisoned. The only way to find out would be to let myself get caught, and I wasn't going to do that. I suddenly felt as though I didn't know myself. I wasn't a mutant like I had always believed, but was deliberately altered to be like this – to have these abilities. On one hand, I was outraged that such a thing was done underhandedly, but on the other, I considered my abnormality to be the most amazing gift ever. I wondered why the geneticist had done it. What was his purpose? Was it to make us better adapted to survival in our Post

Apocalyptic landscape? If it was, he succeeded most magnificently.

"So what do we do about these temporal lobe seizures?" I asked, changing the topic.

"What I will do for now, at least until the Custodians relax their grip on the hospital, is give you anticonvulsant medication to take twice daily. These should stop the seizures. Start taking the tablets tomorrow, and make an appointment to see me again in four weeks. However, instruct your family or workmates beforehand that if you have a grand mal seizure, they must bring you to the emergency department immediately afterwards. They must request me by name."

I nodded as he handed me a prescription.

"There was one more thing I wanted to ask you, Doctor. The images I see when I have these temporal lobe seizures, what are they?" I asked hesitantly.

"They are memories."

"Memories?" I asked, shocked. "But if that's the case, then how come I don't recognise any of them?"

"Give me an example."

"One image was of a polished wooden floor with slippers and boots, none of which I remember seeing before. Another was of a messy bathroom sink that's nothing like the sinks I've ever seen, and stuff like that." I thought I'd better not mention the gun, just in case.

Doctor Nguyen expired thoughtfully. "My guess, young Ethan, is that these memories are from the year you don't remember."

Now that statement baffled me. "But my father told me I spent all of 2120 in hospital."

"Goodness no. You responded very well to the operation and were discharged within a few days, if I recall correctly," he replied.

Fear blossomed deep within in my gut. I suddenly felt very, very disorientated. "So what was I doing for the rest of that year?"

"I suggest you ask your father."

"We aren't exactly on speaking terms at the moment," I admitted reluctantly. "How long was I in hospital?"

The doctor leafed through the pages in my file. You were admitted into hospital on the 16th of November 2120, and checked out on the 8th of December.

I rose slightly in my seat so I could see the hospital patient-discharge form the doctor was examining. I could see quite clearly where it said:

Patient: Ethan Jones
Discharged: 8 Dec 2120
Signed out by: William Jones
Relationship to Patient: Father

I had been in hospital for just over three weeks, from mid-November to early December. So where was I from January till November? Why was my father hiding it from me? And why had the amnesia blotted out a whole year?

The doctor suddenly leaned forward and touched my knee gently. "There's one more thing I need to tell you, Ethan, since it appears your memories are starting to return. Your father insisted that I told you your head injury was caused by a collapsed ceiling."

"That's not what caused it?"

"No, you had been shot, though not when you were brought in. You had been operated on previously, but not by a neurosurgeon," he said.

I sat there for some time, trying to process the distressing information he just dumped on me. I had been shot in 2120! How on earth did that happen? Who shot me? Why did they shoot me? The disorientation I experienced a moment ago threatened to become full blown vertigo.

"I know this is a lot to swallow at once, Ethan, and I wish I could talk with you more, but I have a list of patients to see today as long as my arm. You can stay here in my office for as long as you need. I'll use the office next door for my next patient," Doctor Nguyen said as he rose.

I don't think I even noticed him leave, and I'm not sure how long I sat there in his office, trying to get my head around what he told me. My father said I'd been in hospital from January until December 2120. So what had I been doing between January and November? Wherever I was, and whatever I was doing, it had lead to my being shot.

I had an impulse to rush over and see my father to get the truth out of him, but gave up on the idea. I figured he would probably just throw me out of the house.

I eventually left the hospital and began the slow walk back to my flat. I hadn't taken the prescription to the hospital pharmacy. If I started taking the anticonvulsants the temporal lobe seizures would stop, and so would the memories. And I desperately wanted those memories.

They could be my only chance to find out what happened to me in those missing months.

Chapter Eighteen

Lunch was leftover oden and it proved to be just as delicious cold as when hot. In fact, the flavour was enhanced by sitting in my fridge for a couple of days.

I had just finished and was clearing the table when I heard Nanako and Councillor Okada coming down the walkway towards my flat. I considered opening the door before they got here, but as I was supposed to be hiding my superior hearing, decided against it.

A moment later came the expected knock at the door. Today Nanako wore over-knee socks, boots, jacket, and biker shorts – all black. The black contrasted magnificently with her pink fringe.

"You finished early today?" I asked as she stepped inside, surprising me by planting a kiss on my cheek.

"They didn't request our presence today," she replied, "All the bigwigs have been called to some urgent meeting."

"Probably trying to work out what to do about this new Skel threat," I said, and then, bearing in mind what Michal told me this morning, I turned to Counsellor Okada. "Please join us, Sir."

He hesitated, but then acquiesced and stepped into the flat. "Thank you, Ethan."

"You're looking a lot better today," Nanako said.

She ran a petite hand down the side of my face, her gentle touch breaking down some of the mental and emotional walls I had built around myself over the years. Walls erected to protect myself from getting hurt by Father and Elder Sister.

"Amazing what a good sleep can do for you," I replied.

While the councillor remained in the kitchen and stared out the window, Nanako pulled me over to the sofa and we sat facing each other.

"I dropped by this morning, but you weren't in," she said.

"I had a check-up with the neurologist."

"And how did it go?"

"Well, not so good. I've been having these strange turns lately, and he said they're a form of epileptic seizure."

Nanako's face inexplicably paled. She leaned forward and laid a hand on my forearm. "Oh no! Are they dangerous like the seizures you used to get?"

"They're not much of a risk, apparently," I assured her, since she looked so worried. "And they can be controlled by meds I'm supposed to take twice a day. There's one good thing, though – every time I have one of these temporal lobe seizures, a memory flashes into my mind. And according to the doctor, the memories are from the year I don't remember."

Nanako grabbed my left arm with great excitement, but quickly let go again when I winced in pain. "Sorry," she grinned sheepishly, "but that's wonderful! What have you remembered?"

"Just a bunch of mundane items and places I don't recall having seen before, like a polished floor, a beaten up ute in a factory courtyard, a messy bathroom basin, stuff like that."

"Any memories of people?" she asked keenly.

"No, not yet."

She was clearly disappointed. "Well, keep thinking of those memories, and try to trigger more, okay?"

"Don't worry, I've been pondering them over and over, trying to work out how they fit into that year," I told her. Suddenly I remembered what I wanted to do this afternoon. "Hey, I'm gonna pop over and visit my younger sister, you wanna come?"

"I'd love to, but what about your father?"

"He doesn't get home 'til five. All the same, we're gonna to have to sneak into my sister's room, as I'm not allowed to enter it otherwise, and she's probably too tired to come out and talk to us."

And so we headed over to my parent's place, with the ever faithful Councillor Okada giving us a lift and walking us to the door.

I pulled out my key and then listened carefully, trying to work out where my mother and older sister were. That I could not climb up the back of the building like I normally did was a major inconvenience.

I could just discern sounds in the kitchen — sounds caused by two people. So I slipped the key into the door and opened it noiselessly. Glancing down at Nanako, I held a finger to my lips and crept silently into the house.

To my amazement, she proved to be rather adept at walking quietly too.

We went to the small hallway that lead to the kitchen and the women's bedroom. When the sounds indicated that my mother and older sister were on the far side of the room, we darted into the bedroom.

I quietly closed the door behind us and opened the blinds overlooking the balcony, letting light illuminate the dingy room.

My younger sister opened her eyes and smiled when she saw us. "Hi Ethan, and you brought Nanako too, that's great."

I saw the barely touched plate of sandwiches on the bedside table next to her and sighed. "You told me you were gonna try harder to eat," I chided her.

"Sorry." She avoided eye contact.

Nanako sat on the bed beside her and smiled warmly. "How are you feeling, Meredith?"

"Tired."

Nanako peered closely at the sores at the corner of her mouth, and took one of her hands in hers, brushing her fingertips lightly over the slightly upturned nails.

"Do you sleep well?" she asked.

My sister shook her head.

"Do you get leg cramps? Is it hard to breathe when you walk about?"

My sister nodded in the affirmative for each question.

Nanako looked over to where I stood at the foot of the bed. "She's anemic."

"She's what?" I asked, fearing it may be an incurable disease.

"She has less red blood cells than normal. It's from not having enough iron in her diet," she explained, running a hand affectionately through Younger Sister's unkempt, long hair. "Has she been like this long?"

I nodded. "Too long."

"It's easy to treat," she assured us confidently.

"My father won't take her to a doctor," I said resentfully.

"You don't need a doctor," Nanako replied, and then turned to my sister. "Do you want to be well, Meredith, and be normal like everyone else?" My sister nodded. "You'll have to be brave and eat a special diet, even if you don't like it. And if you do, you'll be healthy like the rest of us in no time."

"I'll try," my sister said hesitantly, which was better than a flat out refusal.

The bedroom door suddenly banged open and my older sister barged in, only to freeze with eyes wide in disbelief. "Ethan! What are you doing here? And you brought that girl with you!"

Mother heard the disturbance and rushed into the room, scowling when she saw us. "Ethan, you know you're not allowed in here."

"We wanted to see Younger Sister," I replied simply.

"Then knock on the front door like normal people," Elder Sister snapped. "How did you get in here, anyway?"

"Walked right past you," I replied, and then turned excitedly to my mother. "Mother, Nanako says Younger Sister is anemic and it can be treated easily with a special diet!"

Mother sighed. "Oh Ethan, you know your father won't allocate any more money for buying food."

"You won't have to, Mrs. Jones," Nanako assured her. "You just need to buy some different foods than what you are used to."

"I can't believe we're even having this conversation!" Elder Sister snapped. "Get out of our room, Ethan, and don't ever come in here again!"

"Please don't stop him visiting me," Younger Sister begged.

"You mean he sneaks in here often?" asked my older sister.

"Mother knows," Younger Sister answered softly, "and she never stopped it."

"Well, I wasn't sure, but I suspected it," Mother answered kindly. Like me, she had a real soft spot for my little sister. "I could not think of anyone else who could be buying you such expensive food so often."

"I thought you were buying that food for her, Mother," said my older sister as she glanced from mother to me, and back again. "I thought you were secretly taking money from Father to buy it."

"Oh, don't be silly," mother scolded her. She fetched a pad of paper and pencil and turned to Nanako. "Please go ahead, Nanako. What changes do I need to make to her diet?"

"You don't have any beef in Newhome, but instead of that you can have chicken, eggs and fish. Always eat whole grain breads and cereals, and also spinach, lentils and peas, nuts, and dried fruits like prunes, apricots and raisins. And give her citrus fruit with each meal, it helps the body absorb the iron better," Nanako said as my mother wrote.

"Thank you, I will incorporate as many of these as I can into her diet, and I'll find a way to do so without Father complaining," my mother replied enthusiastically, "Tell me, how do you know so much about food?"

"It is a Japanese tradition for mothers to instruct their daughters about nutrition and healthy eating," Nanako replied, "Our schools also provide healthy lunches to the children. They are not allowed to bring their own."

After that, Mother and Nanako fell to talking about food and recipes, so I sat with my younger sister and chatted with her, hoping against hope that she would co-operate and eat this special diet and recover from her condition. And if she did, one of the heaviest burdens that had weighed my heart down for so long could lift away.

We left my parent's flat at four-thirty to ensure there was no risk of running into my Father when he came home from work. He was still very angry this morning, apparently.

My Japanese friends drove me home again, and Nanako told me she would come back and cook dinner for me after she had gone shopping.

While she was gone, I lay down for a much needed rest, my mind racing with thoughts about this girl who was taking such an interest in me. It was a most peculiar experience, which both worried and excited me at the same time.

Chapter Nineteen

As she had promised, Nanako made udon when she returned an hour later. It was a Japanese soup with thick white noodles, tofu, seaweed, her hand-made fish cakes, radish, and deep-fried prawns. (I invited Councillor Okada to join us again, but this time he politely but firmly refused my invitation, bowed and made his exit.)

Nanako served the udon in breakfast bowls, with salad and bread rolls served alongside it. "Sorry, the noodles aren't the correct ones," she said as we sat down to eat together, "but they are the closest thing I could find."

"Smells fantastic." I picked up my chopsticks to eat. And while I sucked down the thick noodles with as much decorum as possible, Nanako slurped hers down quite noisily. I was surprised at this sudden display of bad manners, but hid my reaction.

"You like it?" she asked between loud slurps.

"Love it," I replied. "You know, I wish you could cook for me every day."

"You never know, maybe I will." She locked her beautiful eyes upon mine.

My face suddenly became hot, and I don't think it was from the soup. I got the impression yet again that she was interested in me. Yet, that niggling doubt that she was only doing these things to repay a debt for saving her life refused to go away.

"Nanako, there's something I've been wanting to tell you." It was time to get these doubts out in the open. "I don't want you to feel like you owe me anything."

"You mean for saving me from the Skel?" she asked, her eyes sparkling mischievously.

"Yes."

"Is that why you think I'm making these meals and spending time with you?"

"Well...no, that's not what I meant. I just want to make sure you don't think you owe me anything."

She leaned forward, smiling broadly. "That's not why I'm doing these things."

"Then why are you?"

"Because I like you," she replied, and then, looking down at her dinner, she muttered softly under her breath, "*Anata o aishite iru kara.*"

I wasn't supposed to hear that phrase whispered in Japanese, but to my ears, it was as clear as if she had spoken it aloud in English. She had said; "It's because I love you."

Now that was the one answer I hadn't expected to hear. To be honest, that such a beautiful, mysterious girl should profess she loved me, made me feel special and privileged. But it also confused, because we barely knew each other. Not to mention that a relationship between us would never be allowed, thanks to my town's rigid customs.

"But you've known me for less than a week," was all I could think to say.

"As soon as I saw you on Monday – after you had helped Councillor Okada from the car, I knew you."

"What do you mean?"

She reached across the table and laid her small left hand on my right. A thrill raced up my arm and down the back of my spine, melting more of the walls I had built around my heart. "When I saw you, I saw an upright, honest man with a heart for others – a man of passion and capable of greatness."

"I…don't know what to say. No-one's ever said anything like that to me before."

"Then don't say anything." She smiled.

I thought of Father's attempt to marry me off to Sienna King, and once again wished he would contact Nanako's parents to arrange a marriage between the two of us instead. I wished this blossoming friendship could continue yet on a much deeper level. But sadly, it was impossible. My father would never allow it, since he considered it his duty to pick my wife. He also made it clear he was only interested in me marrying a girl who could advance my social standing in the town. Being an outsider, Nanako could not meet either of those hurdle requirements.

It was also just as likely that Nanako's father would not approve of me. This made me wonder what her goals were in pursuing me so openly. I refused to think it was a merely physical attraction, since she said she loved me.

Searching for answers, I decided to try the bold approach. "Nanako, are marriages in Hamamachi arranged by the fathers like here in Newhome, with the children having no say in the matter?"

She shook her head emphatically, her pink fringe swinging from side to side. "In Hamamachi a couple either meets through an introduction arranged by the parents – with no obligation to marry, or they meet and decide to marry entirely on their own, with no input from their parents."

"You're kidding!"

"I'm serious," she said, before lowering her voice and continuing, "Ethan, I've visited several Victorian towns and none of them are even remotely like Newhome. None of them have twelve-foot walls. Their residents are free to come and go as they please. There are no exclusive upper class districts like your North End, and I've never seen anything like your Custodians. They seem more interested in controlling the people than in providing security against external threats."

I tried to absorb what she shared and to be honest I wasn't overly surprised. I had long considered Newhome a prison for a population with very few freedoms.

"Do you know who established this town? Because I'd bet it wasn't someone from Australia."

Now that was a thought that had never occurred to me. "Who else could have established it? We are at the southern end of the Australian continent. What foreign power would have come all the way down here to set up a town?"

"It's a mystery, that's for sure. Councillor Okada is stumped by it too. He believes the submarine moored in the river beside the town may be the answer."

"The submarine's nuclear reactor provides Newhome with its electricity. Do you think it isn't from the Australian navy?"

"The councillor says it's a Soviet built, Whiskey Twin-Cylinder, but that doesn't mean it's from Russia, since they sold them to a number of nations. And are you sure it has a nuclear reactor? The councillor said the Whiskey-class subs had diesel-electric engines."

"All of Newhome's power comes from the sub," I answered. "There's an entire department here devoted to the maintenance of the nuclear reactor. From time to time, they disconnect it from the city's power supply to replace or repair a component. My friend David said it's to make sure no parts of the reactor ever develop cracks."

"So someone down the line must have replaced the sub's engine with a nuclear reactor. Still, our guess is that whoever came here in that sub established this town."

"Interesting." I wondered if there was some way I could find out what nation the sub originally belonged to. I decided to file that topic for later consideration and returned to what we were discussing previously – a topic that was of much greater significance to me personally. "Forgetting about submarines for a moment, I was wondering, at what age you are permitted to marry in Hamamachi? It's eighteen here."

"It's twenty for us," she replied. "However, the age can be lowered to eighteen with parental consent and a magistrate's approval."

I pondered the mindboggling implications of Nanako having the freedom of choosing her own husband. The implications filled me with nervous excitement.

There was one more question I absolutely had to ask. "Nanako, do you have...you know, a guy back home?" I was pretty sure I already knew the answer.

Her confidence faltered and she broke eye contact, her hand from mine. "No. I did have, a couple of years ago, but he...he said he never wanted to see me again."

I looked at her downcast face, and felt sorry for her. I reached out and lifted her chin so that she met my gaze again. "Nanako, if I had a girl like you, I'd never ever, for any reason whatsoever, let her go."

Her eyes filling with tears, Nanako suddenly stood to her feet. "Sorry, I need to go to the bathroom."

She practically ran to the bathroom and shut the door behind her

Great, I screwed up again. I really needed to stop putting my foot in my mouth. As I stood to follow her, with my enhanced hearing I heard her slide down the bathroom wall to the floor and sob quietly. She mumbled the same phrase over and over, "I can't go through this again, I just can't."

And then I knew what weighed so heavily on her heart, why she sat crying so dejectedly on the apartments' roof her first night here. Some fool guy had broken her heart.

I knocked softly on the bathroom door.

"Nanako, please don't cry. Not in there, all by yourself." I wanted nothing more than to help her forget about the guy that hurt her so badly.

There was no response, other than continued sobbing. I didn't want to go barging in there. Determined to give her privacy, I collected the dirty dishes and washed them rather noisily. I put the leftover udon back on the stove and covered it.

Nanako emerged from the bathroom five minutes later, her eyes puffy from crying. Outwardly composed, she bowed. "I'm sorry. We were having such a lovely evening. I'm sorry for spoiling it by getting all emotional."

I reached out and took her left hand awkwardly in mine. "You have nothing to apologise for."

"Shall we watch some TV?" she asked, tugging me after her as she headed for the sofa.

I popped on the TV and we dropped onto the threadbare sofa, which only just barely accommodated two. She sat on my right, turned towards me, and draped her slim, shapely legs on top of mine. The way her thighs flattened out upon mine was simply mesmerising. She laid her head on my shoulder and snuggled her arms against my chest. I hesitantly put my right arm around her, and simply enjoyed being with her. As we cuddled, a serene peace filled me, driving away the disturbing sense of emptiness that had been with me ever since I woke in the hospital back in December 2120.

It was strange. I had never seen my parents cuddle, hug or even touch, but holding Nanako like this felt like the most natural thing in the world. I ran my fingers through her hair and then jerked them back in surprise. "You're wearing a wig!"

"You didn't know?" she giggled.

"I had no idea," I laughed. "Can I see your real hair?"

"Alright." She carefully lifted off the pink and black wig and removed a stocking cap that held her hair flat. That done, she shook her hair out until it fell naturally around her face.

The result was stunning. Her real hair was naturally black and worn in a bob-cut that was short at the back and long at the front. And like the wig, her fringe hung below her eyebrows, which, if anything, further enhanced the effect of the thick eyeliner around her eyes.

"Why the wig? You look just as pretty without it," I declared as I ran my fingers through her hair, which was as smooth as silk.

"I like it, besides, it's part of the fashion," she answered. Then she hesitated before she asked, "Hey, can you give me a leg massage?"

I looked at her in surprise. "A what?"

"You know, massage the muscles in my legs."

"How do I do that?"

"Just start at the ankles and work your way up," she said.

I looked at her legs draped over mine, and at the exposed length of thigh showing between her over-knee socks and shorts, and it seemed to me that what she was asking was quite improper. "Sorry, I really can't."

"Sure you can," she assured me as she rested her head on my shoulder again.

"It...doesn't feel right. I mean, just us being alone together is against the law..."

"Ethan, it's only a massage."

"Right."

Buffeted by guilt because she was an unmarried girl and I was raised to believe this was wrong – a crime even, I hesitated. But the intimacy of her embrace and the giddy realisation that she liked me – loved me, even – sent those thoughts fleeing from my mind. Before I knew what I was doing, my left hand was out of the sling and massaging her ankle and then her shapely calf. All the while, the feel of her body against mine was exhilarating.

I worked my hand up to the back of her knee (and there was no way I was gonna go higher than her knee) when her legs and arms began to twitch. I felt her grow limp against my chest and looked down at her in surprise. She was fast asleep.

I ceased massaging her legs since I felt uncomfortable touching them, and pondered all the things she had done since I met her. Her meaningful glances, making obento for my lunch, the oden and udon for dinner, her gentleness in caring for me when I got wounded, even standing up to my father. All of these things captured my attention and interest. But this! To be so innocent and trusting as to fall asleep in my arms – now she had gone and captured my heart as well.

I knew then that I wanted to be with her forever. And as I held her in my arms, I wanted to scream in frustration because of our rigid customs regarding marriage. I spent my life expecting to be locked in a loveless marriage: it never occurred to me that I would meet a girl like Nanako. Was there anything I could do to be with her?

It occurred to me that if she went back to Hamamachi, I could abscond while foraging and make the dangerous trek alone to be with her there. But with all foraging trips on hold, I wouldn't have the opportunity to leave any time soon. In fact, with the Skel besieging Newhome, I may never have the opportunity again.

Of course, if I did manage to run away, it would be a one-way trip. I would never see my family again, for to return would mean a lengthy prison term. And though I'd miss my younger sister and mother, I would willing pay that price if it meant I could be with Nanako.

Another thought popped into my mind – what if I could find a way to persuade my father to let me marry Nanako? It was a long shot, especially in light of what had happened last night. Then there was the matter of the inexplicable animosity between my father and Nanako.

As I tried to dig my way through this impossible situation, my eyes grew heavy and I too fell asleep.

And began to dream.

Chapter Twenty

Although I was dreaming, my mind entered a state of such clarity that it felt like I was actually experiencing what I dreamed. It was January 2120, and I had only been out of school for several weeks. The next month I would turn eighteen.

Having run away from my foraging team, I was prowling quietly along the front of an old, dilapidated factory in Lilydale, one of Melbourne's easternmost suburbs.

To my left was the factory's car park, overgrown by weeds and wild blackberry bushes. A battered old ute was parked there, but it wasn't the ute that interested me. It was the sound of four young people having a riotous good time – laughing, cackling, and shouting in a foreign language.

I was wary of them – as I was of everything out in Melbourne's ruins – yet at the same time irresistibly curious because I could hear male and female voices together. So I crept quietly through the wild blackberries and climbed, without making a noise, onto the bonnet of the ute. I sat cross-legged and settled down to watch them.

They were teenagers of a similar age – there were two guys and two girls. And they were having a fun watching four small lizards racing through narrow plastic pipes. Whenever a lizard popped its head out the wrong end, they would slap their thighs and laugh boisterously. The little lizards garnered a similar reaction when they appeared out of the far end, but then disappeared back into the safety of the pipe before they could be caught.

I was most surprised and yet extremely fascinated to see girls outside their homes without their mothers to chaperone them, not to mention mixing with boys on even terms.

The shorter of the two girls must have spotted me from her peripheral vision, because she suddenly stood up and whirled to face me, her slightly upturned mouth open as she studied me with a mixture of concern and curiosity.

She was by far the strangest and yet the most intriguing girl I had seen. Her beautiful hair was jet black except for the fringe and some longer strands, which were dark pink. She wore a zebra striped jacket over a black top, a skirt made of lace, and tattered pink and black leggings. She also had a black choker with a silver bell around her neck.

"Hello," she said in English with a broad Australian accent.

"Hi," I replied.

"Have you been there long?" Her dark brown eyes studied me intently.

I nodded. "A while."

"I didn't notice you come. Are you by yourself?" She glanced around.

"I can be pretty quiet, and yes, I'm alone."

Her three companions, who were now aware of my presence, jumped to their feet and stood beside her, clearly worried. The taller girl was dressed similarly, while the boys wore jeans and t-shirts. The tallest boy pulled out a gun and aimed it at me, but the first girl stretched out a hand and pushed it away.

"What's your name?" she asked, peering out from beneath her pink fringe.

"Ethan."

"I'm Nanako. Where are you from?"

"From a town about a day's walk west of here."

"Really? So why are you out here by yourself?"

"I kind of ran away," I replied, hoping the admission didn't make me seem like an immature juvenile.

"From your family?" she asked, clearly surprised.

"No, not from them, from the town," I replied, thinking that should have been obvious.

Her eyes, rimmed with thick, black eyeliner, widened in surprise. "You mean you can't come and go from your town as you please?"

"No. No one is allowed to leave Newhome."

"So how did you get away?" She took a step forward. It appeared she wasn't wary of me any longer.

"I'm a forager. I go out into Melbourne's ruins with a team to collect scrap metal. When no one was looking yesterday I ran off."

She came closer, smiling warmly now. "We're a foraging team too. We collect old mobile phones and such. But hey, I bet you're hungry. How'd you like to join us for lunch?"

"Sounds great," I said as I slid off the ute.

The girl's friends spoke to her in hushed voices in their own language, clearly concerned. But she must have allayed their fears, for they joined her in fetching their lunches from the ute.

Nanako brought out a beautiful lacquered black lunchbox wrapped in a handkerchief, and invited me to sit with her.

Feeling way out of my depth, I accepted her invitation and hesitantly sat beside her. She gave me a rice-ball wrapped in paper-thin seaweed. I had never eaten rice before, and it tasted awesome – a refreshing break from potatoes and bread.

"My friends are Miki, Ken and Hiro. They don't speak English, I'm afraid," she said. "We're Japanese, by the way, from Hamamachi, over near Inverloch."

I nodded politely to the others, and they gave short bows in return. I reflected on my good fortune to have found such friendly people one day out of Newhome.

"Hey Ethan," Nanako said as she passed me a block of scrambled egg wrapped with seaweed. "Why don't you come back to Hamamachi with us and join one of our foraging teams – maybe even ours. We can use all the foragers we can get."

"Can I leave the town when I want to?" I asked, worried that I might be walking into another prison.

"Of course," she answered, and then, after making meaningful eye contact with me, added, "If you want to leave, that is."

My head jerked, tearing me out of the dream. For a moment I was so disorientated I had no idea where I was. Nanako's presence quickly brought me back to reality, though. She was snuggled against my chest, legs draped over mine, still fast asleep.

I don't know how long I slept, but it must have been at least a couple of hours. Apart from the flickering light and shadows caused by the television, the room was almost completely dark.

My mind raced frantically as I tried to process what the dream revealed. It was clearly a memory from my missing year. And a major clue as to what really happened during that time. I had run away from Newhome in January 2120 and headed east, where I bumped into Nanako and her foraging team. After that they invited me to Hamamachi.

I guess I had been willing to run away at that time because it was before my younger sister got sick. Perhaps father lied about what really happened because he was afraid I would run away again if I found out I had done so previously.

I ran my fingers through Nanako's silky black hair and contemplated the most puzzling revelation of the dream, that Nanako and I did not meet on Monday as I had supposed, but three years ago.

Now I understood why she kept staring at me after we saved her and Councillor Okada from the Skel. She must have been so surprised that out of all the people in Newhome who could have rescued her, it just happened to be me. Yet at the same time she must have been so disappointed I didn't recognise her.

But why didn't she greet me by name as soon as she saw me? If I had responded by saying I didn't know her, she could have explained to me how we'd met before. Instead, she greeted me as a stranger. And in all the times I saw her since then, she never once gave me any indication that we met previously. Well, except for the excitement she showed when I told her my memories were returning, and disappointment when I said I hadn't remembered any people yet. She was obviously hoping I would remember her.

The question was, why was she hiding the truth from me? Was there something she didn't want me to find out? I mean, I know she had been in a relationship with a guy two years ago who dumped her and broke her heart. But where did I fit into her life at that time? Were we workmates? Good friends?

Whatever the answer was, she clearly had feelings for me now. She told me that she liked me and whispered under her breath that she loved me.

That I had gone to Hamamachi solved another mystery. Nanako said that everyone in Hamamachi, from seventeen to fifty-five years of age, served in the Militia, so I must have served in it too. That would explain how I learned to use a gun and fight in hand-to-hand combat, confirming King's suspicions that I had been properly trained. It also explained my memory of assembling an Austeyr assault-rifle.

The doctor said I had been operated on before I was brought to him in November, so after I was shot I must have had an operation in Hamamachi. That led to another puzzle I desperately needed answers for. How was I shot?

And this of course led to the next question, and this one was quite significant – who brought me back to Newhome? Whoever it was, they brought me back because they didn't have the means or knowledge in Hamamachi to treat the bad seizures I was having. They must have suspected or known that Newhome had a better hospital and neurosurgeons.

I recalled the discharge paper from the hospital. My father was listed as the one who checked me out. There was also an admission sheet, but unfortunately, I hadn't seen any of the details.

Suddenly, I had to know whose name was written on that sheet. There would be other information in that file I needed to know too. Perhaps even a record or details of how I was shot.

I could sneak over to the hospital right now, pick the lock, and find the information I needed. I considered waking Nanako, confronting her with what my dream had revealed, and asking her if she knew the answers I sought, but would she tell me the truth?

My father lied to me about what happened in 2120 – for two years. And although Nanako hadn't actually lied, she hadn't offered to tell me the truth either. And that meant I couldn't trust either of them. On the other hand, I figured I could trust the hospital records.

I pulled my left arm out of the sling and stretched, grimacing from the pain that stabbed through my chest. I gently lifted Nanako's legs, slipped out from beneath them, and placed them back on the sofa.

After that I changed into black jeans and a black hoody. I stuffed a torch into my belt and armed myself with a set of lock picks I smuggled in from a foraging trip. That done, I slipped out the front door.

Chapter Twenty-One

With my left hand in my pocket to minimize the pain I felt every time I moved the arm, I made my way to the hospital. I had to go to ground twice so that passing Custodian patrols wouldn't see me. If they spotted me, I could spend up to a month in prison for breaking the curfew.

Since Newhome was small size, I was soon in front of the hospital's main entrance, which was of course locked. The emergency department would be open all night, and the entrance was just to the left, so I decided to tackle the front doors. I soon had them open with the assistance of my lock-picks. For the first time I was glad the town council had never bothered spending money to modernise the hospital – the building was decades old, and the locks were very old fashioned. I had picked many such locks out in Melbourne's ruins.

I closed the doors quietly behind me. Taking great care to avoid the hospital's night shift staff and a roving Custodian security detail, I made my way to the neurology department. It was closed and only partially illuminated by the occasional light. Finding my file in the receptionist's office proved quite difficult using only a torch, as there were multiple metal filing cabinets, and piles of papers stacked everywhere. Eventually, I found the cabinet that contained the files of patients admitted into hospital in 2120. Filing by date instead of alphabetically. *What's that about, anyway?*

My hands were shaking when I found and removed my file. I had a good mind to put it back and walk away, but I had to know what secrets it could divulge.

I sat on the floor behind the receptionist's desk and went through the file. As the neurologist said, there were no references to my bio-engineered abnormalities. Nor were there any copies of MRI or EEG scans they had taken.

The first disturbing thing I discovered was the report on the bullet wound, which said I had been shot at point blank range. Fear's cold tendrils snaked through my stomach and into my head. How had this happened? How could someone have gotten that close to me without me knowing about it or trying to stop them? Did someone try to kill me in my sleep? Or while serving in the Militia? With my sensitive hearing, it just didn't make any sense.

I breathed deeply and turned the page. There was no point getting all worked up and worried about something that could not be resolved by guesswork. I kept shuffling through the file, looking for the patient-admission form, and finally found it. It recorded:

Patient: Ethan Jones
Admission: 16 Nov 2120
Signed in by: Nanako Jones

Relationship to Patient: Wife

I don't know how long I sat there, staring at the admission form, simply trying to comprehend the stupendous truth it revealed. And as the truth sank slowly into my mind, my perspective of my life, of myself, slowly unravelled until I felt like I no longer knew who I was.

Nanako was my wife?

That meant I must have married her after I went to Hamamachi. Furthermore, she was the one who brought me back to Newhome to receive the operation that stopped the grand mal epileptic seizures.

But if this was true, why did she leave me? If she was my wife, why did she abandon me and go back to Hamamachi without me? She didn't even wait to see the results of the operation.

Anger at this betrayal slowly turned to rage, driving away the confusion and all other emotions.

I put my file back in the cabinet and stormed angrily out of the hospital, pausing only to lock the front doors.

It was raining incessantly now, and the rain soon soaked through my clothes and bandages, chilling my body but not my mood.

"Why, Nanako? Why did you leave me?" I whispered to myself in an endless loop.

Running on adrenaline alone, I dodged two Custodian patrols and eventually reached my apartment. I barged through the front door and saw the flat was still lost in darkness with the flickering TV as the only light source. I switched on the lights.

Nanako was still asleep on the sofa, a picture of gentle innocence. Yet also the picture of a girl who had abandoned her husband when he needed her most.

She stirred when I stomped over and stood over her, slowly opening her sleep-heavy eyes. She blinked and gasped when she saw me. "What's wrong, Ethan, why are you soaking wet?"

"I just broke into the hospital," I snapped.

"What, why?" she asked, wide awake now, and bewildered by the naked anger in my eyes.

"I dug out my file in the neurologist's office, and you'll never guess what I found. I was signed into the hospital in November 2120 by one Nanako Jones – relationship to patient: wife! Why didn't you tell me, Nanako, why didn't you tell me?" I demanded, deeply wounded and enraged almost beyond rational thought.

Her face paled and her eyes widened in shock. "I was gonna tell you when the time was..."

"Why did you leave me?"

She stepped off the sofa and reached for me. "Please let me explain..."

I stepped back from her angrily. "Why did you bring me all the way from Hamamachi to have the operation and then just abandon me?"

Tears filled her eyes, but she still took a step towards me. "It wasn't like that..."

"You didn't even wait to see the result of the operation," I said. The raging anger began to turn into something else - gut-wrenching heartache. I felt like I was coming apart at the seams, tearing into a thousand pieces. Tears streaked down my cheeks.

"I couldn't..." she began.

"You left me when I needed you the most!" I almost shouted, cutting her off. "I woke up from that operation totally bewildered and confused, with a massive hole in my mind, not knowing how I had gotten there. I knew something was missing but I had no idea what it was. And then I had to do rehab with no one but unsympathetic male nurses. And you went back home to Hamamachi without even leaving me with a letter or memento of you. And now two years later you come back, playing all these mind games, not once telling me that you are my wife!"

With that outburst, the sense of betrayal and heartache grew so strong that I bolted from the apartment. She ran after me, calling my name, but I ran down the stairs and escaped into the welcoming darkness of the night. I quickly lost her amidst the trees and shrubs growing between the blocks of flats.

As I ran through the pouring rain, my thoughts veered slowly into an entirely different direction. From what I had seen of Nanako this week, she seemed so genuinely kind and caring, with a strong sense of right and wrong. Her behaviour this week was at complete odds with the apparent callousness of her actions after I was wounded. When she brought me back to Newhome and abandoned me to my fate.

I slowed to a jog, and wondered if I was reading this situation all wrong? What if she had a perfectly good explanation to why she left me and went home?

And then something she said hit me with the impact of a sledgehammer, driving me to my knees on the wet grass as the full implication of her words sank in. She said she had a man in her life two years ago, a man who told her that he never wanted to see her again.

That could mean only one thing. I was the one who said that to her. I told Nanako I never wanted to see her again. I was the insensitive fool and ugly brute who broke her heart.

Yet even so, Nanako had proven without doubt this week that she was a girl of character who would stand up for me, even going head-to-head with my father. There was no way she would have run back home with her tail between her legs just because I said that to her, especially considering I had said it while gravely wounded and ill. And even more so because I hadn't had the operation yet, the very operation she brought me here to receive.

Something was missing. There was another piece of the puzzle. A piece that would explain everything when I found it.

And then I had it.

The missing piece was my father.

He had obviously been there, and he must have met Nanako. In fact, that would explain what he said when she came to the door. Not, 'Can I help you?' but 'What are you doing here?' And then there was the issue of the considerable amount of animosity between them.

And she had goaded him, asking how he was going to make her leave his home, even asking if he would get the Custodians to throw her out.

That was it. The missing piece. There was no way in the world a girl as devoted and loving as Nanako would walk away from her wounded, sick husband. She would have stuck it out right to the end. And that lead me to the obvious conclusion. My father had her expelled from

Newhome. And then taking advantage of my amnesia, he had the audacity to arrange my marriage to someone else when he knew full well that I was already married to Nanako.

I rose to my feet and headed for my parents' flat. I was going to have this out with him right now – forget the curfew.

* * *

I was utterly drenched, panting for breath, and exhausted, when I reached my parents' flat a few minutes later. Running around at night in the rain was not what I should be doing when I needed to rest to recuperate from the wound.

I banged on the front door with the flat of my hand.

"Who is it?" came my mother's frightened voice a moment later.

"Open the door, Mother, it's me," I commanded her none too kindly.

Chapter Twenty-Two

Mother opened the door and quickly pulled me inside.

"What are you doing out after curfew? You want to go to prison?" she scolded me. "And look at you! You're soaking wet and as white as a sheet – are you trying to get pneumonia?"

"I have to see Father." I stepped past her and strode towards his room.

"If you wake him in the middle of the night there'll be all hell to pay," my mother said as she rushed after me.

"He's the one who's gonna pay." I assured her.

My older sister stood in her bedroom doorway, putting a robe over her gown. I ignored her and barged into my father's room, which until recently had been my room as well. I switched on the light and shook him roughly until he woke.

"What on earth are you doing? Son – do you know what time it is?" he barked angrily as he sat up.

I glanced at the bedroom doorway to make sure Mother and Elder Sister were there. I wanted them to witness this, and then I launched my attack. "Why did you lie to me, Father?"

"What are you blabbing about, Son? Whatever it is, it can wait 'til morning. Now get out of my room!"

"You aren't gonna fob me off this time, Father. Why did you tell me I was in the hospital for nearly a year when you knew it wasn't true."

His anger vanished instantly, replaced by wide-eyed fear. "What are you talking about, Son? I've never lied to you."

"No? Then tell me why you hid from me the fact that I got married back in 2120! You lied and said I spent that year in hospital, as though my wife didn't matter at all!"

His eyes narrowed suspiciously. "You've been speaking to that wretched nuisance of a Japanese girl, haven't you? Don't believe a word she says."

"That 'Japanese girl,' Father, is my wife! And for your information, she didn't tell me. I saw my hospital file today, and it said I was admitted to hospital by a Nanako Jones, with the relationship to patient listed as wife. My memories from that year have also started to come back. Memories of being with her in Hamamachi!"

His face now as white as a sheet, my father climbed out of bed. "Okay, I admit I've been hiding a few things from you, but it was for your own good."

"A few things, Father? You've done much more than that!"

"When that girl brought you back to Newhome you were in a very, very bad way. Not only were you shot while in Hamamachi, but they didn't even have the medical expertise to treat you properly. You were having severe epileptic seizures every day and woke every morning with no memory of the previous day, nor of anything that had happened after you started foraging back in January."

"You had no right to hide any of that from me." I fired back at him.

"There's more," he said, but this time he spoke softly, and with deep emotion. "Every morning when you woke, you were so confused and disorientated from the amnesia. Every morning that girl would tell you she was your wife and everything that happened while you were together. And every time she did, you said the same thing – that you didn't know her and couldn't have married her because you weren't going to marry until you were thirty. Your answer always upset her and she'd start panicking, trying to make you believe her. Then you invariably told her to leave you alone and that you never wanted to see her again. Sometimes the nurses even had to take her out of the room just to calm her down. And when you woke the next morning, the whole cycle started again."

"Father, she was scared out of her wits! She was only eighteen! You didn't even have the common sense or courtesy to bring her home to meet my mother and sisters, did you? And you can't use what I said when I was in that condition to justify what you did to her, and to me."

"What exactly did he do to her?" asked my mother, breaking all convention by actually entering Father's room. She was shocked and enraged that he had hidden all of this from her.

Father wouldn't answer. He just stared at his hands.

"He got the Custodians to throw her out of the town!" I stared daggers at him.

"You did what?" my mother demanded, her face stricken with anguish.

Father's head shot up. "I didn't get the Custodians to throw her out of town. I got them to take her back to Hamamachi."

"What's the difference? You had her forcibly removed from me, her husband! And she's had to wait until now for an opportunity to come back. And Father, you tried to marry me off to Sienna King! When you knew I was already married to Nanako. What were you thinking?"

"It was for your own good."

"You keep saying that. But you know what? From now on, stay out of my life! You hear me?"

"That poor, poor girl," Mother said as she turned to me. "Where is she now, Son?"

With a dizzying sense of dread, I suddenly recalled all the horrid things I said to her.

Ignoring the utter exhaustion that permeated my entire being, I somehow managed to run from my family's apartment. I couldn't get to my flat fast enough! I had to see Nanako and apologise for my insensitive behaviour. But could she find it in her heart to forgive me? Or had I gone and blown it for good?

As I slogged back through the rain, using my superior hearing to avoid a Custodian patrol, it occurred to me that Nanako had been trying all along to tell me that we knew each other. She had been trying her hardest to trigger my memories of her.

She wore the same clothes that she wore when I first met her. She made me lunch and delivered it in her lacquered lunchbox, the same lunchbox she used three years ago when we first met and shared her lunch. No doubt the oden and udon dinners were further attempts to trigger my memories, as was the request to massage her legs.

And her attempts to trigger my buried memories were successful. Starting on the day we had rescued her and Councillor Okada from the Skel, I began having partial seizures, each one accompanied by a memory from my time in Hamamachi. And of course, the dream I had tonight, recalling when I first met her.

So was her strategy to try to help me remember her rather than force the truth upon me? It made sense if that was the case, considering how badly I reacted in the hospital when she forced the truth on me.

I continued to stagger towards my flat. I was so exhausted now that all I could do was put one foot in front of the other. My body ached from my wound as much as from exhaustion.

When I got to my flat, I reached out to open the door, but it swung open as soon as my fingers brushed it. Alarmed, I entered the flat and called out to Nanako, but was met with silence. I hurried past the kitchen and bathroom and into the lounge room come bedroom, desperately hoping to see her waiting on the sofa for me, but she wasn't there. Neither was she in the bathroom.

She was gone.

I sank onto the cold tile floor, fearing the worst. Had my callous accusations pushed her away for good? Had she gone back to North End to share her heartbreak with

Councillor Okada, ready now to return to Hamamachi? A black despair took hold of me and I collapsed against the wall beside the shower. If I could only turn back time and think things through instead of losing my temper and saying such terrible things to her. I still couldn't remember everything about our relationship, but I desperately wanted those memories back and I wanted to make new ones with her – if she could ever forgive me after shoving her away – twice.

I sat there, cold and depressed, when I suddenly remembered what she did the first night she came to Newhome. After waiting two years for an opportunity to see me again, her hopes were crushed when I didn't even recognise her. Downhearted and disappointed, she retired to her apartment's roof to be alone.

I sat up, a glimmer of hope piercing the gloom that overshadowed my heart. Had she reacted in the same way tonight? If so, she could be on the roof of my apartment block right now.

I scraped myself off the floor and stumbled out of my flat for the third time tonight. I headed for the elevator for the first time. I decided under the circumstances, I could break my vow to never use it.

The short walk felt like an hour, and the ride up to the tenth floor an eternity. But the elevator reached its destination at long last and the doors pinged open. Having regained a modicum of energy, I darted out of the elevator and into the stairwell, and up the stairs to the roof.

Doubt and worry assailed me as I reached out to open the door. What if she wasn't here either? What if she had given up on me and gone back to North End or somewhere else in the dark? What if she didn't want to see me again?

I shook my head to clear it and gently opened the door. A massive wave of relief swept through me when I heard the sound of Nanako's voice. Her gentle sobs cut right through me. I hurried from the stairwell housing and there she was, sitting on the roof with her back to the wall. She hugged her knees to her chest, completely soaked by the rain.

She looked up at me, eyes red from crying, black eyeliner streaked down her cheeks, and her hair plastered to her face.

I dropped to my knees, wrapped my arms around her, and rested my forehead gently against hers.

"Nanako, I'm so sorry for all those horrid things I said. I'm sorry I wouldn't listen to you. I should have known you would never leave me by choice. I should have realised my father had the Custodians throw you out of the town. And most of all, I'm so sorry for telling you I never wanted to see you again. I didn't know – I couldn't remember. But I'm remembering now, thanks to you.""

Nanako wiped her tear-streaked cheeks with the back of her hand and turned to face me, hope shining in her eyes. "Do you remember saying that?"

Ignoring the pain in my chest, I cupped her beautiful round face in my hands. "No, but I do remember when we first met, over in that warehouse car park where you and your three friends were racing lizards. You were wearing these very clothes, shared your lunch with me, and asked me to come to Hamamachi with you."

Nanako was shivering from the cold, but she threw her arms around me and hugged me so tight that I thought I'd pass out from the pain. "Oh Ethan, that's wonderful - you've finally remembered me! But how did you find out what your father did?"

"After I ran away from you I started thinking and I put all the pieces together – all the things you said and did, and then it all just clicked. I went to my parents' house just now and confronted my father. He told me everything, even what he did to you. Nanako, I cannot even begin to imagine what you went through back then."

"Before you got hurt, we had everything, Ethan. From the time we met in January, we were inseparable. You lived at my next door neighbours' house but spent nearly every minute at mine with my family and I. You were able to join my foraging team too. We got married on the 7th of March 2120 and moved into our own little flat. We were so happy, but then you got injured in September and suffered from amnesia. You lost all your memories of me and the times we spent together. The seizures you started having were so bad, I was terrified I was gonna lose you. So I spent all of our money to pay someone to drive us to Newhome, hoping the doctors here could help you. They said they could, and your father promised to pay for the operation. I was so desperate for it to be a success – that you would recover and remember our lives together. But then those horrible Custodians turned up the day before the operation, dragged me from your hospital room, and drove me all the way back to Hamamachi.

"This trading venture with Councillor Okada was the first opportunity in two years to return here. No one was willing to make the journey because of the increase in Skel attacks. The guy who took us to Newhome the first time never made it back. I wanted to come back by myself before then, but my family wouldn't let me.

"Ethan, do you have any idea how hard these last few days have been? To finally be with you again after all this time, with my head full of memories of all the wonderful things we did together, but you didn't even recognise me. And then to hear that your father was trying to marry you off, taking advantage of your amnesia."

"I'll never understand what you've been through with all of this," I replied sadly. "There is one thing I would like to ask you, though, and I think I know the answer. When you saw me on Monday, why didn't you tell me who you were, that you were my wife?"

She took my face in her hands and squeezed gently, as though trying to convince herself this conversation was actually happening. "Before I came here," she began, "I suspected you hadn't recovered your memories. If you had, I know you would have come straight to Hamamachi to find me. So when I got here and saw you didn't remember me, I wanted to see if you could fall in love with me again. I wanted to know if you could want to be with me again, not because you had to, but because you wanted to. I tried to trigger your memories of me by doing the same things I did when we met three years ago."

I grinned from ear to ear – I loved this girl. "So you made lunches and cooked dinners for me back then too?"

She returned the smile. "Yes, and anything else I could think of to make you mine." She paused, and added softly, "I want you back, Ethan. That's all I care about."

I took Nanako's small, bronzed hands in mine. My heart, my all, belonged totally to her. "Nanako, if you want me, you've got me. I am yours, now and forever."

"I do, Ethan, I do," she said, rapture glowing through her tear stained face. She lifted her chin, removed the choker from her neck, and slipped off the two gold rings that had been hanging from it. I noticed for the first time that they were different sizes.

Crying again, but this time with joy, she slipped the larger ring onto the third finger of my left hand.

I took the other ring and slipped it onto her corresponding finger.

"Finally." She sighed, a peaceful, contented expression framing her face.

And as the rain sleeted down, we continued to kneel on the wet concrete with our foreheads pressed together and our arms wrapped around each other. Savouring this moment, this reunion.

When her teeth started clattering, I took her hands and helped her to her feet. "We'd better get you inside and into a warm shower before you catch pneumonia."

So hand in hand we made our way to the elevator. I figured I had a good enough reason to break my vow about not using it on this occasion too.

Chapter Twenty-Three

The night's emotional roller-coaster ride and constant running about while already weak from the wound took their toll on me. I was exhausted. I staggered through the door of my flat with an arm draped around Nanako's shoulders. She was so cold that her teeth clattered nonstop, so we went straight to the bathroom. She reached for the buttons on my shirt with fingers she couldn't even hold still.

"Come on, we've got to get you out of those wet bandages," she said, putting my welfare above her own.

I caught her hands and held them still. "A few minutes won't make a difference to me. Our first priority is to get you warm. I'll get the shower going. It's a temperamental little beast."

Nanako nodded and stripped out of her clinging wet clothes while I fiddled around to get the shower to the right temperature, a difficult task at the best of times.

"Right to go." I held back the plastic floral-pattern shower curtain.

She slipped under the steaming hot water and sighed deeply with blissful relief as the water cascaded down her beautiful, lithe body. I stood there drinking in the sight of her, not quite comprehending that she was my wife.

"Don't just stand there." She held out a hand. "Get undressed and hop in."

I didn't need to be asked twice.

* * *

I was rudely awakened when the flat's front door was kicked in. That I didn't wake at the sound of boots outside indicated how soundly I'd been asleep. Lifting my head from the pillow to see the bedside clock, I saw that it was 4:30am and still dark outside. Nanako was lying half on top of me, soundly asleep, with her head on my shoulder, right arm across my chest, and her legs entwined with mine.

I struggled to sit up, waking Nanako in the process. The front door slammed shut and four men with guns rushed into the lounge-bedroom, blinding us with their torchlights.

"Got 'em!" Lieutenant King declared. "Ethan Jones and Nanako, you are under arrest for sexual misconduct."

"No, you've got this all wro…" I protested but got no further before one of the intruders smashed the stock of his assault-rifle into the side of my head.

* * *

I came to with a thumping headache that felt like a red-hot poker was stabbing me in the head. It took a moment to realise I was gagged and on my knees on the floor beside the bed with my hands cuffed behind my back. One intruder stood behind me, holding me upright by my hair and right shoulder.

The lights were on, and by twisting my head a little to the right, I saw Nanako kneeling beside me, similarly restrained. Her eyes were wide with terror. We were both shivering, for she wore only a t-shirt over her underwear, and me only my boxer shorts.

The intruders were all Custodians, but King was the only one in front of us. He stepped closer and leered down at me with undisguised loathing.

"You stupid fool, Jones! Did you seriously think you could cavort and sleep with this girl without us noticing? You're dumber than I thought. Now the normal procedure after arresting you two is to take you to the magistrate in the morning, but we have a bit of a problem with that. The sentence for sexual misconduct is death by lethal injection, but in your case, Jones, the magistrate will transmute your sentence to several years hard labour. Since Nanako is from Hamamachi, he will probably just expel her from the town." He knelt down and stuck his ugly face in front of mine. "And as I'm not happy with either of those options, my friends and I are going to administer the sentences you deserve right here and now. A bullet to the back of the head."

I tried desperately to tell him that we were married, but the gag had been shoved so far into my mouth that I could only make muffled noises.

King stood and drew his pistol. He grabbed my pillow and folded it double. "I'm going to do her first so you can have the pleasure of watching her die, Jones. That's only fitting, isn't it? Payback for what the little cow did to my family's honour."

I flung myself back against my captor, but he jabbed me in the ribs with his right fist and drove the air out of my lungs.

King approached Nanako, but she struggled against her captor with all her might and tried to tell him something, but the gag made her words intelligible as well.

Not caring about our incoherent protestations, King walked behind Nanako, placed the pillow against the back of her head, and pressed the gun into the pillow. Although still winded, I fought desperately against my Custodian captor as well, trying to tear my head from his grip and kick behind me at the same time.

"Hold fire for a moment, Lieutenant," the fourth Custodian said suddenly. Until now he had been standing quietly behind us, content to watch the proceedings, but now he reached out a hand to stay King. He was an Anglo-Australian, as tall as King, with a square jaw, and a very powerful build.

"What is it, Captain Smithson? You said I had your full support in this!" King complained.

"They're wearing wedding bands." The captain pointed out.

I stopped struggling and watched from the corner of my eye as King stepped back to look at our hands, clearly confused. "It's a trick, Sir. It has to be. They weren't wearing them on Friday."

Nanako nodded furiously, desperately trying to speak over the gag.

"The girl's trying to tell us something," Captain Smithson said.

"Yeah, 'don't kill us,'" King snarled angrily.

"Doesn't sound like that at all. Remove her gag."

"But Sir," King protested strongly.

"I know you have issues with her, but it isn't going to hurt to hear what she has to say. Now take off the gag, and that's an order."

King untied Nanako's gag and ungraciously yanked it from her mouth. As soon as it was out, Nanako twisted around to address the captain. Her words poured out like a waterfall as she relayed the entire story to the captain.

"What a load of codswallop," King retorted. "Why didn't you tell Ethan the 'truth' as soon as you saw him on Monday?"

"I didn't want to force the truth on him. I wanted to trigger his memories of me instead," Nanako replied, though to the captain, not to King.

The captain indicated for the Custodian restraining me to remove my gag. "Is what she's saying true, Jones?"

"Yes, Sir! When I went to the hospital yesterday I saw my hospital admission form from November 2120, and it stated that Nanako was my wife. That's how I found out."

"I see. And did she trigger any of your memories?"

"Yes, Sir. Since her arrival, I've had a number of memories of the time I was in Hamamachi. Last night I had a dream where I remembered meeting her for the first time. After things started falling into place, I confronted my father. He admitted he had asked the Custodians to have Nanako thrown out of Newhome."

"Lieutenant King," Nanako said before the captain could reply. "Don't be mad at me for stopping your sister's marriage to Ethan. Blame Ethan's father his deception."

"Can you prove any of this?" the captain asked. It sounded like he was beginning to believe us.

"Have a look at my file in the hospital," I replied. "You'll see I was checked into the hospital in November 2120 by Nanako Jones, with her relationship to me listed as 'wife'."

"You can also ask Councillor Okada," Nanako added. "He knew Ethan very well."

King suddenly had an epiphany. "Nanako, you said Jones went to Hamamachi."

"Yes, Sir."

"Did he join the Militia?"

"Yes, he did, though he was promoted to the Rangers soon afterwards," she replied. "He developed entirely new strategies for dealing with the Skel, and these were adopted by the Militia and Rangers."

"And they were?" King prompted.

"Never fight them frontally but use stealth to get behind them and ambush them."

I'd actually developed my anti-Skel strategies when I started foraging at the age of seventeen. As I was able to detect Skel ambushes using echolocation, it was from there I got the idea to sneak behind them and give them a taste of their own medicine.

"How did you fight the Skel previously?" the lieutenant queried.

"Upon encountering Skel, each squad broke into two teams. One team would provide covering fire while the other advanced."

"I see," King said, nodding his head. As the Custodians were primarily a police force, they probably hadn't learned military tactics such as this.

Captain Smithson looked at Nanako and me, still handcuffed and kneeling on the floor and shivering uncontrollably. He sighed and addressed the Custodians who were restraining us. "Alright, uncuff Mr. and Mrs. Jones and let them go."

Chapter Twenty-Four

Now that we were free, the captain and two Custodian privates strode for the door. In typical form, they did not apologise even though they were about to murder us a moment ago. I was overwhelmed with relief that we were still alive, but also incensed with anger at yet another Custodian injustice. How much longer did I have to live in this prison-town?

Ignoring wrists sore from chafing handcuffs and knees aching from kneeling too long on a hard wooden floor, I stood and helped Nanako to her feet. Like me, she was relieved but angry. She was also shivering uncontrollably from the cold.

But before I could even take stock of our situation, King was back in my face.

"Mention this little 'misunderstanding' to anyone, anyone at all, and there'll be a little accident when you're out foraging one day. You reading me, Jones?" he hissed in my ear.

I wanted nothing more than to smash my fist through his pockmarked face, but that would just give him the excuse he needed to lock me up. With a monstrous amount of self control, I focused on breathing in and out and glared back at him without answering.

King turned and sauntered after his companions, but just as he reached the apartment door, there was an enormous, thunderous boom, which shook the building to its very foundations.

The captain steadied himself against the doorframe. "Earthquake?"

"No, an explosion," I said.

The Custodians rushed onto the walkway and looked about to check if my observation was correct, but they couldn't see anything from there.

All of their radios suddenly sputtered to life. "Code 906. All Custodians report to North End in full battle gear immediately, repeat, Code 906." The message was repeated every few seconds.

"You've got to be kidding!" King exclaimed.

"What's 'code 906?'" I called out as I dressed quickly into trousers, t-shirt and hoody.

"Let's go!" the captain ordered, completely ignoring me.

"Captain Smithson, wait!" I shouted as I darted onto the walkway after them. Again he ignored me, so I reached out and grabbed his sleeve.

"What, Jones?" he practically shouted in my face.

"What's 'code 906,' Captain?"

"Skel have broken into North End," he snapped back.

"What could the Skel possibly gain by doing that?" I asked, trying to prompt him to think things through rather than rush off impetuously. I was working on the assumption that the Skel were much more organised than we had previously thought, and that besieging Newhome was the first stage of some insidious plan. This was obviously stage two. But what was its goal – to cripple the town perhaps? And to such an extent that the population would be forced to leave? If that was the case, then I could think of only two possible scenarios in which the Skel could achieve that end. One was to destroy our electricity supply, and the other was to cut off our water.

Snatches of frantic dispatches bled through the Custodian radios:

"...used a captured Bushmaster to break down the gates..."

"...Skel everywhere..."

"Sir, we've got to go." King pressed.

The captain waved him back and answered me, "Supplies, livestock, slaves, the usual, how would I know?"

"They can get those from any Victorian country town without having to go head-to-head with a few hundred well armed Custodians," I pointed out.

"...taking casualties..."

"...medic!"

"If there's something you want to say, Jones, out with it!"

We could hear the staccato sounds of guns firing in the distance. Custodians were fighting back.

"...building's on fire..."

"...fleeing civilians are blocking my line of fire..."

"Call the security detail guarding the sub and I'll wager my bottom dollar they don't answer," I said quickly, deciding to put my hunch to the test. The Skel were going after the electricity, they had to be.

While the captain made a call to Custodian Headquarters on his radio, Nanako joined us on the walkway. She was dressed in black over-knee socks, shorts and top, and looking a lot warmer.

The captain rejoined us, and was clearly not pleased with what he had heard over the radio. "HQ says they're not responding," he said darkly. "Okay men, we've got a sub to save. Virtually everyone else is already in or on the way to North End, so HQ is sending a couple of squads back to meet us at the western gates. Then we go in and go in hard."

"...bravo company unable to enter North End, gates – the road is clogged by civilians..."

"...get these blasted civilians out of the way..."

"You rush out through the main gates to save the sub and you're all dead." I raised my voice to make myself heard.

The captain was not pleased at my constant interruptions. "And why would that be, Jones?"

"Because they'll have set an ambush outside the gates, expecting you to do exactly that, Sir. May I be so bold as to suggest a strategy?"

"Jones, this is Custodian business!"

"How many times have you fought the Skel, Sir?" I asked, risking a verbal slap down.

"...requesting permission to retreat..."

"...Skel have guns, repeat, Skel have guns..."

The captain glared at me, confirming my suspicion – the answer was never. "Well then, what strategy do you propose?" he finally asked.

"I presume the city has a secret entrance on the west wall?"

"How do you know about the secret doors?" he demanded, shocked.

"I saw a squad of Custodians using one once."

"Well, you're right, there is one on the west wall. It's opposite the bridge, a hundred metres south of the western gates and sub."

"In that case I recommend you send your force out the secret entrance, advance to the river bank and then follow it to the sub. That way you'll come up behind the Skel who are waiting near the gates. When you find them, fire a flare so that you can see them and take them out."

"Sounds good in theory, Jones, but how are we supposed to find Skel hiding in the dark?" he demanded.

I wanted to keep my mouth shut and let the Custodians deal with the situation to the best of their ability, but with such small numbers they'd fail and I knew it. And although my conscience wouldn't be pricked if these particular Custodians met their end out there, what if the city lost power? That would be disastrous for ten-thousand civilians, since we had no alternative power supply. All of the power stations had been destroyed during the war. Without electricity to provide lighting in the green houses, the town would only be able to generate a fraction of the food it needed.

"...we're pinned down here..."

"...fall back, fall back..."

"Put me with the lead squad and I'll take point," I offered.

"You think you can find Skel in the dark, do you, Jones?" the captain asked.

"...walked right into an ambush..."

"... my squad's wiped out!..."

"Yes Sir, no question about it. I know how they operate."

"Sir, I believe he can. He had no problem locating David Chen when the Skel abducted him," King said, surprising me by confirming my abilities. Apparently, he didn't like the idea of fighting Skel in the dark without me.

Nanako pulled me away from the Custodians. "Why do you want to help them, Ethan, after what they just did to us? And you haven't recovered from your wound," she whispered fiercely as she clung to my arm.

I cupped her face in my hand and whispered back. "It's not for them. If I don't do this we may not have a town by morning."

"Then I'm coming with you so I can watch your back."

"There's no way I'm gonna risk you out there," I declared, alarmed by the very thought of her trying to fight Skel ambushers in the dark.

"You don't need to worry about me, Ethan. When we were in Hamamachi you taught me how to fight Skel. I have experience fighting them too. So I'm coming with you whether you like it or not. I just got you back and there's no way I'm letting you go out there against those things without my support."

I saw that arguing would get me nowhere so I nodded my consent, reminding myself that she was in the Hamamachi Militia – which was such a foreign concept to me.

The captain seemed to be weighing up his options, and finally said, "Okay Ethan, let's go. We'll kit you up with a vest and gun when we get to the barracks."

"I'm coming too," Nanako informed him as we hurried down the walkway towards the elevator.

Captain Smithson didn't even bat an eyelid with his speedy response. "Absolutely out of the question."

"Why, because I'm a woman?" she asked as she hurried to keep up with our longer strides.

"Fighting is men's business," he snapped back.

"Not in Hamamachi, Sir. All of our women serve in the Militia one month each year. I am experienced with Austeyr assault-rifles and have fought Skel and raiders both," she said as she stepped into the elevator with us and stared up into his face. "Besides, you need all the experienced fighters you can get."

"As much as it irks me to say this," King butted in, "She's right, Sir."

The captain looked at King, and then back at Nanako. "Fine, you can kit up too then."

I glanced at King, expecting to see gratitude or relief in his countenance, but instead saw cunning anticipation. No doubt he was hoping the Skel would kill Nanako and rid him of a thorn in his side.

Chapter Twenty-Five

Ten minutes later, Nanako and I, along with four teams of Custodians, drove to the secret entrance that was a hundred metres south of the western gates. We had been given Custodian helmets and bulletproof vests, an Austeyr automatic-rifle for Nanako, and a pistol and flare gun for me.

"Right, time is of the essence," the captain announced once we disembarked from the G-Wagons. He pulled open the concealed concrete door and said, "Okay, Ethan, you've got point. Show us what you can do."

"Thank you, Sir. Radios off everyone, and follow me," I responded. Without further ado, I ran straight through the doorway and into the night, with Nanako on my heels. I held the pistol in my right hand, and kept my left hand in my pocket. The flare gun was hanging from my belt.

As I ran towards the riverbank, I let rip with ultrasonic flash sonar, hoping the Custodians didn't have ultrasonic sensors in the walls.

The returning echoes effectively lit up the night, allowing me to see as clearly as in daylight. As I suspected, the Skel had set up an ambush in between the gates and the wharf. There were around two dozen of them, which was far more than I expected. To make matters worse, some had guns, though single shot rifles, not semi-automatics like the Custodians. All the same, twenty-four Skel against sixteen Custodians was gonna be ugly.

We reached the riverbank without incident and crouched down. Spotlights illuminated the town walls but it was so dark out here that without flash sonar I could only just make out the faces of those clustered around me, and silhouettes of those further away. Steel weapons glinted in the starlight.

I could almost smell the fear emanating from the Custodians. They were afraid of encountering Skel in the daylight, so they would be absolutely petrified right now.

"Captain," I whispered, "Give us a sixty second head start, then spread out and follow us as quietly as you can. When you see the flare go up, come on in shooting. Nanako and I will hit the Skel the moment they turn to engage you. Just don't shoot us by accident, okay?"

"Understood. Now go!" he ordered.

Touching Nanako's hand to make sure she was ready, I moved off silently beside the gently sloping riverbank towards the Skel, who were about a hundred metres ahead.

"I'm scared, Ethan," Nanako whispered as she advanced quietly beside me.

"Me too," I whispered back. I'd never been this close to so many Skel before.

"Are the Skel really there, outside the gates? I can't see anything, but you're using your echolocation, aren't you?" she asked.

I almost tripped at that question, and slowed my pace to talk to her. "You know about that?"

"Of course I do, silly."

I must admit it was a stupid question — she was my wife. "There's about two dozen of them, some with rifles, and, oh no!" I whispered in alarm, "They've got an oxy-acetylene torch! They're cutting into a hatch at the stern of the sub. And they've got a whole satchel of explosives. We'd better hurry!"

The submarine and wharf were normally lit up as bright as day but were lost in darkness tonight, so the Skel must have shot out all the lights.

With the sixteen Custodians advancing twenty metres behind us, Nanako and I drew close to the Skel hiding in ambush. The closest were ten metres to our right, with their backs to us. They hunkered down behind trenches hidden behind bushes that faced the town gates, armed with crossbows, old rifles, and the usual assortment of homemade clubs.

I pulled out the flare gun and was about to fire when a Custodian spotted the oxy-acetylene torch flame and shouted, "Captain, they're cutting into the sub!"

And with that, the plan fell to pieces.

Alerted to the Custodians presence, the Skel ambushers spun about and opened fire with crossbows and rifles, dropping a couple of Custodians and wounding others. After that, they grabbed their hideous hand-to-hand weapons and screamed obscenities as they ran towards the now thoroughly frightened Custodians.

I tried to fire the flare so that the Custodians could see their assailants more clearly, but nothing happened when I pulled the trigger. Two further attempts got the same result – the gun was so old it wouldn't fire. Typical Newhome efficiency. Things were not maintained unless they were regularly used, and still not even then.

This was a disaster; the Skel would cut the Custodians to ribbons in the dark.

"It's a dud, it won't fire," I whispered to Nanako as I discarded the flare gun and grabbed my pistol. "I have to save them. Cover me."

Nanako seized my arm, "You can't go running into the middle of that melee! You could be killed!"

"I can see clearly and the Skel can't, that'll give me an edge."

"Ethan..."

"I have to do this."

"Fine. I'll cover you."

So with Nanako at my back, I ran after the Skel as they collided with the Custodians, swinging their lethal weapons left and right like farmers scything through tall grass. Some Custodians screamed in agony and fell while others fired frantic and ill placed shots at the nightmarish skeleton-armoured brutes who hacked away at them in the dark.

Into the midst of this insane swirling melee I ran, the only combatant who could 'see' what was happening as long as I kept shouting ultrasonically. Nanako ran as closely behind me as she could so she wouldn't mistake me for a Skel or Custodian. I fired my pistol, seven, eight, nine times as I ran through the Skel, aiming at their necks and throats. I was careful to avoid the wild shots sprayed about by the Custodians. Seven of the monstrous apparitions went down – seven shots hit their mark while two struck hardened-bone armour and ricocheted off into the night. That immediately changed the odds of the battle, but more Skel were running towards us.

I ejected the empty clip from the pistol, withdrew my left hand from my pocket and grabbed another clip. Before I could slam it home, a Skel smashed a metal-studded wooden club into my stomach. The bulletproof vest took the brunt of the impact and saved my life, but it was still like getting hit with a sledgehammer. I was smashed off my feet and landed on my back, almost passing out from the pain that exploded through my chest from my previous wound. Winded, I rolled onto my side and gasped for breath while I waited for the pain to subside.

The Skel who hit me was a massive brute – taller than Michal and with goat's horns adorning his human-skull helmet. He stepped forward and was about to finish me off when Nanako, wearing a bulletproof vest several sizes too big, darted forward and fired her assault-rifle at him on full auto. She was looking out for me just as she promised. Riddled with bullet holes, the Skel collapsed towards me, but Nanako threw herself against him, knocking him off balance so he fell away from me.

That particular Skel would not be getting up again. I rolled onto my stomach and crawled towards the ammo clip I dropped earlier. I noticed that at least half the Custodians were down, but those still standing were fighting back with almost fanatical fervour, using their guns like clubs and firing whenever they found an opportunity.

Nanako shot down another Skel who charged us, but then her gun made an ominous click as it ran out of ammo. At that moment, a smaller, quick-footed Skel knocked Nanako's weapon out of her hands with a sweep of a converted pickaxe. The Skel bellowed a string of extremely offensive insults in a high-pitched voice, revealing herself to be female. I crawled as fast as I could manage to retrieve the ammo clip so I could come to Nanako's aid.

I saw her duck and dodge two great sweeps of her opponent's weapon, after which she jumped forward and delivered a knife-hand strike to the side of the Skel's unarmoured neck. She followed this with an elbow to the throat, sending her opponent staggering backwards. Although choking and gagging, the Skel shook her skull-adorned head, readied her pickaxe adorned with rusty metal spikes and charged Nanako again.

I retrieved my ammo-clip, slammed it home and put a bullet through the Skel's throat, sending her tumbling to the ground and out of the fight for good.

Nanako retrieved her gun, slapped in a fresh ammo clip, and rushed over to me as I slowly regained my feet. "Thanks, that was too close! Are you hurt?"

"The vest saved me," I assured her. I didn't tell her that the fall had reopened the wound and it was bleeding again. My stomach was going to be black and blue as well.

"We've got to get to the sub, they must be almost through by now," I said as I stood.

"Lead the way, I've got your back." She couched the assault-rifle to her shoulder.

I jogged as fast as I was able for the wharf, firing my pistol at three Skel who tried to stop me. The two I failed to bring down were finished off by Nanako as she followed close behind.

The skirmish behind us had fallen silent. The Custodians had overcome the surviving Skel, although at great cost – only five of them were still standing, and that didn't include Captain Smithson. With King in the lead, the Custodians advanced cautiously behind us. I tried to blot out the disturbing sounds of the wounded and dying who littered the ground like broken, discarded dolls.

I ran onto the concrete wharf to which the submarine was moored, and past the corpses of four Custodians – the security detail that had been guarding it.

As I hurried over the metal decking that lead from the wharf to the sub, I heard Nanako trip and fall, her gun clattering from her hands to the concrete.

"Nanako?" I called out anxiously, terrified she'd been shot.

"I'm okay – go, get those Skel!" she called back.

Holding my pistol before me, I stepped onto the sub and carefully navigated the narrow decking that surrounded the conning tower. I moved quickly between two large missile launch tubes, and then straight for the two Skel at the sub's stern. One was crouching down with the oxy-acetylene torch, which lit up the surrounding area and the two bone-armoured Skel with an eerie glow.

I was tempted to shoot the oxy-acetylene gas tank, but had no idea what effect such an explosion would have on the satchel of explosives. I slowed to a walk and fired a shot at the Skel instead, dropping him to the submarine's decking plate with a clatter of bone upon steel.

The second Skel whirled around, spotted my silhouette in the dark, and madly fiddled with the detonator's timer. I tried to shoot him before he could, but I was out of bullets. While I quickly reloaded the pistol, the Skel dropped the satchel, grabbed a club and charged me.

Afraid that he may have set the detonator to go off any moment, I rushed straight for him while firing my pistol. The first three shots didn't even slow him, but the fourth sent him careening off the top of the submarine and into the water, where he sank like a rock.

I holstered my pistol and fell to my knees beside the satchel. It had a glowing red timer, which was at twenty-two seconds and counting down.

I didn't know if the explosives would damage the submarine if it went off on the upper deck, but I couldn't risk finding out. And that meant I had to fling the bag as far as I could into the river. I stood and prepared to do so, but the bag was heavy and my chest was in such pain that I doubted I could even manage to toss it over the side.

Heavy footsteps bounded up behind me. I turned about and found myself face to face with Lieutenant King – who had his assault-rifle pointed at my head.

We stared at each other for what felt like an eternity, but could not have been more than a couple of seconds. I knew what he was thinking – if he put a bullet through my head now, no one would ever know the truth. He would claim the Skel shot me or that I'd been hit by a stray Custodian bullet. It was an opportunity too good to pass up.

Well, it was until we heard Nanako's light footsteps as she ran up behind King. Even in the darkness, she could recognise what was going on, so she aimed her gun at King and said, "Don't even think it, Lieutenant."

Realising his opportunity for getting away with murder was gone, King lowered his gun. As he did so, my mind switched back to the present and I turned the satchel around to show him the glowing timer, which was down to eight seconds.

In one smooth motion, King dropped his gun, grabbed the bag, and swung it around once and then far out into the river. "Hit the deck!" he shouted, and we complied without hesitation.

The satchel hit the water and exploded in a massive pyrotechnics display, creating a small tidal wave that dumped water over us and rocked the sub violently from side to side.

And then, all was quiet.

Disguising it as a yawn, I lifted my head and let off one last ultrasonic shout as I glanced about, checking to see if any Skel were left standing. Once I saw that they had all been accounted for, I surrendered to the pain and overwhelming exhaustion that wracked my body. I collapsed back onto the sub's deck.

Nanako was at my side in a heartbeat. I tried to convince her that I was okay, but she saw straight through the lie.

After he got his breath King switched his radio on and reported our success to Custodian HQ. They replied with the encouraging news that the Skel had just started withdrawing from North End. They must have had a Smartphone equipped scout watching the battle for the sub, and he must have reported the failure to destroy it to the Skel in the town.

As I lay there shivering in my soaking wet clothes, I pondered how the Skel had managed to get their hands on Smartphones, guns, the oxy-acetylene torch and explosives, even the ability to drive the captured Bushmaster. And there was also the ambush they sprang on Councillor Okada, and their astounding feat of managing to ambush all of our foraging teams on the same morning.

The answer to these questions was staring me in the face – a major player, and quite possibly Hamamachi or perhaps a faction therein, was backing their attacks on us.

All began to go dark as Nanako removed my bulletproof vest to check my condition and discovered that the left side of my chest was soaked with blood. The last thing I heard was her demanding King to get a medic over pronto.

Chapter Twenty Six

I came to slowly, as though waking from the deepest sleep I'd ever had. I was back in intensive care, lying in a hospital bed with a drip in the back of my left hand. There was a bandage around my chest and shoulder, and another around my head, thanks to King smashing his rifle butt against it earlier. In spite of my injuries, I felt little pain, so they must have drugged me on some pretty strong painkillers. I decided then and there not to rush out of the hospital this time, but give my poor body a chance to recover.

It was dark outside and the ward was shrouded in semi-darkness. Every bed I could see was filled and male nurses were quietly checking on patients who were worse off than others. Some patients groaned, others sobbed quietly.

Nanako was lying beside me with her head on my right shoulder. She was fast asleep. I ran my hand through her hair, simply glad to be with her and away from danger.

She stirred and her eyes flicked open. "Decided to rejoin us in the land of the living have we?" she teased.

"Well, you know, thought I'd pop in," I laughed, and then winced. "How long have I been out?"

"About eighteen hours." She glanced at the timepiece on her wrist.

"And what's the prognosis. Will I live?"

"You lost a lot of blood and they had to close your wound again. But you've had a blood transfusion and have been on the drip ever since." Rolling onto her stomach, she propped herself on her elbows. "You gotta be more careful, Ethan. No more heroics from you. Like, forever, okay? You were so pale I was afraid I was gonna lose you."

"Don't worry, you've got my full co-operation there," I promised her.

"They wanted to give you a CAT scan for the blow to your head, but I refused. I had to make up some story that you and I were dead-set against X-ray technology because we believed it would harm us."

"You did well," I said, impressed by her ingenuity. "What's the situation with the town and the sub?"

"After we stopped the Skel blowing up the sub, the rest of them pulled out of North End pretty quick, I was told. But so many Custodians and civilians have been killed or injured. North End's hospital overflowed so badly that they had to bring many North Enders to this hospital, and they're even using a school as a temporary hospital as well."

I shook my head, finding it hard to believe the Skel had become so bold as to attack our strongly defended town so openly, the first time in a hundred years. I hoped they had paid dearly for their audacity.

"Can I ask a question?" I said after we'd been silent for a while.

"Of course you can, silly."

"What was our wedding like?"

She drew herself up onto her knees. "Would you like to see a photo?"

The excitement that rose within me was so strong that for a moment I forgot all about my injuries. "What kind of question is that? Of course I do. Have you got lots of photos of the time I was in Hamamachi?"

She removed the weird goggles that were hanging around her neck. "I do, but I'm hesitant to show them to you yet because I don't want the photos to form the basis of your memories. I want you to keep pushing your mind until you remember these things yourself. I don't mind showing you this one photo, though, it's kind of important, eh?" She put the goggles on and pressed the buttons on the side.

After a moment she pressed them against my eyes – she couldn't put the strap on because of the bruise from King's gun.

I gasped as soon as I saw the image. It was in 3D, with a depth I hadn't thought possible with digital media. We were standing in front of an old brick chapel hidden away in the bush, set in the midst of a landscape of long grass, bushes and the occasional gum tree. It had a slanting slate-tile roof, wooden door, and stained glass windows. It must have been very lovingly maintained over the decades.

But it was Nanako herself who rendered me speechless. She was wearing a magnificent red kimono, embroidered with cranes, trees and mountains in gold, white and green thread. Her hair was put up with golden pins, with a few stray locks hanging loose around her face. The joy and rapture she felt on that day had been faithfully captured by the camera. She was glowing with happiness, complete with joyous smile and sparkling eyes.

I stood beside her wearing traditional Japanese men's attire. It included black-and-white pleated hakama pants, a white undershirt, and black kimono and haori, the latter being a lightweight long coat with wide sleeves.

"You look simply gorgeous. Must have been such a wonderful day. What I'd give to get those memories back," I said when I took off the goggles and reluctantly handed them back. I was delighted to have a concrete image to associate with wedding day.

"It was the second happiest day of my life." She smiled broadly.

I raised my eyebrows, suddenly feeling a little threatened. What could mean more to someone than their wedding day? "Really. What was the happiest?"

She lay back down beside me with her head on my shoulder and took my left hand in hers. "Last night, when you told me that you are mine, now and forever, and we put our wedding rings back on."

I slipped my right arm around her and within minutes, her arms and legs twitched erratically – she had fallen asleep again.

It was hours before I fell asleep, but I didn't mind in the slightest. As I lay with my petite Japanese wife in my arms, I felt content and completely at peace. The ever-present emptiness I felt since awaking from the operation two years ago was gone. And I knew why. That emptiness I felt was her absence.

* * *

"Hey Jones, wake up!" said a familiar voice.

I jerked awake from a shallow sleep and saw my three workmates clustered around my bed. It was just after eight according to the clock on the wall.

"This is new," Shorty said as he appraised Nanako sitting cross-legged on the bed beside me and holding my hand.

"So are the wedding rings." Michal pointed out, observant as usual.

"Did we blink and miss something?" Shorty asked.

"Guys, may I present Nanako Jones, my wife." I grinned like a Cheshire cat.

"Yep, I think we did," Shorty said to Michal, and then to me. "Jones, what on earth are you talking about?"

I spent the next five minutes catching the lads up to speed.

"Man, what a story," Shorty said when I'd finished, "I'm getting a headache just trying to get my head around it."

"Great to see it work out for you two at last," Michal said sincerely. "Make sure you inform the Custodians or they'll get the wrong idea."

"Already have," I assured him, though not quite in the manner he would have assumed.

Shorty and David murmured similar comments, but truth be known, they were clearly uncomfortable with Nanako around. I questioned Newhome's traditions of so rigidly segregating males and females. I remembered how relaxed and natural Nanako and her foraging teammates had been together when I first met her, and concluded that Newhome's Founders had lost the plot when they created our society.

"So how are you three going?" I asked in an attempt to end the awkward silence.

"Saturday was a blast," Shorty said with heavy sarcasm. "I never realised how much fun can be had digging through piles of junk and sorting it into its components."

"Well hopefully the Skel will count their losses and give Newhome a miss for a while," I replied thoughtfully.

"Don't count on it," Michal said.

"Yeah, we need to find a way to drive the Skel out of Melbourne altogether," David added.

"Maybe the Custodians will work out something?" Nanako suggested.

"I don't think they're interested in what goes on outside the city," Shorty said quietly, sending a dirty glance at David.

Nanako noticed the exchange and looked enquiringly at me.

"It's a long story, I'll fill you in later," I said.

She nodded and David looked most relieved. The last thing he wanted was to experience his shame in public again.

"Look, we've got to trot, we just popped in on the way to work to see how you were going," Shorty said. "And you know guys, I don't think we need to look after him anymore, somehow."

"Yeah, we've been superseded by a newer model." Michal smiled bashfully at Nanako.

My workmates bade us farewell and threaded their way past the milling throng of nurses and family visitors.

"Oh no," Nanako said suddenly in a worried voice.

"What's wrong?"

"Your mother and sisters are here."

"Don't worry, you'll be fine," I assured her as I spotted them approaching.

"But what if they're angry because I didn't tell them who I was?"

I didn't have time to reply. Nanako hopped off the bed and walked around to meet them as they approached with concerned expressions. Well, except for Elder Sister, perhaps. Sometimes I wondered if she had any positive expressions in her repertoire.

Clearly troubled, Nanako bowed low and waited. She need not have worried, though. As soon as my mother reached her, she swept her into her arms with tears streaming down her face. "You poor dear, I'm so terribly sorry for the way my husband treated you. You must believe me when I say I didn't know you came to Newhome two years ago. And when Ethan said his father had you expelled from Newhome, forcing you apart from my son, my heart just broke for you, sweetheart. I just wish you'd come to see me as soon as you arrived and then none of this would have happened."

Nanako returned my mother's embrace, and sniffing back tears, answered, "Ethan's father said you refused to see me because you were angry he had married a girl from another town."

"And he said to me that a doctor had forbidden us to visit Ethan until after his operation. And we know why he said that now – it was to stop us meeting you. He would have known I would have accepted you as my own daughter. But, do you know what?"

Nanako shook her head.

"The moment you ran into our home the other night because you saw that Ethan had been hurt, and when I saw how much you cared for him, even standing up to his father, I wished that it was you he was marrying. Not that snooty King girl. So when Ethan told me that you were in fact his wife, I was so overjoyed for him, and for you." She lifted Nanako's head. "I am so happy to have you as my daughter-in-law, and I just wish there was some way I could make up to you the pain and anguish my husband has caused you."

"I'm just glad it's over now."

My younger sister stepped forward and embraced Nanako. "And we're sisters, isn't that just the best? And I'm trying the new diet you suggested and I'm gonna keep at it too, no matter how hard it is."

The new diet was already working. I hadn't seen Younger Sister looking this well for months. I was also overjoyed to see my mother and younger sister welcome my wife into the family with such heartfelt warmth.

The biggest surprise was yet to come.

My heart stopped beating when my older sister took Nanako's small hand in hers and said with the barest hint of emotion, "Welcome to the family, Sister-in-law."

From there my mother and sisters spoke at length with Nanako, trying to catch up on two years of fellowship robbed them by my father's lies. I think they must have remembered I was there, and that I was injured, and should be the centre of attention, but I wasn't entirely sure...

Chapter Twenty-Seven

They discharged me from the hospital on Tuesday morning, and I insisted on walking home to get some fresh air after I was cooped up in there for three days.

When we were back home, Nanako went through the whole flat with a critical eye, considering the paint scheme, faded second hand curtains, towels, sheets, the amenities in the cupboards, even the sofa.

"Do you still want to live in Newhome?" I asked, curious.

"Yep," she answered as she dug through the kitchen cupboards.

"But won't you feel smothered by our laws and traditions?"

"Such as?"

"You know, like young women cannot go to the market without an older woman to accompany them?"

"I know about that rule. I was warned about it when Councillor Okada and I arrived. That's why he's been accompanying me everywhere I go. Are there many laws like that?"

"I'm afraid so." I ran more of Newhome's laws past her, such as women not being able to go to school, work, or even go out after dark. I didn't tell her about our cultural traditions, such as women waiting on men and not speaking during dinner without permission. We would not be observing those traditions in our home.

"That's nuts! What is the penalty if women break these laws?" Nanako wasn't impressed – shocked, even.

"The Custodians would arrest them. Depending on the nature of the 'crime,' they would hit them with hefty fines and possibly prison time," I explained.

"Really? And your women folk put up with this – why?"

I explained to her about the Founders and their goal of establishing a society that would not make the same mistakes the pre-Apocalyptic world made. Mistakes that led to a worldwide nuclear war.

"And restricting women's freedoms is going to prevent another nuclear war?"

"No, it's more a case of men and women having clearly defined and uniquely different roles in society so that there will be less division and conflict. That's what the Founders taught us in school. Sounds crazy, I know, but that's what they believe."

"I think there's a lot more to this than what they're letting on. I really wish we knew what country your Founders came from. I think that would explain a lot." Nanako frowned. "Well, it looks like I'll be asking your mother to come with me when I go shopping."

"Fair enough, but wouldn't our lives be simpler and easier if we went back to Hamamachi? That way you'll be free to do whatever you want," I suggested.

Nanako took me by the hand and led us to the sofa, where we sat down. "We can't ever go back to Hamamachi, Ethan. Not for any reason."

"Why not?"

"Do you know what caused your injury?" she asked carefully.

"My father told me I'd been hurt by a ceiling collapsing while foraging, but the neurologist I saw last Saturday said I'd been shot."

She nodded. "Yes, but not just shot – shot at point blank range."

Fear's icy fingers gripped my stomach and began to twist. I didn't want to hear anymore, but this was something I had to know. "How did it happen?"

"You went out on a classified mission with your squad of Rangers in September 2120. When your squad failed to report in, they sent another squad to find out why. A day later they brought your squad back. Four members were dead, and you were at death's door. After they operated on you they put you in a forced coma, and somehow, you pulled through, although in a very unhealthy state, as you know."

"Did they give you any details on the mission?" I asked, the fear turning and twisting into dread. How could five Rangers be wiped out so easily?

"No," she answered gruffly, "Regardless of how many times I asked or how hard I pushed, they refused to give me any details of what happened, just that you'd been shot in the line of duty. But you know that's impossible, don't you?"

"What do you mean?" The dread was snaking up my spine and spreading its icy tendrils into the back of my head.

"There's no way someone could creep up on you and shoot you in the head at point blank range, is there?"

I knew what she meant, and I agreed – I had already reached the same conclusion. "No, there isn't. No one can creep up on me when I'm awake, and even if I was asleep, the faintest suspicious sound would wake me."

"So what conclusion does that lead you to?"

"I was shot by someone I knew and trusted implicitly." The dread exploding throughout my head.

"Exactly."

"Do you have any idea who it could have been?" I asked.

"No, that's a question I was hoping you could answer. Have any of the memories that returned...?"

I shook my head, "Sorry, apart from the dream, I've only seen fragments. Always of mundane things, not people."

"That's what I thought. So then, do you understand why we can't go back to Hamamachi? Someone there – someone you trusted – murdered your squad and tried to kill you too. If we went back there to live, they may try to finish what they started."

I nodded thoughtfully, and added hesitantly, "Actually, I think it may be worse than that."

"What do you mean?"

"Does Councillor Okada have many enemies?"

"There are those who oppose him in the council, but that's to be expected, right? I'm not aware of him having any actual enemies who'd go so far as to try to harm him. Why do you ask?"

"The whole affair of the Skel ambushing you and Councillor Okada when you came to Newhome doesn't sit well with me," I replied. "I reckon those Skel were waiting for you."

Nanako's eyes widened in alarm. "I thought it was a coincidence, just a case of being in the wrong place at the wrong time."

I shook my head. "A large group of Skel, equipped with bombs powerful enough to blow apart one of your big 4WDs, who just happened to be on the very road you were using? That's too many coincidences for me."

"But if that's true, it means that someone – or someones – in Hamamachi just tried to kill me and the Councillor! And not only that, they must be working with the Skel!"

"That's right, though without any proof it's all conjecture."

"I have to tell Councillor Okada about this," she said.

"I'm sure it's already occurred to him."

"You may be right, but I'll mention it just in case. And oh, one more thing, don't tell anyone else that your memories have started to return. It's possible they didn't try to kill you when you were in the hospital because of the amnesia."

"Okay, but what about Councillor Okada, have you told him I remembered meeting you?"

She shook her head. "No, I told him you found out who I was from the hospital admission form."

"You don't trust him?" Surely she trusted her faithful chaperone.

"Well of course I trust him, but what if he accidentally lets it slip in front of the wrong person?"

"If you don't mind my asking, what is your relationship with the councillor?" I asked. They acted more like family, not like a councillor and his interpreter.

"He was my father's best friend," she replied. "And he's been like a father to my brother, sister and I since our father passed away."

"Oh, I'm so sorry. I didn't know. What happened?" I asked.

She averted my gaze when she answered. "He had cancer, and died a year before I met you. Sorry, can we not talk about this now?"

That answer sent a dozen questions spinning through my mind, but I respected her request and let the matter drop. At a guess, I'd say she'd been very close to him.

* * *

Councillor Okada dropped by our flat on Thursday while Nanako and I were productively engaged repainting my flat's ugly duck-egg blue walls with a refreshing pale golden-yellow. He informed us that he was returning to Hamamachi tomorrow, now that the consignment of goods Newhome was going to trade with the Japanese was finally ready.

We returned to painting after he left, though with some difficulty on my part due to one arm being in a sling.

"You realise you were speaking to Councillor Okada with paint on your nose," I said to my wife.

"That's because you put it there," she replied.

I held up my hands in mock indignation. "Surely not I? Here, would you like me to wipe it off?"

"Please do."

I picked up the small cloth we'd been using to wipe up accidents and spills, and gave her irresistibly cute button-nose a bit of a rub. "Hmm, the paint seems to have dried. I'll have to use a wet rag." I dipped the rag into the wet paint and painted the rest of her nose pale golden-yellow.

"Ethan, you're supposed to be painting the walls, not me!" She admonished me with a touch of mirth as she stepped forward to wrap her arms around me. But as I embraced her with my right arm, I felt a paint roller run down my back.

Nanako stepped back giggling – the first time I'd seen her do so, and it had to be the cutest thing I'd ever seen. It made me wonder how many times we had like this when we were newlyweds.

"These are my best clothes!" I protested in mock indignation.

"Lucky the paint is acrylic then, eh?"

"Absolutely, especially considering your nose is covered in it," I laughed. And then, on a more serious note, I asked "Have I changed much?"

"What do you mean?" she asked as she put down the paint roller.

"You know, from when you knew me before," I replied. "I mean, for me, getting to know you is all new, and I'm loving every minute of it, because you're just the most amazing person I've ever met. But what about you? How do I compare to the Ethan you used to know? Are you disappointed?"

She took my right hand in hers and looked up to make eye contact. "You're still you – the same Ethan I fell in love with three years ago – if that's what you're asking. But there's a depth to you now that wasn't so obvious when you were eighteen. Back then, life was one big adventure, but now you know there's a darker side to it as well. We've both changed because of this trial we've been forced to endure, but now that we're back together again, our wounded hearts can begin the healing process to become whole again. From here it will only get better."

A sharp rap on the door interrupted our conversation. Expecting it to be one of my friends, since I'd heard only one pair of boots approaching, I was most unpleasantly surprised when I opened the door and found our visitor was Lieutenant King.

He tipped his head slightly. "Mr. and Mrs. Jones."

At least he had accepted we were married now. "How can we help you, Lieutenant?"

He removed a sealed letter from his Custodian fatigues and handed it to me. "Orders from Custodian command, Jones."

I read the letter and handed it to Nanako, who was standing beside me now. "Why me, Sir?"

The faintest trace of an empty smile tweaked the corners of King's mouth. "In light of your considerable experience with the Skel and Melbourne's eastern suburbs, I considered you to be the obvious choice to lead the trade convoy to Hamamachi."

"You can't ask Ethan to do this, he hasn't recovered from his wounds," Nanako protested.

Bearing in mind what we had discussed on Tuesday about why we couldn't ever go to Hamamachi, this order from Custodian command was the last thing we needed.

"This isn't an option, Mrs. Jones," he snarled. "And besides, he won't be driving, just directing the convoy where to go."

Nanako looked up at me for help, her eyes desperate. I gave my head the slightest shake. There was nothing we could do. The Custodians' orders were law.

"Fine, my foraging team and I will lead the convoy, Sir, but on two conditions," I replied.

"You aren't in any position to make demands, Jones." King appeared amused I had the presumption to say such a thing.

"Nevertheless, if you want this convoy to be able to fight off a Skel attack, I request that you reinstate me as leader of the foraging team and replace Cooper with Leigh Williams. And we'll need our bows and arrows back. You can hide them under our vehicles' seats if you like."

"Leigh Williams is in prison."

"I need him, Lieutenant. He knows how to hunt and bring down Skel," I said, refusing to budge an inch. Actually, Leigh was the least capable of my team, but this was an opportunity to get him out of prison and I wasn't going let it pass by. "Perhaps Custodian Command could offer him a pardon on the condition he accepts this assignment, Sir."

I could almost see the cogwheels in King's brain turning as he considered my requests. "Fine," he finally grunted. "I'll see what I can do. I will pick up you at five sharp tomorrow morning."

"What, are you going too, Sir?" I asked, suddenly concerned. He was the last person in the world I wanted to accompany all the way to Hamamachi and back.

This time King did smile – a cold, merciless expression. "Oh yes, did I forget to mention it? I'm leading the Custodian team providing protection for the convoy."

"How long will we stay in Hamamachi, Lieutenant?" Nanako asked, her voice wavering.

"We? These orders are for Ethan and him alone," King shot back.

"Sir, until Councillor Okada has returned to Hamamachi, I must continue in my role as his translator," she said.

"I see. Well, the plan is to drop off our trade goods, pick up Hamamachi's, and make the return journey." King's eyes suddenly narrowed. "Now that I come to think of it, with regards to you two, since Mrs. Jones has family there, you're welcome to stay there until the next delivery run," he replied.

I looked at him in surprise – he was going let us stay behind if we chose? What was this, compassion and understanding from Lieutenant King?

"No thank you," my wife replied without hesitation, "We will return with you, Sir."

"Suit yourself," King said, and then took his leave without so much as a goodbye.

After he had gone, Nanako took my hand, her eyes wide and fearful. "We can't go, Ethan, we just can't."

"We don't have a choice when it comes to the Custodians," I said sadly.

"Can we run away then, just the two of us? Get out of the city and go somewhere, anywhere but Hamamachi."

"This town's a fortress designed to do one thing," I answered gently, "and that's to lock its population inside. Except for the foragers, there's no way out."

"Then you have to feign sickness, or break your leg or something," she said, growing frantic, "Please Ethan, find a way out of this. It is too dangerous for you to return to Hamamachi."

"That's not going to work."

"Ethan, you got shot in Hamamachi, remember? Someone there tried to kill you. If you go back there, they will try again! You can't go back."

"I understand that, Nanako, but King's given us a direct order. There's no way around this."

"No! I can't face this, not again!" she said.

I tried to put my arm around her to console her, but she slipped out of my reach and fled into the bathroom, slamming the door behind her.

I stood there, wondering what I should do, but the sound of her mournful sobbing broke my heart, so I opened the door and slipped in after her.

She was kneeling on the floor with her arms against the far wall and breathing so rapidly that she was gasping for air as she wept. If I couldn't calm her quickly she would hyperventilate in no time.

I pulled my arm out of the sling, knelt down beside her and wrapped myself around her back, ignoring the pain in my chest. "It's gonna be okay, Nanako, you have to trust me."

She turned around within my arms and took my face in her hands. "Do you have any idea what it's like to be happily married for just six short months, and then they bring your husband home on a stretcher one day, with such a terrible head wound and covered in so much blood that you can't even recognise him? Can you imagine what that was like?"

"No, I can't," I replied, for I couldn't even begin to visualize what she had gone through. The last two years had been hard on me, but nothing like what she'd been through. I looked at her distraught face and it cut me up inside.

"Ethan, I can't go through that again, I just can't," she said as she broke into tears again, burying her head and arms against my chest.

I remembered how my father said she kept panicking when I couldn't remember her after she brought me to the hospital here in Newhome; sometimes panicking so badly the nurses had to tear her away from me. But this time it was different, because I was with her now and I wasn't gonna let go of her for any reason. So I just held her, and whispered to her reassuringly, "We're gonna be okay, Nanako, I'm never gonna leave you again." And we stayed there on that cold bathroom floor for a long time as I comforted her the best I could.

And it was with quantifiable sorrow that I realised the joy we had felt earlier at the prospect of repainting the flat had completely vanished.

Chapter Twenty-Eight

Nanako had composed herself – well, outwardly anyway – by the time Shorty rang a couple of hours later and reported Leigh had been released from prison. I asked Shorty to bring him over, and then rang David and Michal and invited them over too.

Michal and David arrived first. Michal commandeered the sofa and dwarfed it with his large frame. David leaned against the wall next to the TV – I think he was trying to hide in that corner – but was so nervous he couldn't stop fidgeting. Nanako and I sat on the edge of the bed, and to be honest, I was dreading this pending confrontation between David and Leigh. It could get pretty ugly.

Ten minutes later Shorty knocked on the door and entered with a somewhat dour Leigh trailing behind him. Shorty grabbed one of the two dining table chairs, but Leigh just stood beside the table and stared at Nanako and me. Although he'd only been in prison for a few days, he had lost weight. And his outlook on life had changed too.

"What kind of drongo forgets they got married?" Leigh said finally, looking me in the eye. It would appear Shorty filled him in on current events on the walk here.

"Welcome back, Leigh," I replied dryly.

"He has amnesia," Nanako pointed out defensively. I took her hand in an attempt to encourage her not to take offence at anything Leigh said.

"Whatever," Leigh snapped, and to me he added, "You should have left me there, Jones."

"For another six years?"

"Better there than here," he grumbled.

"I can have you put back in if you like." Sometimes his constant negativity got to me, but honestly, I think it was justified on this occasion.

"Suit yourself."

"David has something to say to you, by the way," I said after a moment's silence.

"Yeah, like what?" Leigh spat, turning to take in David, who was to all attempts and purposes trying to squirm through the wall and escape into the flat next door.

"Leigh, it was me. I was the one who told them," David said softly as he looked at the floor.

"Told who what?" Leigh asked, confused.

"The Custodians. I told them about you and Amelia. Look, I'm sorry, I don't know what came over me. I was angry and jealous and I just blurted it out when I bumped into one of their patrols."

Leigh's mouth dropped open and he glanced at the rest of us, thinking this was some kind of a joke. When we returned his gaze with all seriousness, he realised David wasn't kidding. He exploded into a frenzied rage and flung himself on David, punching and kicking him. David just put his arms around his head and took it without making a sound.

Nanako shook my arm, "Ethan, do something!"

I waited for a few more punches and kicks to land and then asked clearly but softly, "What's happened to us, guys?"

Leigh pulled his last punch and remained where he was, facing David and panting for breath.

"We've always been so close. We've prided ourselves on being closer than brothers, yeah? But look at us now." I looked at Shorty, Leigh and David. "We're letting ourselves be torn apart by jealousy, resentment, hatred and unforgiveness. And yeah, David stuffed up big time, and he'll have to carry this on his conscience for the rest of his life – and that's a heavy burden. But haven't we all stuffed up at some stage or another?"

"Jones, in case you missed it, Amelia's dead 'cause of him!" Leigh snapped back.

I pointed my finger at Leigh. "Don't you dare go placing all the blame for her death on David. If you hadn't been sleeping with her in the first place, the Custodians wouldn't have executed her and put you in prison. Now don't get me wrong, I'm not saying I agree with that ludicrous law, 'cause I don't, but both you and Amelia knew the risks you were taking when you went down that path, didn't you?"

Leigh glared at me.

"Answer the question, Leigh."

"All right! Yes, we knew the risk."

"And yet you did it anyway. How long did you think you could get away with it before her family realised, huh?" I pressed.

"But it wasn't them who reported us, it was him!" Leigh shot back, pointing at David. "Someone who was supposed to be my friend."

"Friends, even family members, make mistakes and do things that hurt one another," I said, and thought of my father and the terrible damage he inflicted on me and my wife. I realised I should be talking to myself as well as Leigh, but I hadn't reached that point yet. "But we have to somehow find it within ourselves to forgive each other and move on. Not one of us is perfect, Leigh. We five, no, we six," I said, putting my arm around my petite wife, "are a family. Let's not let anything come between us, not anything, not ever."

Leigh glared at David and then at me, and said, "You can't fix something like this with words, Jones." And he stomped towards the door.

"Be here by five tomorrow morning – Custodian's orders," I shouted after him as he stormed out the door and slammed it behind him.

"That went really well," Shorty murmured. I honestly couldn't tell if he was being sarcastic or serious.

Nanako hopped off the bed and grabbed David by the sleeve. "Come on. Let's put some ice on those bruises."

All things considering, I guess it went better than I expected. Leigh found out the truth and lashed out at David, but hadn't done any permanent damage to him in the process. How long it would take to mend the rift between them, I couldn't even begin to guess.

When David and Nanako rejoined us, I explained to everyone about our mission to Hamamachi tomorrow, and we discussed the types of dangers we could encounter along the way.

* * *

We left Newhome at six the following morning, while the sun was still low on the horizon. We foragers had been given a modified G-Wagon to drive; it seated five rather than four. Michal was the driver with me beside him to navigate – or rather, be on the lookout for Skel ambushes. To assist me in that task, the Custodians had given me a pair of binoculars, and oh my, they were so much nicer than the ones I hid on the roof of my apartment block. I wondered if the Custodians would let me keep them after this mission. Yeah, right.

Shorty, Leigh, and Nanako sat in the back seat, with Nanako in the middle. A trailer laden with goods and supplies to be traded with Hamamachi was towed by the G-Wagon. A large vinyl bag containing five sets of bows and arrows had also been dumped on the floor between the front and back seats. I was amazed to see that King had caved in to all of my conditions.

Councillor Okada and his large black 4WD came next, with David riding shotgun with him should he need breaks from driving. More items for trade filled the 4WD's boot. Leigh was still looking daggers at David, so I thought it best to keep them separated for our peace of mind. Plus, David was a better driver and was completely obsessed with the big 4WD and its computerised dashboard.

Bringing up the rear was King and his squad of Custodians, riding in their Bushmaster. One Custodian manned the vehicle's roof-mounted machine gun, as usual.

Although we needed to travel east and then southeast to get to Hamamachi, I figured that route was too predictable. So we left Newhome via the western gates, and initially headed west, then north, then east, and finally southeast. I also used minor roads rather than the major thoroughfares. Nanako took over giving directions once we got into the country.

The journey of a 180km would have taken only a couple of hours once, but now took five times as long due to the condition of the roads. We had to slow to a virtual crawl to navigate some of the obstacles we encountered. Sometimes we even had to stop and clear them out of the way.

* * *

We hit the outskirts of Hamamachi just after four in the afternoon, after an uneventful journey with zero Skel sightings. My strategy of keeping away from the main thoroughfares seemed to have paid off.

I was hoping that coming back to Hamamachi would trigger more memories of the time I spent here. Memories of Nanako and of how I'd been shot. Though I wasn't looking forward looking over my shoulder every minute because I didn't know who had shot me.

Hamamachi had no walls, just as Nanako had told me. In fact, the town's outskirts were miles and miles of fenced off fields of grazing cows and sheep. These were patrolled by the Hamamachi Militia, who rode horseback or drove 4WD vehicles, and unlike the Custodians, the Militia wore civilian clothes. No one challenged our progress, so I guessed the councillor must have phoned ahead to advise them he was coming.

As we drew closer, we passed farms, orchards, and fully enclosed greenhouse nurseries. We passed a number of Japanese on the road, some walking and others riding horses or bikes. A few bowed respectfully, but most eyed us suspiciously. I guess the armoured Bushmaster made quite an imposing sight.

We finally hit the actual town itself, and unlike Newhome, most of the houses were one or two story townhouses. Many had Japanese rice-paper screens and doors, which were kept safely behind glass so they couldn't be ravaged by the weather. Roofs were typically made of clay tiles that were glazed in blues, greys, greens and even reds. Compared to the dull greys of Newhome, Hamamachi was a treat to our eyes.

Nanako directed us to the town trade centre, the TTC, which was only a couple of streets back from the beach. It was a large two-story building, and was where all trade with neighbouring towns was conducted.

Upon seeing our arrival, a Japanese Militia squad opened tall wooden gates to the left of the building and ushered us into the loading dock. There was a large parking lot to the left of the dock that could accommodate vehicles of any size. Goods were loaded into the TTC at ground level through three roller shutter doors at the far end. Two roller doors were up, letting me see inside a large warehouse filled with row after row of shelves packed with boxes and crates. Two more squads of Militia stood beside the doors.

TTC workers directed us to drive the G-Wagon and 4WD to within a dozen metres of the loading dock. They brought over two small forklift trucks with pallets to collect the items we brought to trade. Councillor Okada got out to oversee the unloading.

The Bushmaster pulled up behind the G-Wagon but left a big enough space for the forklift to get to the trailer. King got out and stood to one side, watching the TTC workers somewhat apprehensively as they began to place the items we brought on the forklift pallets.

The foragers stayed near the G-Wagon, ready to help if needed, but Nanako took me by the hand and led us to stand on the other side of King. There wasn't much I could do with my arm in a sling.

Councillor Okada walked over to join us. "This is the beginning of a grand new era." He smiled proudly. "A time of goodwill and trade between Victoria's two most productive towns."

"What has Newhome sent here for trade?" I asked. I knew Hamamachi would be sending back a batch of Smartphones, but had no idea what we brought. Any questions presented to King and his men before we left were met with disinterested grunts.

"Newhome has sent biologically altered fruit and vegetable seeds, engineered to grow in Australian soil and at greatly increased growth rates," said Counsellor Okada. "Also tens of thousands of embryos of bio-engineered poultry, and a refrigeration-maturation unit to transport them here and mature them later."

I looked at the wooden crates and plastic and metal boxes dockworkers were unloading from the trailer. "Our chickens are that good?" I asked, surprised.

Councillor Okada laughed. "Your geneticists are quite brilliant, Ethan. From just a few hens and roosters they have given us this batch of modified embryos."

"That's incredible. I didn't know Newhome was doing that," I replied as I watched several Japanese men struggle mightily to push and drag the black refrigeration-maturation unit from the trailer onto a pallet. My mind balked at the sheer weight of the thing. It obviously weighed at least 250 kilos.

An uneasy feeling crept into my gut. Why would a refrigeration-maturation unit the size of a small refrigerator weigh so much? What kind of metals had they built it with? Irresistibly curious, I stepped closer and shouted ultrasonically as loud as I could, disguising it as a yawn.

Trying to hear an echo from inside something metal wasn't easy, but with my hearing, I could normally manage if I was close enough. As this was a refrigerator I was expecting to get back an echo indicating steel, copper, aluminium, plastic and fibreglass, but the most notable echo that returned was something far more dense than lead.

It had to be uranium.

In fact, from what I could tell, the guts of the refrigeration-maturation unit had been replaced by a thermonuclear warhead. A hydrogen bomb no doubt. (I'd seen schematics of them in contraband books I'd read while foraging. I was curious about the things that had destroyed our world.)

Special containers with the chicken embryos, which must have perished since there was no refrigeration, were on a shelf above the bomb. If they opened the unit it would still appear to be the real thing.

The Custodians hadn't come here to trade, but to blow Hamamachi off the map.

Chapter Twenty-Nine

The uneasy feeling in my stomach expanded into a tidal wave of dread that swept right through me. I staggered back a step in shock and my face blanched. I turned my head slowly towards King.

To my surprise, he was watching me intently. He had seen my shocked reaction.

"King, what are you doing?"

"You know, don't you." He glowered at me as though I was evil incarnate. "You're the accursed bio-engineered scum I've been searching for these past two weeks."

"Answer the question, King."

"I'm doing what needs to be done," he snarled.

"There's no justification for genocide, King!"

"It's either them or us. They're behind the Skel attacks on Newhome and you know it. Now back off and keep your mouth shut!" He returned to watching the TTC workers unload the rest of the boxes from the trailer.

"You said Nanako and I could stay here after you left – you're trying to kill us too."

"That was the general idea. Now shut up and let the trade go ahead, and then maybe I'll let you two come back with us."

I had no idea when the bomb was set to go off, but I guessed it would be soon after we left. In which case, there probably wasn't a great deal of time to deal with this insanity.

A dozen scenarios involving me attacking King fled through my mind, but with my arm in a sling there was no way I could carry them out. Instead, I reached back and touched Nanako's hand, getting her attention. Turning my head half towards her so that I could also watch King, I made a massive effort and somehow forced myself to speak entirely in Japanese. "Nanako, quietly and without making a fuss, please go and warn the officer in charge of the Militia security detail that the Custodians have brought a bomb with them."

"What?" Her voice wavered.

"Just trust me."

She nodded and tried to walk nonchalantly towards the Militia sergeant standing near the roller shutter door.

Unfortunately, King noticed our exchange and, putting two and two together, realised I was not going to play along like he had hoped.

In a blindingly fast move he drew his sidearm and aimed for Nanako. I shouted to distract him and knocked his gun aside so that the shot went wide. Nanako threw her arms over her head and flung herself behind the closest forklift while shouting in Japanese to the Militia sergeant.

I tried to disarm King with a knife-hand strike to his arm but he was expecting it this time. He sidestepped my blow and thumped the butt of his pistol on my chest, directly over my wound. Agonising pain speared through my chest and I collapsed at his feet. I writhed about on the ground, trying to ride out the wave of pain and stay conscious.

The secret out, King turned to the Bushmaster and shouted, "Secure the dock!"

The loading dock instantly descended into complete pandemonium.

King fired his pistol at the Militia sergeant, downing him with his second shot. At the same time, the Custodian operating the Bushmaster's roof-mounted machine gun opened up. He cut down two more Militia and forced the rest to scatter. The last two Custodians came running out the back of the Bushmaster and attacked the Militia squad guarding the gates. They shot two and wounded a third, who crawled back around the gates towards safety. Another Militia used the gates for protection and fired at the Custodians, forcing them to duck for cover as well. One used the Bushmaster's rear door while the other hid behind a parked car.

The surviving Militia returned fire, snapping off frantic shots at the Custodians as they hurried towards cover. Two ducked inside the TTC, where they would pop out, fire a burst, and duck back. The rest took cover behind stacks of wooden pallets and the forklift trucks.

Still lying at King's feet as he engaged the Militia, I looked around for my fellow foragers and spotted them crouched beside the G-Wagon, eyes wide with fear and confusion. They had no idea why the Custodians suddenly opened fire on the Japanese.

I made eye contact with Michal and pointed at King and the Custodians, and then made a slashing motion across my throat with my finger. His eyes widened in surprise, shocked by my instructions. I repeated them just to make sure he understood. He finally nodded, opened the G-Wagon's rear passenger door and reached in to remove the bag of bows and arrows.

I looked around for Nanako and spotted her next to the forklift. She was kneeling beside the Militia sergeant shot by King, trying to stem the blood flowing from his chest. But going by her desperate expression, she was fighting a losing battle.

Bullets whizzed past and ricocheted off the Bushmaster as a new Militia squad rushed out of the TTC. Their charge was cut short as they were gunned down by the Bushmaster's machine gunner. The remaining Militia in the courtyard kept firing at the Bushmaster, but without any effect.

I watched King hurry over to the fake refrigeration-maturation unit, unlock it and flip the lid open. He scooped out armloads of small plastic and metal containers that contained the dead chick embryos, and removed the metal shelf beneath them. Still holding to my aching chest, I clambered to my feet to find he was attempting to change the timer on the detonator. It was set at three hours, but he was no doubt trying to make it blow sooner. No wonder he wanted to drop off, pick up, and leave straight away.

Stepping behind the lieutenant, I pulled a small, sharp knife I had hidden in my boot and tried to stab him in the neck. Unfortunately, he sensed my movement and whirled towards me, causing the knife to plunge into his right shoulder instead.

Still, it was enough to distract him from the bomb. He flinched off the next blow I aimed at his bull-like neck and booted me in the stomach, driving me back a few steps. I made to rush back at him, but he grabbed his pistol with his left hand and aimed it at my head.

That would have been the end of me except for Michal, who suddenly appeared behind King and put him in a crushing neck hold, spoiling his aim as he fired. The bullet went wide, but still glanced off the right side of my forehead.

Everything went black.

I can't have been out for more than a few seconds. When I came to, I was laying on my side, facing King and Michal, who were still grappling. In what felt like a dream, I watched King's face go red and the veins on his neck bulge – he had a couple of seconds before Michal's neck hold would render him unconscious. But to my horror, King shoved the pistol behind him, pressed it against Michal's stomach, and fired three shots.

A strange expression crossed Michal's face as he slid slowly to his knees and slumped to the ground, his life fading away before my very eyes.

"No!" I shrieked as I reached for him. Michal glanced at me and then fell still.

I rolled to my knees, and with blood pouring down my face and into my eye, I crawled over to him while King went back to the bomb.

I checked Michal's pulse, but there was none. He was gone.

The enormity of what just happened crashed into me like a tidal wave. Michal, my best friend, had died trying to save me from King. A part of my heart withered and died along with him. I rested my hands and forehead on his shoulder and lamented the loss of a friend who had always been there for me. He had helped me in my moments of inexplicable melancholy, and I had comforted him when his family life sapped him of the will to live. No longer would he join us when we got together on the roof to goof around, no longer would he be the brawn behind our foraging efforts, and no longer could his younger brother and sister look up to him, as he set them a role model worth following.

I couldn't believe this had happened. Today was supposed to be a simple delivery run. The only potential danger was supposed to be from the person in Hamamachi who had shot me two years ago. We weren't supposed to be going up against our own Custodians!

Sitting back on my haunches, I pulled a handkerchief from my pocket and pressed it against the bullet graze on my forehead in an attempt to staunch the blood flow. As I did, Leigh popped up from behind the G-Wagon's trailer, an arrow fitted to his bow. But before he could shoot at King, the gunner on the Bushmaster sent a hail of bullets at him. The arrow went wide and Leigh went down with blood spraying from his chest.

"No!" I screamed in horror at the sight of another close friend shot. A friend I dragged out of prison to come on this mission, thinking I was doing him a favour. It wasn't supposed to lead to his death!

Hearing my shout, the Bushmaster's machine gunner swivelled his weapon around and lined me up in his crosshairs. But before he could shoot, he clutched at his throat and then gurgling and choking, collapsed over his weapon, an arrow through his neck. By facing me he had exposed his back to my lads on the far side of the Bushmaster. It had cost him his life. Good riddance.

With the machine gunner out of the way, I rose and staggered over to King. I had to stop him changing the detonator's timer. But I was so feeble that he fended me off with his right arm, even though weakened by the knife wound. I watched him change the timer to five minutes and activate it. That done, he turned and sent me sprawling to the ground with a strong push.

He grabbed his pistol and aimed it at me. "You've no idea how much pleasure I'm going to get from killing you personally, Jones," he snarled.

"Nooooo!" Nanako shouted in rage as she leapt up from behind the forklift to come to my aide.

Distracted by her shout, King hesitated for only a moment, but it was a moment too long.

Armed with a Militia assault-rifle she had acquired, Nanako charged the lieutenant and unloaded the gun's entire clip into him.

King jerked about like a puppet on strings and collapsed, bleeding from a dozen places. Nanako dropped the gun, ran to my side and knelt down beside me, her eyes wide with horror as she took in the sight of my bloody head. "Oh no, Ethan, please, no, not again!"

I reached out and grabbed her hands. "I'm gonna be okay, Nanako. It looks worse than it is."

"But you've been shot in the head again!"

"It's not like last time, it's only a graze," I assured her. "But quickly, help me to my feet, we've got to deactivate the bomb or its lights out for us all in less than five minutes."

As my wife helped me to my feet, King grabbed my foot. "I win, Jones," he whispered, smiling feebly.

"Not yet," I replied as I kicked his hand away and staggered towards the bomb. And in dramatic contrast to the deafening clatter of the machine guns and ricocheting bullets, the dock had fallen deathly quiet. Another Custodian had an arrow through his throat, and the last one had been taken down by Militia gunfire.

"David! Grab your toolkit and get here pronto!" I shouted as loudly as I could manage as Nanako helped me to the bomb.

"I'm with Leigh, he's been hit," he shouted back.

"Sorry, but I need you here."

David left Leigh's side reluctantly and ran over to us carrying his toolkit.

"What just happened, Jones? Why did the Custodians go berserk?" he demanded.

I pointed to the fake refrigeration-maturation unit and said softly, "David, tell me you know how to deactivate a hydrogen bomb."

His eyes widened further than I thought humanly possible. "The Custodians brought a...?"

I clapped my hand over his mouth before he finished blurting out his question. The last thing we needed was mass hysteria. "David, we've got less than five minutes. How do we disarm it?"

"We can remove the IHE from the physics package or..."

"The what from the what?"

"Sorry, we can remove the insensitive high explosives from the warhead, or we can remove the exploding bridge-wire detonator from the IHE, sorry, the insensitive high explosives," he said with a shaky voice.

"I have no idea what you just said, but can you just do it already?"

David stuck his head in the box and looked inside, "Okay, okay, this is doable. They've put just the warhead and detonator in here. It shouldn't be too hard to get to the IHE if we work quickly." He pulled his head out of the box and reached for his bag.

"Don't move!" commanded a very, very agitated Japanese Militia captain. "Drop your weapons, put your hands on your heads, and lie face down on the ground, or we will shoot!"

Looking up I saw that we were surrounded by several very irate squads of Japanese Militia, some of which had just arrived.

"We've got less than four minutes to deactivate this bomb or we all die!" I shouted back in Japanese.

"Do as I say or we shoot!" Several of them raised their guns, their fingers already beginning to depress their triggers.

"Stop, Captain! These men are on our side!" Nanako tried to explain, but a squad of Militia aimed their weapons at her as well.

I watched the detonator's timer counting down the seconds with an almost morbid fascination, barely aware of the Militia captain shouting at me to lie down.

It was over. For all of us. King had won.

Chapter Thirty

"Stand down!" Okada bellowed, rising from his place behind the G-Wagon.

With that single order, the militia complied.

"We need to hurry!" I cried as Okada quickly joined us.

"What happened – why did the Custodians attack us? What is in that box?" the councillor demanded.

"The Custodians brought a bomb," and I whispered the next part so that only he could hear me, "a nuclear bomb, and it's set to go off in less than four minutes. You have to let us disarm it right now."

"A what?" the councillor asked in sheer disbelief. And then, in seeing that our serious expressions didn't change, he added, "No, absolutely not. I will get in the bomb disposal unit. We will evacuate the town immediately!"

"There's no time to wait for your team, nor any point in evacuating. No one could get far enough away from the blast radius," David replied.

I grabbed the councillor's arm with a bloody hand. "You cannot get a better bomb disposal team than David and I, Sir. Trust, me, we can disarm this."

He stared at me for what felt like eternity, but in reality was only a couple of seconds, and then reluctantly nodded his consent. All the same, as David and I rushed to the bomb, he instructed the Militia captain to call in the bomb disposal unit. The rest of the Militia and TTC personnel moved quickly back from us.

"Right! I reckon removing the exploding-bridge-wire detonator is the best bet," David said. Then, "Shoot! There's a lid screwed over the top. We have to take it off first, but we'll need to get the bomb out of the box so I can see where the screws are. Man, we don't have time for this!"

"Wait!" I said as I leaned on the unit's casing and made a few ultrasonic shouts. I pulled David to me. "Don't argue, just listen. Put your fingers down here, and here. There are two screws there, and two on the other side. Remove them and the lid will come off."

"Three minutes," Nanako announced quietly with a calm I didn't feel.

David nodded and set to work quickly removing the four screws with a combination of touch and his electric screwdriver. That done, we lifted off the aluminium lid, exposing the exploding-bridge-wire detonator.

"Two minutes," came Nanako's countdown to doom.

Armed with the tools he needed, David lay half inside the refrigeration-maturation unit and attacked the detonator wires one by one. Using echolocation I watched him work and marvelled how his fingers could operate so deftly considering what was at stake if he failed.

Finally, he pushed himself off the bomb and slid to the ground, breathing heavily. "It's done."

"The clock's still counting down!" Nanako pointed out in a panic. Councillor Okada had noticed too, his face white with fear.

"Don't worry, the wires are no longer connected to the explosives or the timer, so it's counting down to a non-event," David assured us.

Nevertheless, we all held our breaths and watched the counter tick down to zero.

"Now do you believe me?" David asked.

I wanted to give him a crushing hug, but didn't have the strength. The throbbing pain from my head and chest wounds were taking their toll, so I just sat on the ground beside him and leaned against the trailer.

The councillor congratulated us for disarming the bomb, as did several of the Militia. None of them, however, knew what sort of bomb we had just disarmed.

"David, where on earth did you learn how to deactivate a thermonuclear bomb?" I asked, completely in awe of his abilities.

David stared at me as though it was the first time we had met. "From books and manuals I found in the ruins and smuggled home," he replied. "But Jones, you wanna tell me how you can see through metal?"

Nanako placed a finger against David's lips. "Such questions are best not answered, David."

He nodded and said no more.

The threat of the bomb gone, reality came crashing back to me. "Michal, Leigh!"

"I'll check on Leigh," Nanako said, and she darted away with David at her side.

I staggered over to Michal's prone form and checked for a pulse again. I knew it was a futile exercise. He was gone.

Nanako ran back and knelt beside me. "Leigh's pretty bad, but I think he's gonna make it. Shorty and two Militia are looking after him."

I nodded, despair that we had lost Leigh turning into a sliver of hope. I don't know what I would have done if I lost both of them.

We heard the approach of screeching sirens and several ambulances drove up to the loading dock. Paramedics swarmed out and rushed to treat the many wounded. I was struck by the thought that Hamamachi's peaceful trading centre had been turned into a battlefield. I would never forgive Newhome for this, not ever.

Chapter Thirty-One

Councillor Okada had stopped the militia shooting us while trying to disarm the bomb. However, once Militia Command found out there was a nuclear bomb involved, we foragers were whisked away to be questioned, or rather 'interrogated,' in Militia Headquarters' bleak interrogation rooms.

Paramedics had treated my wound at the Town Trade Centre. They washed it, covered it with a sterile gauze pad and wrapped my head in bandages. After that, they gave me painkillers and declared me fit for questioning. The bullet had apparently glanced off my skull, causing a rather painful flesh wound, a thumping headache, and blood loss, but that was all. And my chest was in so much pain from King's brutal treatment that it hurt to breathe.

The room I was taken to was small, having two chairs, a flimsy wooden table between them, and a large one-way observation window. My interrogator was a stocky, middle-aged Militia major. To lend him some muscle should I become violent, an extremely well built private stood behind me.

The major thumped his fists on the flimsy wooden table that separated us. "Let's go back to the beginning – why were you trying to destroy Hamamachi, Ethan Jones?"

"As I've told you many times, Major, I didn't know about the bomb."

"That answer doesn't work for me. You see, I suggest it was you and your foragers who loaded it onto the trailer, knowing full well what it was and its intended purpose."

I looked into his scowling, darkly tanned face, and wished he would drop these pointless questions and let me lie down somewhere – even on the floor in here. "The Custodians loaded the trailer, Major. The G-Wagon and trailer are Custodian vehicles. We had nothing to do with them apart from driving them here."

"So you say. Okay, next question. Let us reconsider your claim that you didn't know about the bomb, yet expect us to believe you suddenly realised it was in the refrigeration unit because it seemed too heavy to you?"

"It's the truth. I'm a forager and therefore have a pretty good head for judging how much things weigh. That refrigeration unit clearly weighed over two-hundred kilos."

"Very well, let's assume for a moment that you did realise the unit was heavier than it should have been. However, that could not have tipped you off that there was a thermonuclear device in it. So this in itself is proof that you knew the bomb was in the unit, and that you had a sudden change of heart when the enormity of what you Newhomers were about to do hit you."

"If I'd known the bomb was there beforehand, Major, I would have done everything I could have done to stop the Custodians bringing it here. And the proof of that is that my foraging team and my wife took down three of the Custodians and David and I disarmed the bomb," I said wearily. The mention of my foraging team instantly brought back the painful memories of Michal's loss and Leigh's fearful injuries. I wanted to go somewhere quiet and mourn in peace, not sit here while they interrogated me for something I didn't do.

"I find it interesting that you and David knew exactly how to disarm that bomb. I put it to you, Ethan Jones, that you knew how to disarm it because you were Lieutenant King's backup plan in case something went wrong – except your conscience got in the way, didn't it?"

"To be honest, we didn't actually disarm it. We had to dismantle the detonator to stop it going off. If I had been in cahoots with King I would have known the activation/deactivation codes, don't you think?" I shot back at him.

"You honestly expect me to believe a couple of middle-school dropouts knew how to dismantle a thermonuclear device?"

The throbbing pain in my head was becoming steadily worse. "Firstly, David and I deliberately dropped out of school because we didn't want our futures mapped out for us by pompous North End officials. Secondly, I have a gift for finding out how things are put together, and David is a genius when it comes to pulling them apart."

"You've been in Hamamachi before, haven't you, Ethan?" the major asked, suddenly changing tack.

"Yes."

"And you joined the Militia and then the Rangers, correct?"

"Yeah, so?"

"And during your last mission, your fellow Rangers were all mysteriously killed and you were badly injured. From that you apparently developed epilepsy and amnesia, and were consequently taken back to Newhome by your wife to be treated in their hospital," he continued.

"What are you trying to say?" I demanded irritably.

"I put it to you, Ethan Jones, that you are a Custodian spy and were sent here to infiltrate our military, learn everything you could, and then feigned the epilepsy and amnesia so you could be taken back to Newhome without suspicion. And today you came back, bringing with you a weapon with which to destroy us."

The pain was unbearable, so I put my right elbow on the table and rested my head in my hand. "Are you gonna claim I faked the gunshot wound too? And the operation?"

"Sit up, Ethan," the Major snapped.

"Have you forgotten I was shot in the head today trying to stop King detonate the nuke?" My voice came out as a whisper.

The major nodded to the private behind me, who reached forward and slammed me back against the chair. I bit my tongue to keep from crying out in pain as black spots danced in front of my eyes.

"Let me break it down for you, Ethan. Your entire defence is built upon your claim that you determined there was a nuclear bomb in the refrigeration-maturation unit when it was unloaded from the trailer, and immediately asked your wife to warn the Militia on duty. However, as what you claim is impossible, I accuse you of being a Custodian agent who knew the bomb was there. It is on these grounds that you and your foragers will be charged with acts of terrorism and be executed."

I considered telling him that I detected the hydrogen bomb using echolocation. If it came down to my mates and me facing execution or revealing my bio-engineered abilities to save them, then I would reveal them. I hoped I wouldn't have to. I still had no idea who in Hamamachi had shot me or why. Could it be because of my abilities? Had I overheard something I shouldn't have? Was I considered a threat?

The fact was Councillor Okada knew we were innocent, and I was hoping he could sway the Militia to stop this charade and let us go.

I sighed deeply and glanced at the one-way observation window. I wondered who was in there listening to this pointless interrogation. I turned back to the major. "Look Major, you can ask me questions and throw your ridiculous accusations at me all night, but I really, really need to lie down, or I'm gonna pass-out. Some more painkillers wouldn't go astray either."

Before the major could respond, he paused and listened to his earpiece. He nodded, and then turned back to me, scowling. "Looks like you get your wish. Private, escort Mr. Jones to his cell and have a doctor see to him."

I wondered if Councillor Okada was in the observation room and if this reprieve was thanks to him.

The private nodded and pulled me roughly from my chair, sending pain shooting through my chest. I was too sore and tired to walk, but the promise of a bed was so appealing that I somehow found the strength to put one foot in front of the other.

Chapter Thirty-Two

I woke in the middle of the night from a fitful, nightmare-plagued sleep. The clicking sound of the metal bolt sliding back was the culprit. My first thought was that it was the assassin, come to finish what he started two years ago, but those fears evaporated when I saw Councillor Okada and another man standing there. Before either of them could speak, however, Nanako pushed her way between them and darted to my side.

"You're so pale, Ethan, are you okay? I can't believe they haven't given you proper medical treatment, considering what you did for them today," she said angrily.

I pushed myself to a sitting position and regretted it instantly as pain stabbed through my head. I took her small hands in mine, simply relieved that she was unharmed. "That's not the way they see it, apparently," I replied.

"You two will have ample opportunities to talk later, but right now you have to go," the councillor said as he stepped back from the cell door.

"Where are we going?" I asked as I left the small concrete-walled cell with one arm around my wife's shoulders to steady myself. Out in the corridor, I was glad to see Shorty and David waiting for us. They nodded in greeting, but appeared as bewildered as I was.

"My nephew, Ken, will drop you off a couple of kilometres from Newhome," Councillor Okada explained as we hurried down the prison block's corridor towards the entrance.

"Why are you doing this, Councillor? Won't you get in trouble?" I asked.

"All video surveillance has been disabled, and there has been an error with the prison staff shift change. None of this will be traced to me," he replied. "As to why am I doing this? It's because I know you are innocent of complicity in the Custodian's plan, because I owe you my life two times over, and because you're my friend."

We left the prison and stepped into the brisk night air. An old, weathered 4WD was parked at the curb with its engine idling.

"But what of Leigh? We can't leave without him," I protested.

"Leigh is still in critical condition and cannot be moved. Do not worry. I will keep a watch over him."

"But…"

"Ethan, the council is understandably in an uproar over this. All they can see is that the people from Newhome tried to destroy the town with an atomic bomb. They cannot differentiate between the Custodians and foragers, not even after I tried to explain it to them. Even the fact that you foragers took out the Custodians and disarmed the bomb does not allay their suspicions."

"Ethan," Nanako said with a sense of urgency bordering on panic, "Some of the councillors are convinced the foragers are Custodian spies and are demanding you be tortured and, whether you confess or not, executed. So please! Get in the car, we have to go."

Ken was already behind the steering wheel, so Shorty, David and Nanako quickly clambered into the vehicle. Shorty in the front and the other two in the back. I held back for a moment and reached out to shake Councillor Okada's hand. "Thank you, Sir, I won't forget this."

"Take good care of Nanako, young Ethan," he said softly so that only I could hear him. "She is not as tough as she seems."

The councillor cared for Nanako like a daughter, and obviously knew something from her past I didn't. The information did not come as a surprise to me though. I had already seen that side of her – and loved her all the more for it.

"You can count on me, Sir," I assured him as I climbed into the vehicle and sat next to my wife in the back seat.

The councillor's nephew took off as soon as I closed the door, accelerating to 80-klicks in an instant. I glanced out the rear window as we set off and saw the councillor hurrying towards his black 4WD.

"Someone wanna tell me why we're going back to Newhome?" Shorty asked, as he twisted around in his chair to meet my gaze.

"Somewhere else you'd rather go?" I asked.

"Anywhere but there."

"I wanna go back," David added, earning an evil look from Shorty.

"Our families are there," I reminded him.

"Exactly," David agreed.

"They'll do just fine without me. No, they'll be thrilled to bits if I don't come back," Shorty said. "Why are you so keen to return, Jones?"

"As I said, my family's there. More specifically, my little sister needs me. As I told you before, until she returns to full health, leaving Newhome ain't on my list of things to do. However, there is another reason – one that affects us all."

"And that is?" Shorty demanded.

"What do you think the Custodians will do when they find out their attempt to nuke Hamamachi failed?"

"They'll try again," Nanako said, joining the conversion.

"Exactly," I agreed.

"What's that got to do with us?" Shorty asked.

"Excuse me?" Nanako blustered. "That's my home, my family, my people – possibly the last Japanese on earth."

"Shorty, don't you care if the Custodians succeed in nuking Hamamachi – in murdering a whole town of innocent people?" I asked, meeting his gaze.

"Of course I do, but what can we do about it?"

"I say we go back to our jobs but keep our eyes and ears open to what's going on in the town. Besides, as foragers, we should be the first to know if the Custodians are going to mount another attack on Hamamachi. And if they are, we can work out then how to stop it."

"Still rather we'd go somewhere else," Shorty mumbled.

"Fine! But tell me this, though – what are we gonna tell the Custodians when we get back?" Shorty asked.

"We'll tell them that we got ambushed by Skel on the way back," I replied. "We'll work out the details later to make sure our stories match."

"And if they don't buy it?"

"They will, don't worry."

As darkened houses, buildings, and sheds flashed past in the night, I put my arm around Nanako and she rested her head against my shoulder. I looked down into her lovely round face and at the mixture of determination and concern etched there.

"We're gonna get through this, okay? And one day we're gonna live our lives without the worry of our two towns trying to wipe each other out – or of people trying to kill me," I assured her.

She searched my face for a long moment and said, "I'm going to hold you to that."

We sat there in the darkened interior of the 4WD as the councillor's nephew drove over the weed overgrown freeway through an eerie, nighttime landscape. As we went, I wondered what was in Newhome that was such a threat to the Skel and whoever was backing them – a faction in Hamamachi perhaps? – that they wanted to destroy it.

Love never gives up. (1 Corinthians 13:7)

New Living Translation Bible
Copyright© 1996, 2004, 2007, Tyndale House Foundation

Infiltrator, Book Two in the Forager Trilogy, now available on Amazon Kindle. For Ethan Jones, Nanako, and the surviving foragers, the trip back to Newhome is a nightmarish journey fraught with danger. When they do get back to Newhome, they fall afoul of a senior officer of the town's draconian Custodian police force. More memory fragments from Ethan's missing year surface, bewildering him with their horrific implications. A Hamamachi Ranger stumps Ethan when she asks if Nanako has told him the dreadful things that happened to her after she was dumped back in Hamamachi two years ago. What are these disturbing secrets from her past that Nanako is hiding from him?

Expatriate, Book Three in the Forager Trilogy – the thrilling and final chapter in the Forager trilogy, now available on Amazon Kindle.

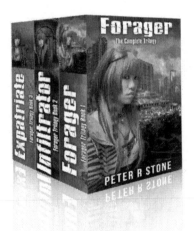

Forager - the Complete Trilogy – grab the complete Forager Trilogy for one low price.

Other Books by Peter R Stone

<u>*The Clockwork Mechanical,*</u> now available on Amazon Kindle, is a middle grades children's book, ages 7 to 12, and has 88 pages. Join Brad on his frantic quest to disable the space station's force field generator and save the world. See him team up with some unlikely companions - a swarm of little clockwork butterflies, a mechanical spider, and a girl with ADHD - as he tries to outsmart the Clockwork Mechanical.

The Ring of Fire (Mechanicals Book 2) now available on Amazon Kindle. Bradley Millner and his friends have completed the mission the Orb gave them, but instead of taking them home, it dumped them onto an oil rig that's drilled a well deep into the belly of the Earth. Worse, there's an evil Mechanical onboard that's planning to drop a powerful bomb down the well. A bomb that will cause over four hundred volcanoes in the Ring of Fire to erupt.

High Altitude Airship (Mechanicals Book 3) now available on Amazon Kindle. The Orb has taken Brad and his friends to a high altitude airship, which is over Antarctica. A Mechanical onboard is using it to enlarge the hole in the ozone layer. They have to stop it, for without the ozone layer, humanity, the animals, and most of the earth's plant life, will die.

Clockwork Mechanicals - the Complete Trilogy now available on Amazon Kindle. Clockwork Mechanicals -

the Complete Trilogy - a middle grades book for one low price. 33,902 words and 287 pages.
Includes:
The Clockwork Mechanical.
The Ring of Fire.
High Altitude Airship.

Acknowledgements

Thank you, Lord Jesus, for always being with me.
Thanks also to:

Alice Kurata, the amazing model pictured on the book's cover to represent Nanako.

Juliet Lauser, for her invaluable critique, suggestions, and editing.

David Hamono, for the time he put in to creating such an amazing full jacket book cover.

Ben Hamono, whose enthusiasm to read my work motivates me to write faster, and for his helpful editing.

Faith Blum, for her editing, and comments that had me in stitches.

Hannah Stone, for all the priceless chats we had while reading the book to her.

Tim Steen, for his amazing eye for spotting so many errors while editing the book.

About the Author

Peter R Stone is an award-winning writer, winning the Faithwriters Writing Challenge on three separate occasions, as well as frequently being a Faithwriters Editor's Choice top ten winner. His winning entries include The Medal and Dreams Forsaken.

Peter R Stone, an avid student of history, was reading books on Ancient Greece from the age of four. Periods of interest include the ancient world, medieval era, Napoleonic times, and the Second World War. He still mourns the untimely passing of King Leonidas of Sparta and Field Marshal Michel Ney of France.

A product of the Cold War Generation, Peter Stone studied the ramifications of a nuclear missile strike when he was in his senior year of high school, learning the effects of nuclear fallout and how to (hopefully) survive it. He has ever been drawn to post-apocalyptic and dystopian novels and films, and eagerly devoured The Day of the Triffids and John Christopher's Tripod Trilogy when he was a child. He is also an avid fan of science fiction, and his favorite books include the Lensmen Series by E.E.Doc.Smith, anything by Alastair Reynolds, and the Evergence trilogy by Sean Williams.

Peter Stone graduated from Melbourne School of Ministries Bible College in 1988. He has been teaching Sunday School and playing the keyboard in church for over twenty-five years. His wife is from Japan and they have two wonderful children. He has worked in the same games company for over twenty years, but still does not comprehend why they expect him to work all day instead of playing games.

Forager Online

http://foragertrilogy.blogspot.com.au/
Forager on Goodreads
Forager on Facebook
Forager on Amazon

Made in the USA
Middletown, DE
26 November 2016